THE HEIRESS

KISANE SLANEY

Disclaimer

This is a work of fiction, albeit inspired by real events. It is intended for entertainment purposes only, hoping to inspire the reader to dig deeper into the historical events that shape our world. While certain long-standing institutions, agencies, and public offices are mentioned, all the names, characters, businesses, places and incidents in this book are fictitious or the product of the author's imagination. Any resemblance to actual persons, living or dead, events and locales is purely coincidental.

ISBN: 978-1-7635978-1-5
ISBN: 978-1-7635978-0-8 (eBook)

https://kisaneslaney.com.au

Book Cover Design by ebooklaunch.com

CONTENT WARNING

Reader Discretion is advised. Proceed only if you are comfortable with potentially sensitive topics. This novel contains explicit sex scenes, references to child physical and sexual abuse and material that certain readers might consider religiously controversial.

DEDICATION

In memory of my daughter Candice, who would have been so proud that I finished writing and publishing my first novel.

ACKNOWLEDGEMENTS

Without the support and encouragement of the following people, I would never have finished this book.

My sister Alex told me I should write a book and then read every chapter and listened to me read the rewrites. That's sister love for you!

My daughter Katherine gave me valuable critical feedback and support during the publishing phase, and my son Sam and daughter Elizabeth's positive feedback encouraged me to keep writing.

My writing group members, Tessa, Denise, Margaret and Fran, patiently listened to me read chapter excerpts, blurbs and synopses. Michelle and Barry read the entire book to give me feedback.

My editor, Polly Phillips, provided insightful feedback and suggestions that were vital to improving the quality of the final manuscript.

My sincere thanks to them all.

CONTENTS

PART ONE

THE FAMILY

CHAPTER ONE

Tiana slammed the taxi door, flew up the front steps, through the main entrance and raced down the oak-panelled hallway to the cloakroom. Checking her face in the mirror and the precious piece of paper in her blazer pocket, she darted back into the hall and peered both ways. *All clear.* She was halfway down the corridor to her classroom when a voice echoed down the hall, bringing her to an abrupt halt.

"Tiana," called out Sister Agnes, "what *do* you think you are doing? Is this any way for a young lady to behave, a *Marymount* young lady?"

Tiana froze, then bowing her head, she turned towards Sister Agnes. "Oh, Sister, I'm so sorry," she said, her eyes fixed on her shoes. I've just come back from the dentist." She slowly raised her head and said, "And I was hurrying because I don't want to miss class—Modern History."

Sister Agnes's brows snapped together as she gave Tiana the once-over. "Your face does look somewhat swollen, Tiana. Very well, proceed, but at a walking pace, please."

"*Thank you*, Sister," Tiana said as she turned with a quick sigh of relief and headed for her class.

Entering the classroom, Tiana slipped into her seat next to her best friend, Veronica. "Vron," Tiana whispered, "you'll never believe what I saw at the dentist in Tatler." She gave Veronica a lopsided grin. "I tore out the page. Show you after class."

Tiana and Veronica became best friends when they were eleven years old. They first met at Harrods whilst getting their uniforms fitted for the London Marymount International School. Walking into the large fitting room, Tiana saw Veronica kneeling on the floor whilst an assistant crawled around her, pinning up her skirt so it sat precisely at the bottom of her knee, barely skimming the floor. Looking at Tiana, Veronica mouthed the word "Help" before rolling her eyes and going cross-eyed. Tiana burst out laughing, and that was the beginning of a life-long friendship.

"Come on then," Veronica said the minute class was over, "cough up."

Tiana pulled out the page ripped from Tatler and said, "Look, isn't that the most sophisticated thing you've ever seen?"

Veronica gazed at the spot where Tiana was pointing. "Oh, Lordy, I don't believe it."

"Yep," Tiana said in awe, "she's smoking a cigar. A *cigar*."

"Wow, she looks so worldly. I've never seen a woman smoking a cigar before. Cigarettes, of course, but *never* a cigar."

"I know," Tiana said. I adore the aroma of cigars, but I never expected to smoke one myself. Don't you love it?"

"Yes, imagine whipping out a cigar and lighting up on a date just like Lady Scott-Fernsby in Tatler. Oh, shock, horror!"

"Totally, I knew you'd be all for it, Vron. So, how old would you say she is?"

"Mmm, mid-twenties."

Tiana shook her head. "Far too long to wait. I'm thinking of eighteen to make our debut. We should start practicing. The problem is, how? Papa keeps his cigars in a special box and cuts and lights them up in a special way. We'll have to persuade him to help us, teach us."

"Goodness, Tiana, do you think he would?"

"Well, maybe. I think I know how to persuade him. Papa has been telling me about our business interests, and one of them is importing cigars. I'll tell him

I want to learn more about that aspect of the business. *Then*, I'll let on about wanting to learn how to smoke them."

"Sneaky."

"Strategic. Papa told me it takes five years or more to go from tobacco seeds to handmade cigars, and actually, I am interested in learning more about the process."

Veronica laughed, "Okay, you've convinced me."

"I'll talk him into it," Tiana said with a determined nod. "Just as soon as I get home for the summer hols. After all, it's the seventies, not the fifties."

"Go you, make Germaine proud."

***

Tiana adored her papa. He was a cigar connoisseur, and she pictured him in his study, sitting by the fire in his leather chair, cigar in hand. The glow of the table lamp cast its light onto his book as logs shifted in the vast fireplace, sending up tiny showers of sparks.

His grand study took up the whole ground floor and was by far Tiana's favourite room in their elegant six-storey apartment in the exclusive Sixteenth Arrondissement in Paris. It was in this room that her papa sat at his vast burr walnut desk, with towering floor-to-ceiling bookshelves filled with leather-bound volumes as its backdrop, and oversaw his global business empire. Whenever she walked into the room, the familiar scent of cigars, rich leather and freshly polished wood filled her senses.

One afternoon, when Tiana was six years old, she escaped from her Nanny and went to visit her papa in his study. That was when their afternoon ritual started.

"Come in, come in, darling," he would say when he saw her peeping around the door. "Sit, sit," and she would scramble into the corner of the enormous leather Chesterfield sofa in front of the log fire. Then her father would enquire about her day, and, with the occasional puff on his cigar, he would listen attentively whilst she told him of her little triumphs and troubles.

Then he, in turn, told her stories about the places he visited, the people he met and the fascinating things that he saw. She learnt about her great-grandfather and how he came to receive the beautiful blue and white Ming Dynasty dragon jar vase sitting on the Chippendale side table. "It was a powerful man in China who gave your great-grandfather that beautiful vase Tiana."

Her father introduced her to her paternal grandfather, who had died before she was born, through the story of the Jaques Anderssen boxwood and ebony chess set. "Your grandfather gave it to me for my twelfth birthday. Then he taught me how to play. When you are twelve, I'll teach you how to play, and it will be your chess set one day. It has great sentimental value for me and is also extremely valuable, so I trust you to take good care of it when that day comes."

In the summer, they retreated to the opposite end of the vast room and looked out at the small courtyard and trees beyond through the four elegant ceiling-to-floor windows on either side of the glass-panelled French doors.

On hot afternoons, Tiana loved sitting outside in the courtyard, filled with the intoxicating perfume wafting through the air from the two potted Frangipani trees. The gentle sound of water bubbling up and trickling over the little cherub in the fountain provided a peaceful, hypnotic backdrop to the soft murmur of their voices. By evening, the courtyard would be awash with the addition of a heady mix of aromas from the honeysuckle and jasmine that had for years been scrambling and entwining over the trellis that covered the courtyard walls.

At three o'clock each afternoon, their conversation would be interrupted by the arrival of Dominique with a tray of homemade lemonade for Tiana, her papa's pot of his favourite black coffee, no sugar, and an afternoon treat baked by their cook, Maria. When her papa wasn't visiting their head offices run by his CEOs in Paris, London and Greece or flying overseas, these late afternoon father-daughter visits became the highlight of Tiana's day.

Once Tiana was at boarding school and returned home for the school holidays, the first thing she did on arrival was call out, "Papa, Papa, I'm home." And regardless of what he was doing or whom he might be with, he would come out of his study to greet her, arms open wide. "Tiana, my darling, welcome home," he would say, sweeping her into a bear hug, and she would - inhale.

After Tiana's fifteenth birthday, her father explained some of the intricacies of the family companies, dealing with their cruise line, resorts, boutiques, luxury goods and cigar import and distribution. Tentatively, they began to explore whether she would like to play a role in the business in the future or choose to go in a different direction altogether. "But there's no rush, Tiana; we'll continue this discussion over the next three years until you graduate from Marymount."

***

Tiana loved her mother, too, but there had always been a distance between them. Whereas her papa was openly affectionate, her mother was *restrained* when it came to demonstrations of affection.

As long as Tiana could remember, her mother had an air of sadness about her. At times, it would be barely noticeable, but at other times, it seemed to overwhelm her.

Is it my fault? Is it something I've done? Tiana dared not ask her mother.

But the situation had changed for Tiana during the previous half-term break when she'd walked into the drawing room and found her mother crying. Quickly brushing away her tears, her mother had turned away, giving Tiana the strong message that she did not wish to discuss her emotions with her daughter.

That's it, Tiana decided after leaving her mother. *I can't go on like this. I can't stand not knowing what's making maman so sad. I'll ask papa; he must know.*

Tiana headed straight to her father's study, and before he even had time to greet her, she blurted out, "Papa, please tell me what makes maman so sad?"

"My darling, I'm not sure," he said, looking startled. "I've asked her, but she is so evasive. I can only guess that it has something to do with being unable to have more children."

This upset Tiana even more. "So, it *is* my fault, Papa, that maman is so sad. I knew it had something to do with me."

"Good Lord Tiana, what on earth makes you think that?" her father said, looking shocked as he gazed at his distraught daughter.

Tiana burst into tears. "Having *me* must have caused the problem."

"No, no, Tiana, you must not think that any of this is your fault. Your mother would be even more upset if she thought for one moment that you were thinking like this," her father said, putting his arms around her and stroking her hair.

Tiana was still not convinced. After seeing her father, she went to the telephone and rang her former Nanny, with whom she kept in touch.

Her Nanny repeated what her father had said, assuring Tiana that whatever had happened was most certainly not her fault. "Chiquita, I had no idea this is what you were thinking. So, this is what you must do: you must speak to your Aunt Vivienne. If anyone can tell you what's upsetting your mamá, her sister is the one. Promise me you'll do that."

"Si, Si, I'll speak to Aunt Vivienne during the next holiday break."

***

Tiana was just two weeks old when her adored nanny, Nanny B, took over the routine tasks of raising a child from babyhood until she went to boarding school.

Elena Belasco was Spanish and came from a large, loving family. But in 1957, there was little work for women in Spain. "You know I can't stay, Papá," Elena told her father. "I've been looking, but there simply aren't any jobs. Sofia has written to me suggesting I go to France, where she's sure I'll find work as a nanny."

"My only consolation," her father said, "is that you'll be living in Paris with your cousin whilst looking for a job."

A week after her arrival, Sofia came home looking excited, "Elena, I've just learned from one of the other nannies that Madame Adelia Manning is interviewing for a full-time nanny for her baby daughter Tiana. It sounds like it will be a long-term position."

Elena went for the interview and rushed home to tell Sofia, "Can you believe it? I got the job!"

When Elena first held Tiana in her arms, she gazed down at her for the longest time before lifting her up and whispering in the baby's tiny ear, "I'll teach you Spanish songs and Spanish prayers, Chiquita. We'll have a wonderful time together."

***

Once Tiana was old enough, she would sneak up to the maids' quarters on the sixth floor of the apartment and sit and listen to Elena and her friends gossiping and laughing together. It was easy for Tiana to imagine she was in Spain, with the Spanish music playing on the record player, everyone talking in Spanish and the food, always the aroma of the delicious food. Tiana's favourite was paella, a colourful mix of rice, seafood and spices. In the summer, she loved to have the cold gazpacho. When she was older and well-behaved, she was permitted to have small sips of sangria as a treat. Gradually, it became apparent that Tiana had a natural talent for languages, and by the time she was eleven, she was fluent in Spanish as well as French and English.

Tiana cried when she was about to leave for London to board at Marymount International School for the first time. "Oh, Nanny B, I'm going to miss you so much," she said, her eyes brimming with tears. She knew that this meant Nanny B would be leaving the household, a momentous shift in her young life. "You absolutely swear that you will come and visit when I'm home on holiday?" she asked as she hugged her Nanny close.

"Sí, Sí, Chiquita, I promise."

***

Whilst Nanny B took care of Tiana daily, it was Tiana's mother, Adelia, who bore the responsibility for ensuring that Tiana always displayed the 'breeding' bestowed upon her at birth. She must learn to dress appropriately, when to speak and remain silent, and how to act like a young lady, especially when it comes to good manners. "It is my duty," Adelia informed her daughter, "to ensure that you are fully prepared to take your rightful place in Paris society."

Adelia was the quintessential Parisian woman of style. She had the tall, slender body that would be the envy of any Dior model. Her thick, dark brown, glossy hair was cut in the short pixie style made so famous by Audrey Hepburn. This was the perfect cut to draw attention to her large, brown, almond-shaped eyes, framed by straight eyebrows that tapered off like tiny wings. Adelia applied her favourite lipstick, Pink Champagne, with stunning effect, shaping her naturally arched lips into the fashionable cupid bow.

As a young member of Le Tout-Paris, the fashionable and affluent elite, Adelia always sat in the front row of the fashion shows held at the Maison's of Chanel, Givenchy, and Dior, her three favourite fashion designers. But of the three, her favourite was Givenchy, who would one day have the honour of designing her wedding dress.

Adelia dressed Tiana exquisitely from the moment she was born. In Paris, she was regularly seen shopping at Baby Dior. When Tiana went to boarding school, they shopped in London at Harrods after each of Tiana's fittings for her school uniform.

Alan, Tiana's father, had insisted that their daughter attend an international school where she would mix with students from all over the world. "I want her to be open-minded and aware of what's happening in the world. I will not have our daughter grow up to be a snob who has no concept of how people less fortunate live," he told Adelia.

"Bien Alain, I agree, as long as she goes to Finishing School once she graduates."

"Or Oxford or Cambridge," Alan replied with a smile.

***

Whilst her father's study was his private domain, Tiana's mother held court in the drawing room on the first floor. This was the most elegant room in the house, with its bank of floor-to-ceiling windows and double French doors that opened out to a balcony fragrant with lemon and orange trees in large ceramic pots, lush ferns, a mixture of white hydrangeas, and cascading flowers in baskets falling over the wrought iron railings.

Formerly, the entire room had been painted in *blanc de roi*, royal white. However, Adelia wanted to redecorate and decided that all the intricate and ornately carved boiserie and mouldings on the walls, ceiling and tall double doors should be highlighted in gilt.

"I think adding the gold will bring the room alive, Alain."

"Dearest, you have impeccable taste," her husband assured her. "I'm sure it will look wonderful."

The result was spectacular, transforming the room to a level of opulence and sophistication it had not previously possessed. The glittering crystal chandelier and ornate carvings on the marble mantle were now complemented by shimmering gilt highlights, and the massive mirror above the marble mantle gleamed.

A pair of matching three-branch silver candelabra stood at either end of the mantelpiece. Adelia made sure the candles were lit when they entertained important guests for the evening, adding a magical flicker to the already opulent atmosphere. And it was in this room that Tiana's mother held one of her own weekly afternoon rituals.

***

Every Monday afternoon at three o'clock precisely, a priest, who might well be a Bishop or Cardinal, visited Adelia in her drawing room to share afternoon tea and discuss the charities she supported. When her guest arrived for the first time, Adelia would enquire, "China or Indian?" before pouring the steaming tea of choice into delicate Limoges porcelain teacups. An assortment of delicious little sandwiches, scones, clotted cream and damson jam, chocolate éclairs and glacé petits fours were offered and eaten midst the murmur of serious conversation.

Once Tiana was ten years old, her mother insisted she make a brief appearance in the drawing room after school to meet her guest and respond politely to enquiries about her health, school and so forth before excusing herself. Tiana would then dash down to the kitchen where Maria, their cook, would have her tea and hot, buttered raisin toast waiting for her on the scrubbed pine kitchen table. "Phew, I'm glad that's over for another week," Tiana would say to Maria with a cheeky grin.

When Tiana was older and home for the school holidays, her mother still expected her to come and make polite conversation whilst afternoon tea was brought in and laid out. She told Tiana that it was good training for the future. "It is essential that you know how to speak to people at all levels of society, Tiana, including how to address the clergy hierarchy."

"Oui Maman," Tiana responded, wondering how many more weekly meetings she would have to endure as part of her mother's training.

She decided she had to figure out an escape plan. *There must be a way to get out of these boring conversations.*

***

Driving home from the airport to start her summer holiday, Tiana was busy rehearsing how she would start the conversation with her papa about smoking cigars when André, the family chauffeur, told her that her father had left on an emergency business trip. "He said to tell you, mademoiselle, that he is *very* sorry and will make it up to you when he returns."

"Darn it, André, I had something very important to talk to papa about."

"Never mind, Mademoiselle Tiana, there's always afternoon tea with Madame," he teased.

Tiana sighed, "Just my luck. I must come up with an escape plan, André. Maman would kill me for saying it, but they're all so old and incredibly dull."

"Well, Mademoiselle, Madame has a new priest visiting her today."

"Really? As old and decrepit as all the rest, no doubt?"

"Well, I wouldn't say that exactly."

"No?" Tiana said, puzzled by the amusement she saw in André's eyes in the rear-view mirror.

But André' would say no more.

"Well, you've got me curious, André," Tiana said.

Once home and wanting to end the ordeal as soon as possible, Tiana hurried up the stairs to the drawing room, leaving André to take her bags to her bedroom.

"Good afternoon, Maman, I'm home," she said as she walked in. All she saw was the back of the black soutane worn by the priest talking to her mother as she moved to sit in her favourite chair.

"Ah, Tiana, your home at last. Do come in," her mother said, at which point her guest turned around.

***

Tiana stared in complete shock. *Holy cow!* Her thoughts whirled around in her confused brain as she stood there, immobilised, staring.

Her mother looked shocked. "Tiana," she said, "mind your manners please, prêter attention." Then, turning to her guest, she said, "Father, allow me to introduce my daughter, Tiana. Tiana, I would like you to meet The Very Reverend Philippe Gagnon. Father Gagnon is filling in for Father Aubry, who is currently in hospital."

It wasn't the words so much as her mother's *tone* that snapped Tiana out of her trance, only to be completely let down by her body. She could feel the blush slowly creeping up her neck and willed it to stop. But no, it kept rising until her cheeks were suffused with a reddish glow. She felt mortified.

Tiana felt her throat constricting, forcing her to clear it. "Ahem, Ahem," - swallow. Finally, she managed to whisper, "Father."

And then she experienced the ultimate betrayal: her hands. *Oh, please, no,* she prayed. *Don't let him take my hand.* But her prayers went unanswered. Stepping forward gracefully, Father Gagnon took her sweaty palm in his strong, cool hand and then placed his other hand on top.

Tiana felt an electric charge go through her body, giving her sensations she had never experienced before in places she had not known existed and for which she had no words. She could barely raise her eyes above his chin. But then she saw the slight quiver at the corners of his lips and just knew that he was making every effort to restrain them from a full-blown grin.

"Tiana, how lovely to meet you. Will you be joining us for tea?" he said, his voice washing over her like warm treacle.

"Oh no!" Tiana blurted out, looking imploringly at her mother, who immediately stepped in.

"As Tiana has just arrived home from the airport, Father, no doubt she would like to go and freshen up," she said, glaring at Tiana.

"Of course. Well, Tiana, it's been a pleasure."

She glanced up at him, confirming that he was the most handsome man she'd ever seen in her entire life, let alone a priest. "Father," she said, bobbing her head and turning; she willed herself to walk, not run, from the room.

Once outside the drawing room, she rushed upstairs to her bedroom and threw herself onto her bed. Rolling over onto her back, she stared at the delicate floral design in the ceiling, replaying what had just happened at her mother's 'Monday Afternoon Tea'. *I could die of embarrassment. Oh, mon dieu, what a fool I made of myself. What must he think? 'Stupid child'! Maman will be furious that I embarrassed her. Holy shit.*

***

On the other hand, Adelia looked horrified as she watched her daughter respond to meeting Father Gagnon.

Why wasn't I warned that a younger priest would be coming to replace Father Aubry this week? Oh, if only Alain had been here, I could have sent Tiana to him instead. She doesn't understand the danger. Never again.

CHAPTER TWO

Tiana couldn't stop thinking about Father Gagnon. She daydreamed about him at the oddest times, especially before she fell asleep at night. *His blond hair against the black soutane, My God! It's just not fair for a priest to be that handsome. I wonder what he looks like in ordinary clothes.*

Lost in one of her daydreams, Tiana didn't hear her mother enter her room until her mother's stern voice broke her reverie.

"Tiana, I'm speaking to you."

"Oh, excuse-moi Maman, I didn't hear you."

"Clearly. Tiana, pack your bags. I've just spoken to your papa, and we'll meet him in Greece. We'll stay with your Aunt Vivienne and the family on their yacht."

The news was completely unexpected, and for a moment, Tiana felt bitterly disappointed. For the first time ever, she had been looking forward to attending the next 'Monday Afternoon Tea'. She was longing to see Father Gagnon again.

Tiana's eyes dropped as her eyebrows drew together, and the shadow of a frown slipped across her face as her mother watched her.

Oh well, Tiana reasoned, *at least now I get to see papa and talk to him about smoking cigars.*

And then she remembered that she also wanted to talk to her aunt. *Perfect, I can speak to Aunt Vivienne about maman.*

***

Her father was there to greet them once they boarded the yacht, and Tiana couldn't wait to get him to herself.

"Papa, can we escape from the family? There's something I want to talk to you about, well, two things actually."

"Of course, darling, we'll go ashore tomorrow morning for breakfast, and you can tell me all about it."

The following morning, after ordering breakfast, Alan said, "So tell me, darling, what is it that's so important to discuss?"

"Well, Papa, I've decided I want to learn about the cigar distribution side of the business."

"Good heavens, Tiana, what brought this on?"

"Well, I love the aroma of cigars, and I've seen how much you and your friends enjoy smoking them. From what you've told me, what goes into making them sounds fascinating."

"Oh, come on, Tiana, I know you too well. There's more to it than you're telling me, although I can't imagine what."

"Well, there is something."

"I knew it."

Tiana opened her bag and pulled out the page from Tatler.

"I want to be like Lady Scott-Fernsby and smoke cigars. Look Papa. It's all the rage."

"Good God, Tiana, are you serious?" he said, a look of utter amazement on his face.

"Yes, Papa."

Alan sipped his coffee, and there was a lengthy pause.

"You understand there's more to it than simply lighting up?"

"Yes, of course, Papa."

More silence.

"And if I were to agree to this, Tiana, I would have to be sure that you genuinely loved every aspect involved in producing the final product, the perfect handmade cigar. Cigars are a passion for those involved in the industry, both the creation and the smoking of them."

"I know how much you and your friends enjoy smoking cigars, Papa."

"Yes, Tiana, but it's a long journey from planting the seeds to smoking the cigar. Once the seedling becomes a mature plant, the next step is the curing barn. When the plant goes in, it's a verdant green, and then, as the plant dries out, it turns into a rich brown.

"Tell me if I'm boring you."

"No, no Papa, go on."

"Then, after removing the ammonia through fermentation, the tobacco is packed into bales of cardboard or wood and left to age and mature and further round out the flavours. Some warehouses will have tobacco that's five or six years old. All the tobacco leaves used to come from Cuba, but now they might come from Puerto Rico, Colombia, Nicaragua, or the Dominican Republic."

"Gosh, so many steps. So how does it become a cigar?"

"Well, the leaves have to be blended. Often, cigar factory managers create new blends. It's an absolute art, Tiana. It may take two years of experimentation, combining different leaves to develop a new and unique blend that is the perfect marriage of texture, flavour, and balance.

"Then, once the blend has been selected, the buncher will combine the leaves using a traditional method, and the roller turns the leaf into a cigar. Amazingly, one cigar roller can make up to five hundred cigars in a day. But that's extreme. It's more usual for rollers to produce one hundred and fifty to two hundred a day."

"Goodness, I'd love to see them do that."

"It's amazing to watch," Alan said. "But that's not all because, for the next six months to two years, the cigars are placed in a cedar-lined ageing room. Finally, they're banded, boxed and ready to be shipped off, and that's where we come into the picture."

"Wow, no wonder the whole thing takes so long."

"Well, if you're truly serious about wanting to be involved in this aspect of our business, then I'm prepared to consider taking you on as a trainee."

"Oh my God, *really*?"

"Yes, but you must be prepared to learn everything about the process, and we haven't even touched upon how to store, light up, and smoke a cigar yet."

"Oh, I will, Papa, I will, I promise."

"One reason I'm prepared to do this, Tiana, is because the women in the families involved in the cigar business will often smoke themselves. So, I can hardly, in good faith, ban you from smoking. Of course, you will not be smoking anything until you're eighteen and have graduated from Marymount. Is that clear?"

"Yes, Papa."

Secondly, I can't imagine anything more wonderful than involving you in this part of our family business."

"Oh, thank you, Papa."

"It so happens that last year, a friend introduced me to a cigar created by the Arguello family. Because I loved it so much, I decided to extend my business trip to the United States to visit the factory in Ybor City in Tampa, Florida. There I met all the family. Since then, Juan Arguello and I have become good friends, and we're discussing becoming one of their European distributors.

"I think it would be a good idea for me to take you to visit the family on one of your school holidays. There, you would learn from the Master. You already speak Spanish, thanks to Nanny B, so that's a real bonus. What do you think of that idea, Tiana?"

"It's a brilliant idea, Papa. I'm so excited. But what about maman, do you think she will approve?"

"You leave your mother to me."

"Definitely," Tiana said.

***

After ordering a fresh pot of coffee, Alan said, "So Tiana, what was the second thing you wanted to talk to me about? I seem to remember you said 'two' things."

"Oh, yes." Tiana hesitated, then said, "I wondered if you believe in love at first sight."

"Goodness me, you *are* full of surprises today," Alan laughed.

Tiana couldn't help grinning, "Well?"

"I do."

"Really?"

"Yes, Tiana, really. When I first saw your mother, it was love at first sight."

"Oh my *goodness*, you never told me that before."

"Well, you never asked me that question before."

"So, how did it happen?"

"Well, it was in Monaco, and I had been invited to a party. The sun was about to set, and I saw your mother standing on the terrace, looking out at the ocean. She was a vision, tall and slender, with a golden suntan. She wore a long, floaty, white dress with shoestring straps, and it was synched in at the waist with a wide, long blue sash tied in a soft bow at the back. Her hair was long then, and she had it pulled up in a ponytail, and she wore large, gold hoop earrings. She took my breath away."

"Holy cow, Papa, I can't believe you remember so much detail. You're such a romantic."

"It's a vision locked into my memory, Tiana. There and then, I said to myself, *that's the woman I will marry.* There was a fragility about your mother, and I wanted to protect her and take care of her forever."

"I can't believe I've never heard this story before," Tiana said, gazing at her father in awe.

"Well, it's true, and we were married within a year. But you're only fifteen, Tiana. Surely you haven't lost your heart to someone already?"

"Oh no, Papa. It's just something that Veronica and I were discussing. You know whether or not it could happen."

The lie slipped out so fast that Tiana barely registered a twinge of guilt.

I can't speak to anyone about this, only Vron.

***

Adelia was waiting to speak to Alan when they returned to the yacht. "So what did our daughter have to say, chéri?"

"Oh, she just wanted to discuss possibilities for becoming part of the business. We're in the early stages of the discussion. But she did say something unexpected. She asked me if I believed in 'love at first sight'. Can you believe it? I, of course, answered in the affirmative and told her about the first time I saw you, my love, and fell head over heels."

Adelia looked shocked.

"What is it, darling? Are you alright?" Alan asked.

"Yes, yes, just a little taken back, like you," Adelia replied. "Did she mention any person of interest?"

"No. It's just something she and Veronica discussed, as no doubt teenage girls do."

"I see," Adelia said.

***

Leaving her husband, Adelia hurried down to their cabin. She collapsed into a chair, overcome by dizziness and nausea, triggered by Alain's account of Tiana's 'love at first sight' question. *Mon dieu, this is far worse than I thought.* Suddenly, the memory of seeing Nicolas for the first time flashed into her mind, and her eyes widened in fear. *This is the first treacherous step and must never go any further.*

***

Back on board, Tiana left her father to look for her Aunt Vivienne. She found her on the top deck reading and said, "Aunt Vivienne, can I speak to you about something important in private?"

"Of course, my dear," Vivienne said, looking surprised. "How about we go down to my cabin? I want to get changed anyway."

***

Once in the cabin, Tiana said, "Aunt Vivienne, I'm so worried about maman. A while ago, I walked into the sitting room, and she was crying. She is so sad sometimes, and then at other times, she seems fine. As long as I can remember, she's been like this. I don't understand why, and I think it might be because of me."

Vivienne looked stunned. "Oh, Tiana," she said, "what on earth do you mean it might be something to do with you?"

"Well, papa said he thought it might be because maman couldn't have more children. So having me must have caused the problem."

"Well, Tiana, I know your mother wanted a large family, which may be why she gets sad. But Tiana, the fact that she can't have more is purely a medical issue and certainly not something you should blame yourself for."

"That's what Papa and Nanny B said. But Nanny B thought you might know another reason for maman's sadness."

"No, chérie, I don't. I think the best thing you can do is show your mother lots of love and stop blaming yourself for something that has nothing to do with you."

Since all three adults had responded the same way, Tiana took their advice and let that guilt go. But demonstrating her love would be a challenge.

I'll have to get creative, she decided.

***

Later that evening, Vivienne took Adelia aside and said, "I have to talk to you alone - now!"

"Goodness, Vivienne, what on earth's the matter?" Adelia said, following her sister, who walked briskly to the other end of the deck.

Vivienne repeated her conversation with Tiana. "But the worst part was that I had to lie through my teeth, Adelia," Vivienne said, her expression reflecting the anger Adelia heard in her voice.

"Mon dieu, I had no idea Tiana was even aware of how I felt. She did walk in on me a while back and caught me crying. It was the day of the anniversary of the loss, Vivienne. The pain and guilt never goes away."

Frowning, Vivienne said, "Well, I thought you should know that Tiana is taking it all very personally and is worried about you."

"That's terrible. I promise I'll be more discreet. I'm so sorry you were put in such a frightful position, Vivienne, especially after all the support you gave me."

"It's been so long, Adelia. I thought you would have come to terms with it by now."

"I wish it worked like that, Vivienne. I do."

Her voice softening, Vivienne said, "Well, now that you're aware of how Tiana is feeling, I know you'll find a way to reassure her."

"Bien sûr, I'll give it some thought. She mustn't know that we talked about this. I'll come up with a plan."

After her sister left to join the family, Adelia stood on deck, grasping the railings and gazing out to sea. *Am I still being punished for my sins, but now through my daughter? This is my wake-up call. I've burdened her with my pain and sorrow. I have to make it up to her. We must become closer so I can protect her.*

CHAPTER THREE

It was 1953 when sixteen-year-old Adelia first set eyes on Father Nicolas Brune. He came out to stand next to Father Allard, the parish priest of Notre-Dame de l'Assomption de Passy. Adelia was sitting in the pew between her mother and her best friend, Olivia when she saw him. She dug her elbow into Olivia's ribs, and they both turned to each other and grinned.

As soon as they left the Church, Adelia told Olivia, "I didn't expect we'd get such a young priest. Can you believe how handsome he is, Liv?"

Olivia laughed. "I won't tell Charles you said that. Come on, let's give him the once over."

They walked to the adjoining garden, where a 'welcome party' was being held for the new assistant priest. Adelia watched Father Allard skilfully guide Father Brune through the crowd of parishioners, ensuring he met the most influential families.

"He looks rather uncomfortable," Adelia said. "I don't think he likes being the centre of attention."

"Well, you don't have time to rescue him. If we don't hurry, we'll be late for the cinema, and Charles and Damien will be furious with us for making them miss the start and BB."

"Charles is obsessed with Brigitte," Adelia said. "He can't stop talking about her after we see her films. 'She's *so* sexy,' he raves. He wants me to dress more like her."

"What does that mean?"

"You know, those tailored polka-dot pants, the off-shoulder neckline."

"Oh, are you going to?"

"Yes, but not because of Charles. I like that Brigitte has her own style and dresses the way she wants now. I'm sick of looking like a younger version of my mother. Have you seen those boring photos in Elle? I want to look awesome like Brigitte."

"Well, I love the gingham dresses she wears," Olivia said. "Who would think that gingham could look so à la mode? It's so weird, though, seeing her up on the big screen after seeing her growing up in the neighbourhood."

"I know. Maman and her mother, Anne-Marie, were friends from church. A couple of years ago, we were in Saint-Tropez, and we bumped into the Bardot family. They were a little 'avant-garde', maman said, but otherwise just like us."

"Damien thinks Brigitte is incredibly sexy, too."

"Has Damien asked you to do it yet?"

"No, what about Charles?"

"Not yet, but I expect him to pressure me once I've left school. You know, 'Come on, Adelia, so and so is doing it'. They want you to have sex, but they want to marry a virgin; it's so not fair."

"Guess what? Damien told me that Paul and Lucile have done it."

"No way. How does he know?"

"Paul told him. Lucile will be mortified he's telling everyone, especially if it's not true. Oh look, Father Brune is looking at you."

Adelia glanced back at Father Brune, and he gave her a shy smile. Caught off-guard, Adelia blushed.

"Oh my goodness, look at you two," Olivia said, laughing.

"Don't be absurd," Adelia said.

***

Adelia was in her final term at the Institut De La Tour and was focussed on her studies. She was an average student and had no desire to pursue higher education. The fact that there would be limited opportunities to pursue a career after she graduated was of little concern to her. She enjoyed a privileged life that meant she was free of any concerns for her material welfare. She could do whatever she wanted until she married, provided it met with her parents' approval.

She continued to see Father Brune through the regular activities and events at the parish. Then, one Saturday, they had an unexpected encounter at the local markets. It was a warm summer's afternoon, and she was busy rummaging through the books at a second-hand bookstall. She was searching for volume one of The Second Sex when she heard a voice behind her say, "Hello again." She turned to see Father Brune standing there with his shy smile.

"Hello, Father, what are you doing here?"

"I'm looking for books on the afterlife and counselling the sick and dying. Facing judgement after death and being sent to either heaven, hell, or purgatory is a scary concept, and I think my pastoral care skills need improving."

Adelia was taken aback by his honesty and found it touching. All the priests she had known seemed to perceive themselves as dwelling in an all-knowing, rarefied atmosphere well above the laity.

"Why are you here, Adelia?"

"Well—umm, I'm just looking around to see if there's anything interesting." She lied, knowing full well that the church had banned the book she was looking for.

"Do you enjoy reading Adelia?"

"I do; I read a lot."

"What else do you enjoy doing now that you've left school?"

"Oh, all the usual things: shopping, tennis, the cinema, parties. We have a country house we go to in les Yvelines, and in the winter, my parents take the whole family skiing. My elder sister Vivienne, brother-in-law and young nephew all come with us. It's a family tradition, things like that."

"It sounds like a very full life."

And then, just as Adelia was about to ask Father Brune about himself, he said, "Well, I'd better be on my way back to the parish. See you in Church, Adelia."

But in the new year, there was a subtle shift in their relationship.

***

It started when Adelia was cycling in the Bois de Boulogne on a crisp spring morning and suddenly saw Father Brune ahead on his bike. She called out, and he stopped and waited for her to catch up.

"Adelia, how are you?" he asked.

"Great, thank you, Father."

They chatted for a few minutes, and then Adelia said, "Would you like to get a cup of coffee, Father?"

"Good idea. Let's get out of the cold for a while."

Once settled, she asked, "Did you see your family during your holiday, Father?"

"I did. I saw my mother; she's in hospital. She hasn't been well this last year."

"Oh, I'm so sorry; I hope she's feeling better. Is your family far from here?"

"The family have a farm in North Champagne."

"Do you have brothers and sisters?"

"I have, or had, nine older brothers and sisters. I was the last to arrive."

"Wow, and did you like living on a farm?"

"No. My father worked from dawn to dusk and expected the same from my older brothers. But I knew I wanted something different, although I wasn't sure what that might be. Of course, my father expected that I would someday join my brothers.

"But that all changed in 1940 with the war. After the north of France was lost, we found ourselves in the German Occupation Zone. My father and four of my brothers were taken prisoner and sent to the work camps in Germany."

"Oh, how terrible. What did you do?"

"At first, we were completely devastated, but my mother said we had to keep the farm going for when they came back. My three older sisters and brother were all teenagers in 1940, but she trained them. My brother Jules was thirteen, and he used to drive the horse and cart, taking my mother and sisters out to the fields. We were lucky we didn't lose our horse to the Germans. I was ten in 1940, and my brother Claude was eleven. We both went to school, of sorts, but we had our chores, too. We all did our best to keep it together."

"Your mother sounds amazing. My parents don't talk about the war at all."

"When the Germans first arrived, it was complete madness, Adelia. Our nearest large town was Reims, and they took over all the champagne houses. The soldiers were stealing millions of bottles of champagne, getting drunk and causing utter chaos. They had to bring in a top-brass German to bring it all under control.

"I've never heard that story before."

"The Germans took over many of the school buildings, completely disrupting the schooling system. Claude and I went to a school set up in the house of one of the wealthy farm owners. There wasn't enough paper, so we used slates and chalk! And then there was the food shortage, even for us living on the farm. We were always hungry."

"I'm lucky I was only three when the war began. What happened after the war? Did your father and brothers come back?" Adelia asked, completely absorbed in Father Brune's account of his experiences during the German occupation.

"Three of my brothers eventually returned after liberation, but not my father and eldest brother Henri. They died somewhere in Germany."

"Oh, I'm so sorry, your poor mother. How old were your other brothers?"

"Well, by 1945, Charles was twenty-five, Antoine was twenty-three, and Gabriel, a twin, was twenty-one. My mother had two sets of twins. So, after the war, my four older brothers decided to keep the farm, expand operations, and run it together. Jules was eighteen by then.

"They joined JAC, the Catholic Agricultural Youth, and attended numerous educational activities that taught them how to organise themselves in cooperatives. Then, they started to modernise the farm and use new techniques to improve the farm's production. Two of my sisters married and left to live on their husbands' farms. My sister Jeanne, Jules' twin, worked as a hairdresser in Reims. Claude was sixteen, and I was fifteen, so we were still at school."

"So, when did you decide you wanted to be a priest?"

"Goodness, Adelia, I don't think I've ever talked so much about my family," Father Brune said softly. "But I have to get back to the parish, so I'll save that part of the story for another time."

"I'd like that," Adelia said, smiling up at him as he rose to leave.

***

Adelia continued to see Father Brune, but there was no opportunity for a private conversation. Then, one day, he said, "Adelia, I have a day off next week; maybe you'd like to join me for another coffee?"

"That would be lovely. I have to go to the Ninth Arrondissement to see if my father's barometer will be fixed when my parents return from America. Maybe we could meet at the café at number two, Rue des Martyrs, and you can tell me the next part of your story."

He laughed.

"Very well, number two, Rue des Martyrs it is. Shall we say ten o'clock?"

"Perfect."

***

Since Father Brune had invited her to join him for coffee, Adelia had been thinking about him a lot—so much so that she was finding it difficult to sleep. She thought him handsome when she first saw him at Mass, but now, as she got to know him better, her attraction had become very physical.

She could feel the energy flooding her body as she became more animated around him. She wanted to touch him but, of course, could not. The strength of the sexual energy frightened her at the same time as she longed to be closer to him.

What if he touches me? I'd faint! What if he kisses me with those beautiful lips?
She shivered with delight at the thought of it.

Father Brune was taller than Adelia, well built, and fit from taking boys for
sport and riding everywhere on his bicycle. He kept his dark brown, wavey hair
short at the sides and longer on the top, which resulted in the occasional strand
falling onto his forehead. She found it endearing. But it was his voice that got
her heart racing.

His voice, the way it softens when he talks to me. It's so - intimate.

She could hardly wait for the day when they would meet for coffee. And then
she had a sudden, shocking realisation - *I've fallen for him.*

***

When the day finally arrived, just the thought of what to wear to meet Father
Brune threw her into a turmoil of indecision. Finally, she decided that a 'soft and
feminine' look would be most appropriate. She settled on a pale pink sleeveless
shirt and a softly pleated mid-length skirt in a Liberty floral print in pastel
colours. It was still cool in the mornings, so she wore her white mohair cardigan
with pearl buttons down the front and then slipped into her taupe ballerina
flats. She added her Hermès bracelet and a light dab of pink lipstick as a final
touch. Now confident in her choice of clothing, she cycled to the métro and
arrived at number two, Rue des Martyrs, just before ten o'clock, and Father
Brune was waiting for her.

"Adelia, right on time," Father Brune said as he got up to pull out her chair.
"What coffee would you like?"

"A café crème please Father."

After placing the order, Father Brune said, "You mentioned you have to see
if your father's barometer is ready."

"Yes. It stopped working, and my father was upset when my mother removed
it, saying she'd put it into storage. But of course, she hadn't. She's getting it
repaired as a surprise for him when they return from their trip to America.
Gillery is one of the few craftsmen in Paris who can restore mercury barometers.

They need special weights and fine barometer needles; it's all extremely exact. He also gilds old frames and mirrors. It's important to know where you can get such work done."

"I'm impressed by how knowledgeable you are about barometers, Adelia."

Adelia laughed. "It's all part of my mother's training, Father. But enough about barometers; you promised to tell me how you decided to become a priest."

"Did I decide? Well, as I mentioned, my brothers joined the JAC, and I joined the JEC, the Christian Student Youth. I also used to go on holiday camps, which were supervised and run by priests through the French Catholic Youth Association.

"One day, one of the priests asked me if I'd thought of becoming a priest. I was stunned by the question and said, 'No, Father, I have not'. He said I should pray to God and ask him to show me if I had a vocation. He also said he would like to speak to my mother, which he subsequently did. She was over the moon at the idea that one of her sons might become a priest."

"She must have felt so proud that the priest showed interest in you."

"Yes, she was. Of course, if my father had been there, it would never have been an option. I felt special being approached by the priest, an experience I wasn't used to having. So I did pray, although I had no idea how I would know if I was being 'called' to God or what to expect if my prayers were answered. I was then faced with the decision to go to the lycée and eventually join my brothers on the farm or go to the seminary and become a priest. I picked the seminary.

"Of course, I had no concept of what it meant to dedicate my life to the priesthood. I was thinking of it more as an alternative to life on the farm. I've never told anybody that before, Adelia. Not exactly a 'Road to Damascus' story!"

She smiled and said, "Please go on, Father."

"So I went to the seminary at Lille."

"What was it like being in the seminary?"

There was a lengthy pause as Father Brune slumped and his shoulders hunched as he stared at the table.

Finally, his voice hushed, he said, "I think I could learn my pastoral care skills from you, Adelia. You've got me thinking and talking about things I've never allowed myself to examine deeply before, and I've certainly never spoken about them to anyone, even my confessor."

"Was it so awful?"

The look of distress that washed over his face and settled in his eyes broke her heart.

She reached out and put her hand over his. The look he gave her was so full of emotion that she held her breath. They sat gazing at each other until he finally looked down at their hands.

He lifted her hand, turned it over and ran his finger around her palm, sending tiny shivers down her spine, before he gently placed her hand back down on the table.

"Adelia," he said, in that voice she knew he reserved only for her. "Adelia, we cannot do this. I cannot do anything that might put your soul in danger. I would rather die than cause you harm."

"It's too late," she whispered. "I've fallen in love with you, Nicolas. I have to keep seeing you."

She held his gaze, her eyes shining with love, until he said, "My sweet Adelia, I've never felt this way. I can't bear the thought of bringing you harm, but, dear God, I can't bear the thought of not seeing you again. I don't know what to do."

"It *can't* be a sin to love someone," she said.

"But I'm a priest, Adelia. You know what that means. If anyone should find out -"

"We won't let anyone find out. We'll be careful. No one will know, just us."

"All my life, Adelia, I've only known loneliness despite my large family. I've ached for connection and thought that's what I'd find when I finally heard God call my name. I waited and waited, but I did not hear the call."

Adelia leaned forward, her eyes glued to his face.

"I thought it would happen when I was ordained at Reims Cathedral and received the grace of the Holy Spirit. I thought my prayers would finally be answered, and my spiritual nature would be permanently changed, and I would *experience* that change." His voice became a whisper, "But I felt nothing, Adelia."

Adelia felt tight in her chest as she listened to his desperate search for proof of his calling.

***

Looking down, Father Brune paused and took another sip of coffee before he continued. "I studied hard all through the seminary. I wanted to please God Adelia, so I submitted to the strict observance of the rules and the deferential obedience to superiors in a profoundly hierarchical system."

"It sounds terrible. Did you make any friends there?"

"I did, but they were superficial friendships. We were not allowed to touch or hug each other or enter into the room of another seminarian or novice. We were warned of the dangers of sexual attraction and feelings that had to be suppressed. What does that tell you about life in the seminary? The only way sex was discussed was in terms of self-control and sin. That didn't stop some boys from becoming enamoured with each other, of course, but I kept away from them.

"Once I got to the Catholic University of Lille, I loved the academic side of things, my studies in philosophy and theology. I was inspired by the teachings of Glorieux and Cardijn and 'Catholic Action' and the movement to rechristianise French society through the apostolate of the laity. I was successful in my studies and felt less of a failure. I dreamt of becoming part of the missionary role of the church, developing instruction among the working class."

"Oh goodness, how did you end up here with us then?"

"I was given no choice. A different path was chosen for me within the church's hierarchical structure, which felt threatened by the new movement. So the rising desire I'd felt to save souls was crushed. Of course, we were constantly told to heed God's call and to stay faithful to our vocation. One teacher spoke of having a love affair with our Lord. Oh, how I envied him.

"I thought that after I was ordained, I would find companionship amongst other priests, but I've found the priests barely speak to each other. I now see that despite all my study and training, I had no idea what the life of a parish priest would be like, the pastoral demands, the lack of intimacy. I've met a few priests now who've turned to alcohol or gambling to cope. And through it all, the loneliness has been like a hard stone that sits inside me."

"Oh, Nicolas," she whispered.

"And now you, Adelia, have opened my eyes with your gentle questions and revealed the truth of who I am. I am a fraud."

Adelia was devastated by his words.

"Oh Nicolas, no, no, you must not say that. Oh, I can't bear that you would judge yourself so harshly. How could God not love you, not hear your prayers."

Father Brune sat with his head bowed and finally said, "I've never seen myself with such clarity, Adelia. But that's only one part of the revelation." Taking her hand in his, he looked at her distraught face and said, "I love you too, Adelia. I must have done from the moment I first saw you in the church garden."

Adelia would have thrown herself into his arms but for the table between them and the curious eyes of those sitting nearby.

"We have to talk in private," she said. My parents left for Havre yesterday and sailed for New York in the Liberte today, so I have the house to myself for the next ten weeks, apart from the servants. Promise me you'll come tonight so we can decide what we should do together. Come at eight-thirty, and I'll let you in the front door."

"Adelia, are you sure?"

"Yes, yes," she said, "I'm sure."

CHAPTER FOUR

By the time Adelia got home, she'd worked herself into a panic. *Suppose he changes his mind and doesn't come? Oh, I couldn't bear it.*

To calm her nerves, she focused on the preparations. She asked Lili to light the fire in the study at five o'clock and make sure there was plenty of wood for the evening.

"I'll have an early supper by the fire in the study; thank you, Lili. I won't need you after that."

"Very well, mademoiselle."

But when Adelia's supper tray arrived, her anxiety had returned, and she barely touched her meal. Jumping up from the sofa, she busied herself, adding another two logs to the fire. Then, as soon as Lili had been to remove the tray and they'd said goodnight, she turned off the brighter light, leaving on the two table lamps that gave a soft glow to the room. As long as Adelia could remember, her father had his hyacinth bulbs blooming once a year in his study, and now the heady perfume of allspice, wood and vanilla filled the room.

As it approached eight thirty, Adelia lit the candles on top of the three different-sized wooden candle holders on the mantlepiece above the fireplace as a final touch.

There, she thought, stepping back to admire the romantic atmosphere that she'd created; *it could be a scene in one of Brigitte's movies.* Now, her anxiety was replaced with excitement at the thought of seeing him again.

Just before eight-thirty, she ran down the hall and swung open the front door, and there was Father Brune cycling towards the apartment.

***

She waited until he was inside the door and stepped straight into his arms.

"Adelia," he said as his arms circled her, drawing her into him. She tightened the grip of her arms around him, pressing her cheek against his chest.

"I was frightened you wouldn't come," she whispered.

"You've changed my life, Adelia, my love. How could I not see you tonight?" he said. Then he kissed her. She melted into him, savouring the longed-for, the forbidden.

His lips are so soft.

His second kiss was more intense, and her lips parted. She felt the touch of his tongue against hers, sending an electric current surging through her body.

Adelia drew apart and grabbed his hand as they walked to the study, where she pulled him down beside her on the sofa in front of the open fire.

"What shall we do?" Adelia asked, her face close to his as she gripped his hand.

"I will speak to Father Allard."

"When?"

"Tomorrow."

***

The thought of what Father Allard might say when Nicolas told him that he didn't want to be a priest anymore made her sick with worry.

"Oh, Nicolas, I'm so scared for you."

"Don't be my love; it will all work out," Father Brune replied as he kissed her on the forehead, then again on her lips as his hand slowly slid down to her breast.

Caught between her fear and desire, Adelia froze and wasn't sure how to respond.

"Adelia," he said, "are you sure you want this?"

"Oh yes, yes, but - "

"What is it?"

She pulled him closer to her and said, "It's my first time, and I wasn't sure what to do next."

"It's my first time, too," he said, "and I'm just as nervous as you!"

They laughed together with relief.

"Come," he said as he got up and threw another log on the fire and then grabbed a cushion and put it down in front of the fireplace. "Lie down here, Adelia."

Adelia did as she was told.

Hearing the gentle sound of the logs crackling and seeing him gazing down at her in the soft glow of the lamps and flickering candlelight, she felt her body relax.

She remembered a scene from one of Brigitte's films, and she started to undo the buttons of her blouse. He knelt between her legs to help her and then slid one side of her bra strap off her shoulder and pulled down her bra, releasing her breast.

"You're beautiful, so beautiful," he murmured.

He bent to kiss her again before moving down to kiss her breast. His lips found her raised nipple, and he ran his tongue over its hardened mound. She closed her eyes as she felt her back arch and press towards him as the physical charge shot down from her nipple to that secret place between her legs.

Eyes still closed, she felt him remove her shoes and fold up her skirt. She raised her body so he could pull off her panties, and then she opened her eyes.

So he does wear boxer shorts! Oh my lord, it's so big. She stared and inhaled sharply.

"Adelia, are you sure?"

"Yes, yes."

Oh, mon dieu, he can't get it in!

She helped him and then clung to him, her body rising to meet his with each deepening thrust until a searing pain rocked her body, forcing her to cry out with shock before biting down on her lip.

He paused -

"Don't stop, don't stop," she said, clamping her teeth together to prevent herself from crying out again.

He continued to thrust a few more times, then gasped, shuddered, and suddenly it was all over. As he withdrew, he looked shocked.

"Adelia, you're bleeding."

"Don't worry," Adelia replied, "I was told it could happen the first time."

Getting up, she grabbed her panties and shoes and said, "I'm just going to the bathroom."

***

In the bathroom, she peered in the mirror, trying to see if she looked any different now that she was a woman. *Will my friends know when they see me?*

She ran her fingers over her lips, remembering how soft his lips were when he first kissed her and then how aroused she'd become. It was all going so well until - *Damn, the pain of the first time. Thank God that part's over now. Next time, it'll be so much better. I'll be like Brigitte. He's mine now.*

When she returned, he was dressed and standing by the fireplace.

"Adelia, are you alright?"

She smiled, reached up and kissed him and said, "I wanted you."

Taking her hand, he said, "I will speak to Father Allard first thing tomorrow. I entered the priesthood for all the wrong reasons, and I'm not worthy to be a priest. I have sinned against God and the Church. You are *not* to be involved, Adelia."

"What will happen next?"

"I don't know. I'll let you know what Father Allard says I must do."

"I'll be waiting. Telephone me, or I can come and meet you."

"Yes, I'd better get back now. I love you, Adelia."

As she watched him cycle away, a dread swept over her.

Dear God, please forgive us for our sins tonight. Holy Mary, Mother of God, please help us, she prayed silently.

Once back at the rectory, Father Brune quietly opened the front door and carefully closed it on the inside. He turned, and there, sitting on a chair in the hallway, was Father Allard.

***

The next day, Adelia waited and waited to hear from Nicolas, but by late afternoon, she had heard nothing. It was too late to go to the Church, and she dared not go to the presbytery.

Maybe he'll telephone me tonight.

But he did not.

She spent a sleepless night and waited impatiently for when she could go to Sunday morning mass.

Once at the Church, she sat waiting for him to come out next to Father Allard. But he didn't.

Then, Father Allard said that he had an announcement to make. He informed the congregation that Father Brune had been called to another parish to stand in for an elderly priest who had suffered a heart attack.

"It's unlikely Father Brune will be returning," he said. "We shall all miss him."

Adelia felt sick and had to lean forward and grip the pew in front whilst she took deep breaths to prevent herself from fainting.

"Are you alright, my dear?" an elderly lady asked.

"Yes, thank you," Adelia managed to reply.

She left the Church in a distraught daze and barely got herself home.

The 'not knowing' ate her up inside as the questions circled in her head.

What did Father Allard say to Nicolas? Where have they sent him? When will I see him again?

But most of all, she was desperate to know why he hadn't contacted her. *Is he alright? What have they done to him?*

And then -

I've committed a terrible sin, and this is my punishment.

As the days stretched into a week and then another, her despair drained the life out of her. She knew she should repent and confess but could not since that would implicate her Nicolas. So, she suffered the guilt and agony in silence.

***

Adelia could not imagine her life getting any worse, but the nightmare had only just begun. She missed her period, but in her torment, she hadn't noticed. Then came the bleeding and then the cramps.

I'm dying.

There was only one person she could turn to, her elder sister Vivienne. She barely made it to her sister's apartment.

Vivienne looked at Adelia and said, "Mon Dieu, Adelia, what's wrong?"

As soon as Adelia described what was happening to her, Vivienne said, "That's exactly what happened to Simone last month when she miscarried."

The two sisters stood staring at each other in shocked silence.

"*No*, Adelia, you can't be...*can* you?"

Adelia stood twisting her hands together, her huge eyes full of terror. "We were only together once, Vivienne," she whispered.

"Oh, Adelia, darling, how could you be so naïve? So, I'm at a loss for words. I didn't even know you were seeing someone. Who *is* he?"

Adelia turned deathly white, clutched her stomach, and sank to the floor with a soft thud as the cramps gripped her body.

Twenty minutes later, the family doctor arrived, and soon after, she miscarried.

***

Adelia refused to tell her sister the name of her lover and swore her to secrecy about the miscarriage. It was a blessing that their parents were still away and would not be back for another six weeks.

"I just don't understand Adelia. Why on earth won't you tell the father? Surely, he would want to know?"

"I can't discuss it, Vivienne. It's too complicated."

"This doesn't make sense. Unless...is he *married* Adelia, is that what it is?"

"Vivienne, please stop. I can't talk about it."

"But look at you, Adelia, you're thin as a rake, you don't eat, you won't leave the house."

"Because I can't bear to see pregnant women or mothers and babies, Vivienne. It's too painful, the loss is too painful, and I feel so guilty. I killed my baby," and Adelia's frail body shook with her sobs.

"Oh darling, don't be so foolish. These things happen; look at Simone. Don't blame yourself like that, Adelia. Is there *anything* I can do? How can I help?"

"Nothing, there's nothing you can do."

"Maybe if you saw a priest?"

"No, absolutely *not*. I don't need a priest, Vivienne."

When her parents returned home, they looked shocked when they saw how frail she'd become.

"Adelia, you look so ill; what *is* the matter?" her mother said. "Your father and I are so worried about you."

"No, I'm not ill Maman. I had a terrible cold and cough whilst you were away, and it's just taking a while for me to recover," she lied.

Adelia made a supreme effort to pull herself together through fear that her parents would continue to ask questions and, worse yet, call in the family doctor. She forced herself to eat and contacted Olivia to say she'd returned from her visit with her sister. Stepping back into her social set, she was seen at all the fashionable spots in Paris, went to the theatre and cinema, gossiped with all her friends, and holidayed in the South of France. She put on the performance of her life, always praying, hoping he would contact her.

***

One year later, when Adelia was in Monaco on holiday with her friends, Olivia said, "There's someone I want you to meet, Adelia. He's English and incredibly wealthy, and I think you will like him. His name is Alan Manning."

Reluctantly, Adelia agreed to be introduced, and it wasn't Alan's wealth or his yacht that impressed her; it was his gentleness and warmth that touched the tips of her splintered heart.

Alan was slightly shorter than Adelia when she was in heels, and he had a solid build. She wasn't surprised to learn later that he had been one of Eton's top rugby players. He was an excellent host, genuinely interested in his guests, and she could see why he was such a successful businessman. He made her feel special and safe.

Over the next two weeks, Alan invited Adelia and her friends to his yacht, took her to lunch and dinner and barely left her side. Olivia took Adelia aside and said, "Mon dieu, Adelia, this man is crazy about you. Everybody thinks so. The way he looks at you, it's so touching. And when it comes to picking your maid of honour, remember that I'm the one that introduced you, your very best friend."

"Oh, good grief, no pressure!" Adelia said, laughing at Olivia. "But I do like him."

The following week, Alan flew to Paris to see her father. Having received his blessing, he returned to Monaco with the ring and proposed. Adelia accepted.

Ten months later, they were married in great splendour, and Adelia and her 'Alain' moved into his Mayfair townhouse. Two months later, Adelia fell pregnant.

When she called and told them the news, her parents sounded ecstatic. "Do come and visit," Adelia begged. I miss you both so much."

"We miss you too, darling. Of course, we'll come. We'll get the Night Ferry tomorrow evening."

"Wonderful, we'll be at Victoria Station to meet you."

Then tragedy struck. On the way to the Gare du Nord railway station, Adelia's parents were involved in a head-on crash with a truck that took a turn too fast. They both died at the scene of the accident.

***

After the funeral in Paris, Adelia said, "Please, Alain, please, can we move to the Paris apartment? I need to be near my sister and friends right now."

"Whatever you want, darling," Alan said, looking anxiously at Adelia. Anything to protect you and the baby. It makes no difference to me anyway, with half my clients in Europe. I can run the business just as easily from Paris."

***

Adelia carried the baby to full-term but had severe complications during the delivery.

When Vivienne went to visit Adelia in the hospital, Adelia told her, "I can't have any more children."

"Oh darling, I'm so sorry."

"No, no, you don't understand Vivienne. I'm so relieved. I was terrified all through the pregnancy that God would punish me, and I'd lose my baby, or it would be born with a terrible deformity. I can't believe how perfect she is. But I couldn't bear to go through that again."

"Oh, Adelia, why didn't you tell me? My poor darling."

"And now Tiana is my gift to Alain for saving me. She will love and adore him unconditionally as he deserves to be loved."

"He's already absolutely besotted with her," Vivienne laughed. "But darling, surely you love Alain?"

"I do. Of *course* I do. It's just..."

"Not the same?"

"Yes," whispered Adelia.

"Adelia, you have a devoted husband and a beautiful baby daughter; you must stop comparing and living in the past."

Adelia's eyes filled with tears. "I know, I know. I try, I do."

But hard as she tried, one question remained in her mind: *Why didn't Nicolas contact me after speaking to Father Allard?* Not knowing the answer to that question nearly destroyed her.

CHAPTER FIVE

"So, we've agreed, Tiana, we'll approach your mother as a united front,' Alan said, "and put forward our Florida proposal."

"Yes, Papa, fingers crossed."

"I think we should plan to go at the end of March next year, just as soon as you break up for the holiday. We must be mindful of your exams this June and December, Tiana. After that, over the next couple of years, I'll familiarise you with the distribution and sales side of things. But the focus has to be on your studies for your A Levels."

"I know Papa and March sounds perfect. Should we speak to maman this evening after dinner?"

Her father cleared his throat and said, "Yes, that's as good a time as any."

Tiana couldn't help laughing at her father. "Papa, you sound almost as nervous as me!"

**

After dinner, Alan said, "Adelia darling, Tiana and I have something we'd like to discuss with you."

He then told her about Tiana's interest in becoming involved in the cigar distribution side of their business and his idea about taking her to meet the Arguello family in Florida.

"It would be a wonderful way to immerse Tiana in the passion that creates the perfect handmade cigar, and it's never too early to start building a business relationship."

There was a brief silence, and then, with a big smile, Adelia said, "Well, I think that's a fabulous idea!"

Tiana stared at her mother, a look of disbelief on her face.

"You do?" Alan said in surprise.

"Bien sûr Alain. I would love to come too. We could pick you up straight from school, Tiana, and fly out from Heathrow. And then, if there's time afterwards, we could fly to New York and shop."

"That's a wonderful idea, darling; we'd love to have you join us," Alan said, looking delighted. "And we can definitely squeeze in a few shopping days for my two favourite women. I'll speak to Juan and then book our flights."

'Brilliant,' Tiana said, beaming.

***

When she returned to school after the holiday, Tiana couldn't wait to tell Veronica that her father had agreed to teach her about cigars and the distribution side of the business. "And when I'm eighteen, I can start smoking, so then we can learn together."

"Wow, Tiana, I can't believe you pulled it off."

"I have to learn all about the business first, and, you won't believe it, we're flying to Tampa in Florida to meet the Arguello family and see how handmade cigars are made in their factory. Papa loves their cigars and wants to add their brand to the ones we sell on our cruise line and in our resorts."

"That's amazing. When are you going?"

"During the holidays, March next year."

"What does your mother think about it all?"

"Well, that's the weirdest thing, she's all for it, and she's even coming with us to Florida. We couldn't believe it when she agreed to the whole idea."

"Gosh, that is a surprise."

"One thing, though, we're not allowed to start smoking until after we've left school."

"Well, I couldn't see your papa or mine letting us smoke before then anyway. And also, what would - "

"Yes, I know; what would Sister Agnes say?" They both burst out laughing.

"So, did anything else exciting happen on your holiday?"

"Yes, I fell in love," Tiana said with a grin.

"You're kidding."

"Nope, I met the most gorgeous man you've ever seen; talk about dishy."

"God, you're having all the luck. Where? In Greece?"

"No, at maman's 'Monday Afternoon Tea'."

"What? I thought her guests were always boring old priests."

"Well, he's older, but not old, and he is a priest," Tiana said.

"Tiana, that's positively wicked."

"I only met him once, but if he wasn't a priest, he could be a Hollywood movie star."

"Well, I hope you're joking about the 'in love' bit because that's a dead-end street."

"Of course, I'm joking," Tiana replied quickly. "But he is handsome."

"Ha," Veronica said.

Despite passing off what she had said as a joke, Tiana was shocked by Veronica's comment about a 'dead-end street'.

She's right, of course. What am I thinking? What am I doing falling in love with a priest?

The reality of the situation hit her.

What would everybody think? What would papa think?

She remembered how she'd lied to him and imagined the look of shock and disappointment on his face when he knew the truth.

My God, I can't bear to think about it.

And maman, she would never understand, and she would be so angry with me. She shivered at the thought of facing her mother.

And Father Gagnon, he probably doesn't even remember meeting me, and I made a complete fool of myself on top of it. I've just got to keep busy and stop thinking about him.

Tiana threw herself into her schoolwork with a vengeance, pushing all thoughts of Father Philippe Gagnon to the back of her mind.

In no time, the school term had flown by, followed by the Christmas holidays, which were always a busy family affair.

***

Back at school in the New Year, Tiana studied hard. She genuinely enjoyed schoolwork and school life. She and Veronica were 'A' students and the top two students in their class. But as the end of term approached, Tiana began counting down the days until she and her parents would fly out to Florida.

Finally, the day arrived. Her parents came and picked her up, and they headed off to the airport. It was then that her father told her that the trip nearly didn't happen.

"I was sad to learn last month that Carlos, Juan's father, died at the age of seventy-two," Alan said. "Carlos founded the Arguello Company in 1924, Tiana. He was a Spanish immigrant, only twenty-three years old. He ran it until he retired at sixty-eight, and that's when Juan took control of operations.

"Of course, I rang Juan and said we would postpone our trip until another time, but he insisted that we still come to Florida. He wants to discuss the new cigar they're creating in memory of Carlos. Everyone is very excited because it's to be created with his father's special blend. It will probably take a couple of years till its release, so we have until 1975 to get ready for the launch. Juan and I agree that it will be the perfect cigar to introduce the Arguello brand to our European customers and overseas visitors."

"That's so exciting, Papa. But sorry to hear about his father."

"It is exciting, Tiana because you have the opportunity to see the creation of a new handmade cigar right through to its introduction to the market."

***

The visit to Florida was a huge success. Tiana's enthusiasm and willingness to muck in and help wherever needed impressed everyone. The fact that she spoke Spanish further endeared her to them all.

Isabella Arguello taught Tiana the correct way to cut and light a cigar. Tiana had seen her father cutting and lighting his cigars hundreds of times, but it looked different to see a woman light up. She also taught Tiana how to judge the quality of a cigar. "You must use your eyes, fingers, and nose," she said.

But the absolute highlight of the trip came entirely out of the blue.

"Alan," Juan said, "I have a most unusual request to put to you."

"Fire away."

"We're about to launch a new cigar, and we'd love to have your beautiful wife in the advertisement."

Alan looked stunned.

"Well, Juan, you've taken me by surprise. But goodness me, I think Adelia would be thrilled with the idea. Have you asked her?"

"We thought we should run the idea past you first, Alan."

"Well, if Adelia is happy to do it, so am I."

Adelia was flattered to be asked to be in the advertisement and threw herself into the project.

"Tiana, you must help me decide what dress and jewellery to wear," she said, smiling. "How fortunate that we decided to go on to New York, so I've brought evening gowns with me."

"Holy cow," Tiana said. "This is *so* exciting!"

"I was thinking my green Dior chiffon would be perfect. What do *you* think, Tiana?"

"Absolutely, off-the-shoulder dresses are so sophisticated. Then you could wear the emerald and diamond necklace papa gave you as a wedding present, together with the matching earrings."

"In that case, I think I'll put my hair up; now it's a little longer," Adelia said, expertly pinning her hair into a loose French chignon, leaving tiny whisps of hair trailing her neck.

"How do I look, Tiana?"

"Oh, Maman, it's perfect, you look beautiful. Papa is going to die when he sees you."

The setting for the photographic shoot was the Siboney Room in the famous Columbia Restaurant, where Spanish dancers and musicians entertained the guests. The male model was the one smoking the cigar, and Adelia was his partner.

Juan and Isabella thought Adelia and the model looked fabulous together. "Your wife has the beauty and sophistication that only French women possess," Juan told Alan with a broad smile.

"Thank you, Juan," Alan said, beaming with pride.

That evening, they had a magnificent meal in the restaurant and then danced the night away. "This has been one of the best nights of my life," Tiana told her parents. "You both look so happy."

Alan was equally enthusiastic. "This could not have been more perfect," he told Adelia. "The foundations have now been laid for Tiana to step into my shoes one day."

"Decades away mon chéri, Adelia said."

***

Back at school, Tiana told Veronica about her trip and her mother's starring role in the advertisement to launch a new cigar on the market.

"Oh My God, Tiana, that's amazing."

"I know. She looked so glamorous, Vron. And you should have seen papa's expression when he was watching her during the shoot. It gave me goose-bumps."

"So romantic," Veronica sighed.

"Oh, and by the way, papa is still adamant that we can't start to smoke until we're eighteen. He says we must slowly develop our palate by trying different mild cigars until we've developed a taste for a particular brand."

"What would be far out is if we could smoke a cigar at our graduation party," Veronica said.

"Well, I'll tell papa that we would like to have that as a goal and see what he says," Tiana replied. "Talk about the shock factor. We might even get into the newspapers. That might be good for business—the publicity!"

"Ever the devious one," laughed Veronica.

***

The following two and a half years of school flew by for Tiana. School life was packed with study, exams, sports, field trips, student volunteering and educational tours. The tours gave students first-hand experience of how their knowledge was linked to the real world. It was precisely what her father had hoped for when he chose Marymount for his daughter's education.

Tiana only thought about Father Gagnon when she was home on holiday and wondered if he might be the guest at 'Monday Afternoon Tea'. But he never was.

Maybe this time, she thought, when she returned home for the last holiday before her final graduation term at Marymount.

***

"...and now he's gone to Rome to become a Bishop no less," Maria said.

"That doesn't surprise me," André said.

"Who has gone to Rome to become a Bishop?" Tiana asked, walking into the kitchen.

"Mademoiselle Tiana, I didn't hear you come in," André said, jumping to his feet.

"Sit down, André, please. I just came down to see if there's any raisin toast on offer."

"Of course, Mademoiselle. Take a seat, and I'll put the kettle on," Maria said with a warm smile.

"So, you were saying?"

"You remember meeting Father Philippe Gagnon once, Mademoiselle?" André said.

"I think so," Tiana said, trying desperately to appear calm at suddenly hearing his name.

"Well, Maria was just telling me that he's gone to Rome. He's to become a Bishop, and I said I wasn't surprised."

Tiana saw him in her mind's eye, resplendent in a black cassock with a purple sash and a shock wave ran through her body. She sat down abruptly on the kitchen bench.

"Well," she said, "well, that's, that's great. Where did you hear about it, Maria?"

"I overheard two nuns discussing his departure, Mademoiselle. He is so handsome and charming. I think all the nuns in the parish are secretly in love with him."

An intense longing overwhelmed Tiana, followed by pure hatred towards the nuns.

Maria set the pot of tea and hot, buttered raisin toast on the table in front of Tiana, who then took her time filling her cup, sipping the tea, and slowly eating both slices of toast, hoping to calm her nerves. She prayed that Maria and André hadn't noticed her trembling fingers. She smiled and nodded as they continued their conversation, but she could not have told you later what they talked about.

Breathe, keep it light.

Rising from the table, she said, "Thank you, Maria, that was great. I can hardly believe it's my last school holiday, and next term, I graduate."

"Time flies so fast, Mademoiselle. It seems like only yesterday when you would rush down to the kitchen for tea and toast after you met with Madame's weekly guests."

They all laughed, and Tiana left them both, praying that she'd given no indication that she had just been hit by a bombshell, resulting in an insane bout of jealousy.

I'd done it, you were out of my mind, and now it's ruined. You're back in and in Rome, and I'm stuck with you again. Damn, you and your besotted nuns. Damn you to hell.

***

Tiana threw herself into her revision and preparation for the vital upcoming examinations with a single-minded intensity.

This drew a comment from Sister Agnes, who said, "Tiana, my dear, please take some time off to relax. You look so pale and drawn and seem to be losing weight. If you keep this up, you will be too sick and exhausted to sit your final examinations."

That's what love sickness does to you, Tiana thought bitterly.

Even Veronica looked worried when she said, "Come on, Tiana, lighten up; you're making me look bad by comparison. We all know you're going to score top marks, but at this rate, you'll kill yourself in the process."

"I have to make sure my marks are good enough to give me the choice of any college or university I want, Vron," Tiana said, knowing full well that this was only half the truth. But she didn't dare confide in Veronica after she received such an abrupt response to her first confession about falling for a priest.

"Okay. Well, will you at least talk about our graduation party?" Veronica said.

"Yes, of course, Vron. Sorry. Everything's organised so far as the Ritz goes; maman's checked already. Just about everybody has replied to the invitations. Now all we have to do is get our dresses," Tiana said. "It's a shame papa didn't go for us smoking a cigar at the party. But, once we've officially graduated, we can start developing our respective palates."

"Can't wait, and we should still aim for a photo in Tatler."

***

During the mid-term break, the two mothers took Tiana and Veronica shopping for their dresses, and Tiana was caught up enough in the excitement of it all to forget about 'The Bishop' as she now thought of him. Adelia and Suzanne, Veronica's mother, double-checked that everything was organised to perfection for their daughters' big celebration. Both women were determined that it would be the party of the year and their daughters would have a wonderful time.

Alan had said, "Spare no expense. I want this to be a special occasion that Tiana will never forget. I want her to know how proud we are of her."

Nobody was surprised when Tiana got the highest ranking in her graduation class, with Victoria a close second. "I'm so proud to be chosen to give the Valedictory Address Vron, but so nervous," Tiana confessed.

"Rubbish," Veronica said. "I've heard you rehearse it enough times, and it's great. Your parents are going to be bursting with pride."

***

On Graduation Day, Tiana and Veronica were in the St Croix Boarding House running through the schedule leading up to the ceremony when Sister Agnes entered the room.

"Tiana, would you come with me, please? The Headmistress wants to see you."

"Goodness, what have I done now?"

"Nothing Tiana. You haven't done anything wrong."

"Then why does she want to see me?"

The expression on Sister Agnes's face puzzled Tiana. She couldn't quite put her finger on it.

"Just follow me," Sister Agnes said.

"Stay here, Vron," Tiana said. "I won't be long."

***

Sister Agnes was walking so briskly that Tiana had to jog to keep up.

Goodness, she's in a bit of a rush to get there. She's very odd today.

When they arrived at the door to the Mother Superior's office, Sister Agnes gave a soft knock, and they heard Sister Bernadette say, "Enter."

As they walked in, Sister Bernadette got up from behind her desk and came around to meet Tiana.

Once again, Tiana was taken by surprise.

That's so weird; she's never done that before. What gives?

CHAPTER SIX

S tanding in the Mother Superior's office, Tiana's heart was beating faster, and a flutter of anxiety swept through her as she stared at Sister Bernadette, fearful of what was coming next.

"Please sit down, Tiana," Sister Bernadette said, pulling up a chair opposite her.

Weirder and weirder, what on earth is going on? Tiana's chest tightened.

Looking straight at her, Sister Bernadette said, "Tiana, I am so sorry to have to tell you that your father had a massive heart attack three hours ago, and, my dear, he did not survive. He died at the hospital."

Tiana couldn't drag her eyes away from Sister Bernadette's face. She stared at her in dead silence.

What is she talking about?

Finally, she said, "Oh no, that can't be true. Papa and maman are coming to the graduation ceremony."

"I'm so sorry, dear, but it is true. Your father died shortly after he arrived at the hospital. Your mother phoned me, and arrangements have been made to fly you back to Paris. Everything has been arranged."

Tiana's green eyes grew huge with fear, and her hand flew to her mouth, but no sound came out.

"Sister Agnes, please get a cup of tea for Tiana whilst we wait for the taxi to come to take us to the airport. I will accompany you, Tiana, to ensure you get on the plane safely."

***

Tiana was in shock and did not remember getting to the airport, boarding the small private jet, and flying to Paris.

She could not accept what Sister Bernadette had told her.

I have to go to papa's study. I know he will be there sitting in his leather chair. This is a terrible, terrible mistake.

Sister Bernadette had told Tiana that André, their chauffeur, would be at the airport to meet her.

When she walked through to the main terminal of the Paris Orly Airport, she stood there in a daze, looking around but seeing a blur. Everything was happening in a slow-motion haze.

Suddenly, there he was, striding towards her, The Most Reverend Philippe Gagnon. She stared in disbelief, seeing him there only adding to her sense of unreality. "Your Excellency, what are you doing here?" she stammered.

"I'm here to meet you, Tiana, and take you home," he said

"But what are you doing *here* in Paris?"

"Oh, I see, I'm here on Compassionate Leave. Come, Tiana, let's get you to the car." She felt his hand circle her elbow as he guided her through the crowded airport to the waiting car.

Tiana had the sensation of landing in a parallel universe where nothing was as it should be.

Looking distraught, André opened the car door and said, "Mademoiselle Tiana, on behalf of myself, Maria, and all the staff, may I offer you our deepest condolences?"

"Oh, André," she said, "it can't be true," and she burst into tears.

André looked helplessly at His Excellency, who quickly walked around to the other side of the car and got in next to Tiana. He handed her a white cotton handkerchief, and André started the car and drove into the traffic.

"Tiana, this has been a terrible shock for you and your mother. It is a tragic loss for you both to lose your papa like this."

"Oh My God, maman." She looked at His Excellency in utter dismay. "I haven't given her a thought," she whispered. "Not since Sister Bernadette told me what happened to papa."

"That's because you've been in shock, Tiana. It's completely understandable."

"I have to go to papa's study. I have to see for myself."

"Of course, whatever you need, Tiana."

"What will I do? What will I do without him?" she said, looking imploringly at His Excellency.

"Right now, Tiana, there is only one way to get through this, and that's one step at a time. First, you get through today and then tonight. Don't think beyond that. And then tomorrow, you do the same. And you keep doing it, day by day, Tiana, and gradually it becomes easier, and you come to accept the new reality."

She just stared at him, trying to take in what he was saying to her.

"But I *need* him."

"I know. But Tiana, you have courage, and you will find the strength you need to grow through this. Pray with your mother, and you will be in my prayers every day."

"Oh, poor maman, it's just not fair. He's too young to die, and now she's all alone."

"It's a mystery why good men like your papa die so young, Tiana. But for eighteen years, he was a gift to you."

She looked at him, so lost and forlorn. In the desolate days ahead, she would remember all his words and be filled with gratitude for the time that she had with her beloved papa—but not now. Right now, she was acutely aware of Bishop

Gagnon's physical presence, sitting so close to her, and the sound of his calm, soft voice, which made it possible for her to hold herself together barely.

André caught the eye of His Excellency in the rear-view mirror and gave him a tiny nod of gratitude.

The minute they got home, Tiana ran straight to her father's study. She threw open the door. *Let him be there, please let him be there,* she prayed.

Someone had lit the fire, and every fibre of her being longed to see her father sitting in his chair, smoking his cigar and turning to welcome her home.

But he wasn't there.

A sob rose in her throat. She was cold and so utterly alone.

She walked over to his empty chair and curled into it, smelling his cigar in the leather. Pushing her face into it, she wept.

***

She had briefly fallen asleep and awoke with a jolt. It was starting to get dark, and the fire had burnt down. Entirely disorientated, for a brief moment, she was in that blissful space between awakening and remembering, where everything was as it was before. She called out, "Papa, Papa".

And then she remembered, and the desolation washed over her.

Now cold and stiff, she got up, threw a couple of smaller logs on the embers to get the fire going again, and turned on two of the table lamps.

There was a gentle knock on the door. "Come in," she said.

She looked over, hoping to see His Excellency.

The door opened, and there stood Nanny B. Tiana rushed over, throwing herself into Nanny B's arms. Nanny B held her, stroking her hair, murmuring little endearments.

Eventually, they moved to sit together on the sofa and just sat watching the flames grow as the new logs caught alight. "How did you know to come?" Tiana asked.

"It was His Excellency; he telephoned me with the tragic news and then sent André to pick me up from the airport."

"Oh, he knew, he knew I would need you."

"He did, and now Maria is sending up a tray, and you must eat Tiana to keep up your strength. And then we will go to your mother, she's waiting to see you. Your Aunt Vivienne has been with her all afternoon, and the doctor has given her a sedative to help her sleep after you've talked."

"Oh, poor maman. I must be there for her now. Nanny B, I'm so grateful you're here. Can you stay?"

"Of course, Chiquita, as long as you need me."

"If it wasn't for you and His Excellency, I don't know what I would have done. I miss him so Nanny B. This is the worst day of my life. Nothing will ever be the same again."

Nanny B's eyes filled with tears.

"And Nanny B, do you know what the worst part is? I didn't even get the chance to tell him how much I loved him. And now..."

***

Tiana sat on the sofa, shoulders hunched, staring at the table before her but seeing nothing. And then she saw it. A box-shaped object came into focus. It was gift-wrapped and tied with a cream satin bow. Propped up against it was a cream envelope, and on it was written 'Tiana' in her father's handwriting.

Her hand shook as she reached out to pick up the envelope. She looked at Nanny B, who nodded in encouragement. She opened the envelope and took out the card. It was a 'Congratulations' card upon her Graduation. It read ...

Tiana, My Darling,
Words cannot express how immensely proud your mother and I are
of your outstanding achievement of being named Valedictorian
of the London Marymount International School, 1975 Graduating Class.
I have loved you, my darling, since the first moment I held you in my arms,
and it has been the joy of my life watching you grow over the last eighteen years
into the loving, beautiful, intelligent young woman you have become.
The world is your oyster now, Tiana, full of exciting possibilities.

My greatest wish for you is that you find your passion and pursue your dreams.
Whatever you decide to do, you have my full support and my love, always.

Papa

P.S. One word of advice: warn your escorts before you light up!

Tiana pressed the card to her chest as warm tears slid down her cheeks. She sat silently for several minutes before handing the card to Nanny B to read.

"It's beautiful Chiquita. Such a loving father; you have been truly blessed."

"I can hear papa's voice saying those beautiful things. It's like he's come back to me," Tiana said, smiling weakly.

Nanny B smiled, too, and handed Tiana the gift to open.

Tiana quickly removed the ribbon and wrapping paper, feeling a sudden surge of excitement. Inside was a russet-coloured box. Engraved in gold on the top of the box was the inscription S.T. Dupont. She opened the box and, sitting inside, nestled in the cream satin, sat an exquisite, solid gold lighter. It had a delicate weave pattern, and down one side, her name 'Tiana' was spelt out with tiny diamonds.

"It's so beautiful," Tiana said, taking it out and holding it gently in her hand. "Each time I light up a cigar, papa will be there with me."

Just then, there was a knock at the door, and Dominique wheeled in the supper trolley. Tiana was surprised to find that she was famished. Her papa's card and gift had enabled her to feel his presence again, and her deep sense of loss had lifted, if only for a brief moment.

***

Adelia and Vivienne sat together on the sofa in the drawing room. Taking Adelia's hand in hers, Vivienne said, "I can't begin to imagine what this has been like for you, darling, losing Alain like this so suddenly."

"Oh, Vivienne, I was terrified," Adelia said. "I heard him crying out for me, and I ran to the study. He was so pale, and he was walking up and down, up and down, clutching his left arm. He said, 'Call an ambulance, Adelia.'

"He said he had terrible pain in his chest and was having trouble breathing. And then, he just collapsed onto the floor. I rang for the ambulance and, Oh Vivienne, I was so scared for him. I was on the floor holding his hand, and I kept telling him how much I loved him and that the ambulance would be here very soon.

"By the time it got there ten minutes later, Alain was unconscious. Then we were in the ambulance, driving like mad to the hospital.

"I wouldn't let go of his hand, Vivienne and just kept telling him I loved him, and we would be at the hospital soon. I was praying he could hear me. A priest was there waiting for us when we arrived, right there at the entrance. A doctor said, 'he's gone into Cardiac Arrest.' Then the priest performed the Last Rites, and then he was gone; Alain was gone. They had to pull my hand out of his because I wouldn't let go. Oh, Vivienne, my poor Alain." Adelia started to sob.

"Oh, my darling," Vivienne said, now in tears herself.

Adelia finally stopped crying and said, "I had to call Tiana's Headmistress. Just before it all happened, we were about to leave for the airport to attend Tiana's Graduation. Mon dieu, can you imagine Vivienne getting such news on your Graduation Day? I asked the Mother Superior what would be best for Tiana, and she said being told face-to-face that her papa had died would be less traumatic than being told over the telephone."

"Mon dieu!" Vivienne whispered.

"I booked a private jet to fly Tiana to Paris. Then I rang home to tell the staff the terrible news. I told André when to go and pick up Tiana from the airport. After that, there were so many telephone calls and arrangements to be made, and then I called you."

"How could this have happened, Adelia?"

"I still don't know. There was no warning, no way of knowing."

"Thank God a priest was there to give the Last Rites."

"Well, that was thanks to His Excellency Bishop Gagnon."

"Bishop Gagnon?" Vivienne said in surprise

"Yes, apparently, he arrived at the house shortly after we left in the ambulance and found everyone in total shock. They told him what had happened and, realising how critical the situation was, he immediately rang the hospital. He spoke to the priest there and asked him to meet the ambulance and be ready to administer the Last Rites."

"Oh, my lord."

"And then he said he would stay there until they had news about Alain. I'm so grateful he did because everyone was devastated when I rang to say Alain had died. He then offered to accompany André when he went to pick up Tiana. André told me later that he didn't know how he would have coped had His Excellency not been there to support Tiana, who was in a terrible state of shock."

"Oh, Adelia, what would you have done without him being here?"

"And that's not all. Then he organised for Nanny B to be brought here for Tiana."

"He did that. So thoughtful, that poor child."

"Yes. Nanny B and Tiana are together now in Alain's study. I thought it best to let Tiana do whatever she needed when she got home. I asked Maria to send up supper for them both, and then Tiana will come and see me."

"She'll have appreciated that so much. What about His Excellency? Will he be coming again?"

"No, tomorrow he flies back to Rome. It was extraordinary circumstances that enabled him to be here at this time. He lives in Rome now, as you know, and a week ago he flew back to Paris for his mother's funeral. He had come by to pay me an unscheduled visit to drop off some documents from His Excellency Archbishop Armand. They were about one of my charities and needed my signature."

"Well, you were both blessed to have Bishop Gagnon here to act on your behalf."

"Yes, we were. I shall write him a letter of thanks tomorrow. Will you be able to stay, Vivienne?"

"Of course, darling. I've already told Spiros and the children to expect me when they see me," Vivienne said, taking her sister's hand.

"Thank you. You've always been there for me."

"And I always will be."

"I made a terrible mistake, Vivienne."

"What do you mean?"

"It was Alain, Vivienne. It was Alain who was the love of my life."

***

Later that evening, after Tiana had left to try and get some sleep, Adelia wondered what impact His Excellency might have had on her when he picked her up from the airport.

What he did was incredibly thoughtful and kind. Oh, if only he was older, lacking in charm and looked like poor Father Aubry, she thought, smiling wryly despite herself.

Has this reawakened the infatuation of a schoolgirl? Does she now think of him as her 'Knight in Shining Armour', so perfect that nobody else can compare?

***

Over the next few days, Tiana repeated her mantra whenever the magnitude of the funeral preparations and ongoing adjustments overwhelmed her.

She told herself, "I am my papa's daughter. I can do this."

She finally understood the purpose of her mother's training. Watching in admiration, she saw how smoothly and elegantly Adelia took control and oversaw all the arrangements. Her mother knew exactly what had to be done and was brilliant at delegation, always choosing the perfect person for the job at hand. She was treated with the utmost respect, and everyone couldn't do enough to support her.

The Vigil was held at home and was attended by family members and thirty of her parents' closest friends. Listening to the Eulogies, Tiana cried. There were so many stories about her papa's kindness and generosity in private and public life. Adelia and Tiana both agreed that his casket should be open at the Vigil, and Tiana finally told her papa how much she loved him and said goodbye.

The following day, three hundred and seventy-four guests attended the Funeral Mass. They had flown in from all over the world. Alan had been loved and respected by friends and business associates alike.

When the funeral was finally over, Adelia told her daughter, "I am so proud of you, Tiana, for the way you conducted yourself, and your papa would have been so proud of you too."

Tiana felt closer to her mother now than ever before. This made it far easier for her when Nanny B left to go home.

"The time has come for us to finally sit down and discuss what we're going to do with all our business enterprises, Tiana," Adelia said. "Your papa has already left you a sizeable fortune, and I already have this apartment and now your papa's London townhouse.

"He was meticulous in his business dealings, and all the adjustments are running like clockwork, as he planned they would in the event of his death. So now we must decide whether to keep or sell our various interests."

"Do we *have* to decide now, Maman?"

"No, we don't have to at all. If you like, we could take a year off and return in twelve months to make our decisions."

"Yes, let's do that. I don't feel ready yet to make such big decisions."

"So, what are your plans for the next twelve months, darling?"

"Well, as you know, Vron and I had already decided to take a year off before Oxford. We planned to be based in London, and Vron's parents are allowing us to live in their Chelsea flat, which they rarely use. Vron has moved in already. But now it's so close to Christmas, and she'll spend the holiday down south with her parents.

"So, I'll stay here for Christmas and wait until the New Year festivities are over before returning to London to join her. Christmas is going to be so hard, Maman. Thank goodness we have the support of the whole family. But I'm worried about you. Will you be okay when I go?"

"Bien sûr, darling. I have Aunt Vivienne, my close friends, and all my charity work. In the new year, I'll attend periodic board meetings to keep in touch with what's happening on the business front. All that will keep me busy. I'll be fine. Don't worry."

"Okay, as long as you're sure. I'll telephone Vron tomorrow and tell her what's happening."

***

Over the weeks following her father's death, Tiana had given her all to support her mother and conduct herself in a way she hoped would have made her father proud. But she had been living a double life. Her emotions had been split, running along two divergent tracks from the minute she walked into the Orly Airport and saw His Excellency striding towards her. On the one hand, her grief at the loss of her adored papa and, on the other hand, the reawakening of the overwhelming attraction she felt for Bishop Gagnon, who had indeed become her *Knight in Shining Armour*.

The sudden reappearance of 'The Bishop' in her life at such a critical moment was like a burning match thrown onto her suppressed longings, causing them to erupt into flames. The more she replayed how he had come to her rescue, the more she longed to see him again. The touch of his hand under her elbow and his proximity as he guided her through the airport, his kindness and gentleness on the drive home at precisely the time of her greatest despair. All fused into a depth of emotion she could not resist. The infatuation of a schoolgirl had now become the burning desire of a young woman.

She had possessed the strength leading up to the funeral to set these emotions aside, telling herself, "I'll think about him later, after the funeral and Christmas."

During the funeral mass, she prayed silently to her father. *Please forgive me, dearest Papa, for lying to you. I know you won't approve and will worry for me. But I can't help it. I love him, Papa.*

The guilt of keeping such a dark secret from her mother weighed heavily on her, but it was no match for the feelings that now consumed her. She was determined to devise a plan to see him and longed to hear his voice again.

I'll think of something, she vowed to herself, *once I get to London.*

PART TWO

THE PRIESTS

CHAPTER SEVEN

Archbishop Armand glanced at his watch as the car drew up outside the Church of Santa Maria dell'Anima. A tall, imposing man, he emerged from the car dressed in a superbly tailored black suit. Resting upon his black clerical shirt beneath his Roman collar, he wore a magnificent fourteen-carat Pictorial Cross hanging from the equally impressive fourteen-carat gold chain. The cross and chain had been a gift from his family upon his ordination as a bishop.

His Excellency wore his aristocratic heritage like a cloak that subtly broadcast superiority. It was not intentional on his part but bred into him. His thick, white hair was side-swept, and although he never admitted it to himself, he took great pride in it. He had penetrating blue eyes, which he used to affect when he wished to intimidate the person standing before him. But the one thing that surprised people who did not know him well was that he possessed a subtle sense of humour that emerged at unexpected moments.

Walking rapidly down the cobblestoned Via della Pace, he reached his favourite ivy-covered café, known locally as Bar della Pace. The historic café had first opened its doors in 1891. This history appealed to His Excellency, who had been visiting the café regularly over the past ten years, ever since he discovered it upon his arrival in Rome in 1965. Over the years, he had come to know the owner and all the staff very well, and he was always welcomed like an honoured family guest.

On this December morning, he went straight inside and was surprised to see that Bishop Martin had arrived. The staff had seated him at the Archbishop's favourite small, marble-topped corner table.

"Ah, Edmund - no, no, please don't get up. Am I late?" he asked, smiling as he reached to shake the bishop's hand.

"No, Excellency, I managed to get away early and only just arrived," Bishop Martin said, half rising from his chair to greet His Excellency.

In contrast to His Excellency, the Bishop was barely five foot tall, portly, and, despite his best efforts, always looked slightly dishevelled. His short, cropped, greying hair was complimented by his metal round-framed glasses, contributing to an overall impression of a studious, somewhat distracted cleric. He was much liked for his easy-going nature, but he also had an incisive mind, which many underestimated to their detriment.

"Good, good. Now, how do you like your coffee, Edmund? And I highly recommend the cannoli," His Excellency said, quickly stepping into his role as host.

The order completed, His Excellency leaned forward and, in a hushed voice, said, "I'm worried, Edmund, about these accounts I'm hearing of child sexual abuse. What concerns us at Social Communication is the potential for scandal, especially via the printed dailies."

"It concerns us too, Excellency. I've heard that one of the Committees has stirred things up a bit. They raised the issue of an article that appeared in an American newspaper a year ago about a priest said to have molested over two hundred boys in a School for the Handicapped. The article said the abuse went on from 1950 to 1973. Naturally, there was no comment on the article by the archdiocese."

"Naturally," His Excellency murmured.

"Late last year, graduates of the school, now adults, informed the local law enforcement agencies of the abuse. However, the police and County District

Attorney expressed doubt about the credibility of the allegations. Added to that was the issue of statute of limitations. So, they decided not to proceed."

"What happened to the priest?"

"He was given an extended leave of absence and currently lives at his mother's house."

"I see. Of course, in the fifties and sixties, they didn't have to deal with the press we have today. Even before that, back in 1933, the Holy Father quickly understood the threat of the press in terms of spreading scandal. I don't know if you're aware, Edmund, but two years after the Vatican radio started broadcasting, he imposed 'the secret of the Holy Office' on all stories involving child sexual abuse, effectively cutting off the spread of information at its source."

"Far-sighted indeed. But maintaining that silence is becoming increasingly challenging. I don't envy you, Excellency. Now you also have to deal with the television and cinema."

His Excellency gave an appreciative nod.

"Exactly, it's a big problem and a huge responsibility. I tell you, the ever-growing possibility of publicity about the clergy and the problem of child sexual abuse is giving me sleepless nights, Edmund. We must maintain the Church's credibility, and the fact that these allegations are now emerging worldwide doesn't help. The last thing we need is for the Church to look like it's under siege. I've even heard there are rumblings about the problem in Australia."

"It's true," Bishop Martin said, leaning closer to His Excellency as he added, "and I'm particularly concerned about four St Isidore Brothers Provinces in Western Australia."

"Have there been complaints?"

"Yes, and the first complaint goes back to 1919. It concerned a St Isidore Brother at a school orphanage for Catholic boys. We know about this case because it's a rare example of a brother receiving a gaol sentence. He pleaded guilty and received three years. Following the trial, they brought in a new superior and staff."

"Hmm, 1919, that doesn't surprise me."

"Well, Excellency, after the St Isidore Brothers' Congregation Leadership Team moved to Rome in the early nineteen sixties, they discovered earlier correspondence between the Superior General and the Provincial in Australia."

"Interesting," His Excellency said. "Any revelations?"

"Yes, the documents were extremely revealing, disclosing that child sexual abuse was a recurring and persistent problem for the Congregation. The relevant provincial councils knew about the allegations against brothers in their institutions around Australia. Correspondence about the Farm & Trade School at Baile, north of Perth in Western Australia, referenced allegations of sexual *and* physical abuse of boys going back *decades*."

Bishop Martin paused to remove his glasses and rub the bridge of his nose before replacing them. He took another sip of coffee before continuing.

"Apparently, in the forties, they referred to the sexual abuse of a child as 'interference', and in the fifties, they referred to a brother having a 'weakness' or 'moral lapse'. They also knew that such 'lapses' tended to reassert themselves and did not quickly die, which they considered a danger to the brother.

"They knew about the ongoing impact on children too, that it would be hard to forget anything of that nature," Bishop Martin added, looking visibly flustered.

"Well, it's not like this issue is new to us. You are, of course, familiar with the cases from 1629 Edmund."

"Ah yes, where they *promoted* the priests who were sexually abusing children and then moved them to new schools to avoid their superiors finding out."

"Yes, exactly, those are the ones. And when it kept happening with more priests, it eventually became a policy. I forget what it was called."

"Promoveatur ut amoveatur."

"That's it - *promotion for avoidance.* I recall they eventually shut the Order down but later re-instituted it. The history of the sexual abuse of children by priests and brothers goes back centuries, not mere decades. Rome, the bishops, the priests, they've all known that it's a problem. The only difference now is that the laity are starting to hear about it."

"So, how did the Provincial Council in Western Australia deal with the brothers?"

"Censure, canonical warning, verbal advice. Some brothers continued to have ongoing access to children, which was the case at Baile. Others were transferred from a residential facility to a day school, but no explanation was given. Some were transferred and had no further contact with children, whilst others were recommended for dismissal."

"And over the last decade?"

"There was less mention of cases in the sixties. Possibly, a decision was made not to record them."

"What about cases involving *priests* in Australia?"

"Well, Excellency, after learning what had been happening with the brothers, I started to make discreet enquiries, and it seems that bishops there see sexual abuse as a *moral* failing, a sexual *sin* rather than a *criminal* offence. It's about repentance, forgiveness, and restoration. Bishops are extremely loyal to their priests, especially when they profess innocence or swear they'll not re-offend if given a fresh start and a clean slate."

"A father-son relationship then."

"Exactly, and the way they protect the Church's reputation is by keeping everything 'in-house' and private. The last thing they want is a scandal that would make people think badly of the clergy, the bishop or the institution. I'm told that's why they don't report allegations to the police or get involved in the criminal justice system. It's the alleged victims or their parents who choose to go down that path."

"So, how *do* they deal with the complaints they receive?"

"Again canonical warnings, a granting of leave, send them to a thirty-day penitential retreat. But from what I hear, the most common response is to transfer them to schools or parishes in other locations, somewhat like the 1629 policy example, but without the naming and promotion. Transfers could even be interstate or overseas. Recently, some priests have been sent for treatment or reflection, the purpose being healing rather than punishment. In Australia, bishops are willing to give their priests the benefit of the doubt."

"Hmm, the priest you mentioned from the school in the United States was put on extended leave. I don't even dare think about what's happening in that country. But you know Edmund, it's the follow-up in that case that worries me the most. So many of the former residents of institutions, or students of priests and so forth, are now adult men and women, and their stories are starting to seep out into the press. I can feel my blood pressure rising at just the thought."

His Excellency paused, and then, with a faint smile as he signalled for the waiter to come over, he said, "I think we need another coffee and more cannoli to help us deal with this, Edmund."

***

Revived by his coffee, His Excellency took the conversation in a new direction.

"Incidentally Edmund, I've been meaning to ask, you know Bishop Gagnon, Philippe, don't you?"

"Oh yes, Philippe and I have been good friends since we were students at the Pontifical Gregorian University. Why do you ask?"

"Well, I had a brief conversation with Philippe the other day. He had been over in Paris for his mother's funeral. He dropped by to inform me that Madame Manning, one of the most generous supporters of our charities in France, would be mailing me the documents I'd sent with Philippe for her signature.

"Anyway, he said he leaves for Melbourne, Australia, early next year. He's being sent there to set up a canon law course within a Victorian theological college.

"I've heard on the grapevine that the Holy Father thinks very highly of Philippe, which is probably why he's supporting the Archbishop of Melbourne's request for this appointment. The Archbishop got to know Philippe when he spent time here in Rome."

"It doesn't surprise me, given his Doctorate in Canon Law. I hated canon law, so incredibly dry."

"Well, now that we're having this fruitful conversation, Edmund, I'm wondering if we should inform Philippe before he leaves about the approach being taken by bishops in Australia.

"It worries me that if we get more and more adults coming forward accusing priests or brothers of having sexually abused them as minors, then eventually, we will start seeing more and more of them standing up in civil courts as sex offenders. And I dread to think what the press would do with that."

"What a horrifying thought, Excellency. I'm starting to think that the Australian bishops are not well informed about how to proceed under canon law when dealing with allegations of child sexual abuse. Maybe in Australia, they never saw the 1922 instruction *Crimen Sollicitationis* or the updated document reissued in 1962.

"And if that's the case, then they don't know the procedures the local dioceses and tribunals should adopt when dealing with child sexual abuse."

"A distinct possibility, Edmund."

"And *that* makes me wonder, Excellency, whether the bishops know that in 1974, the *Pontifical Secret* was applied not only to the start of an investigation following an allegation of clerical child sexual abuse but also to the *allegation*, the complaint itself. The Pontifical Secret binds the bishop who receives the complaint not to reveal it to *anyone,* given that in our canonical system, the trial *starts* with the *allegation*.

"Anyone associated with the tribunal in any way must maintain strict confidentiality and keep the secret for the rest of their lives," Bishop Martin said.

"So now we are getting to the crux of it, Edmund. A lack of knowledge of canon law and canonical procedures could be a problem in Australia.

"And from what you've discovered, it seems clear that the bishops are taking the *pastoral* approach to child sexual abuse whereby a diocesan bishop has an over-arching responsibility to the individual priest."

"Yes, but in doing so, it seems they're failing to understand, or choosing to ignore, that whilst child sexual abuse is a moral matter, it is just as much a canonical crime as soliciting sex in the confessional."

"Exactly. It's the application of the *Pontifical Secret*, the strictest confidentiality, that should prevent bishops from going to the police with allegations, not simply a desire to keep the matter 'in-house'.

"What we need, Edmund, is for the Australian bishops to start taking swift and decisive steps to commence preliminary investigations and *be seen* to be taking action, or I fear the whole situation will backfire on us. *That* is how we stop our priests from being hauled before the civil courts and how we stop the spread of scandal."

Bishop Martin leaned forward, a look of anxiety on his face. "Indeed, Excellency, but there is one significant roadblock to all this causing *me* sleepless nights."

He paused to adjust his glasses, which had slipped down his nose, and in a hushed voice, he said, "It's an administrative challenge, Excellency.

"The instruction in 1971 that bishops could partition us at the Vatican for an administrative laicisation, a dismissal of a priest for the sexual abuse of a child without going through a church trial, has resulted in a large backlog of worldwide cases, including some from Australia.

"Admittedly, we at the Congregation do favour an administrative process rather than a judicial one because of its speed and simplicity. The preliminary investigation ought to take only a few days.

"But then, if we start getting more reports of all that's been discovered after preliminary investigations, and we then have to decide if there are grounds to proceed with a canonical prosecution, a procedure which could take months or even years, not to mention possible delays well, I just don't know how we'll cope."

Bishop Martin sat back, a look of consternation on his face as he said, "People just don't realise that we have such a small team here at the Congregation, and sometimes we have hundreds of cases pending worldwide."

"Good Lord Edmund! Well, that process needs to be streamlined immediately. In the meantime, we agree that Philippe would benefit from our briefing."

Bishop Martin slowly nodded his head.

"Yes. It would certainly give him some ideas for his curriculum. It will also prepare him for what he's up against if articles start appearing in the press in Australia, given it's the Church hierarchy that will have to deal with the fallout."

"Yes, and hopefully, he will be able to keep us abreast of what's happening on the ground."

"Exactly. Though I must say, I'll miss Philippe when he goes. There are so few of us here in the Vatican who aren't members of 'The Parish'," Bishop Martin said with a wry smile.

"Oh yes. Well, let's face it: gay priests have always received a better welcome in the Church than we have. If they all left the Church at once, we'd be up the proverbial 'creek without a paddle'! We need to stick together, what with all the rumours, gossip and settling of scores that go on at Vatican City.

"And you know Edmund, just between you and me, I have wondered if some of the gay cardinals and bishops who are sexually active are so fearful of their homosexual acts coming out as a consequence of a scandal involving child sexual abuse that they'll do anything to make the allegations go away. Homosexual acts are, after all, grave sins, immoral and contrary to the natural law in the eyes of the Church. Yet another layer to this issue, where the potential for scandal is endless. I swear I'm going to age before my time."

"I certainly hope not, Excellency," Bishop Martin said, his laughter causing the inevitable slip of his glasses down his nose.

"Needless to say, discretion is the key, and that's one of the reasons I like to meet here in the café. If Philippe accepts our invitation, I'll invite him to join us. And thank you, Edmund, for this conversation. We've certainly covered a lot of ground. Knowing what action to take next is always so helpful."

"Not at all, Excellency. Not at all.

CHAPTER EIGHT

When Bishop Gagnon entered the Bar della Pace, he was delighted to see his good friend Edmund, an unexpected surprise. But he was ill-prepared for the briefing he was about to receive. His coffee was forgotten whilst he listened in stunned silence to Edmund's account of decades of child sexual abuse perpetrated by priests and the St Isadore brothers in Australia. This was followed by His Excellency's account of his fear that scandal would result from Australian bishops failing to proceed with a preliminary investigation when there was sufficient evidence to justify doing so.

Wanting to clarify for himself that he'd understood the complexity of what he'd just been told, he said, "So Edmund, my understanding is that you believe Australian bishops are taking a *pastoral* approach when they receive an allegation of the crime of child sexual abuse committed by one of their priests. And in the case of brothers, alleged offenders are being moved around and given canonical warnings, and so forth, and presumably few recommendations for dismissal are being made to Rome, to the Superior General.

"Regarding bishops' response, you think it could be due to their lack of knowledge of canonical trial procedures in cases of this type, and they may lack an understanding that the *Pontifical Secret* covers all aspects of the preliminary investigation, including the allegation itself. Consequently, both you and His Excellency believe that should it become public knowledge that the Church is failing to hold offenders accountable through our own judicial processes, there's little doubt there would be a scandal."

"That's it *exactly*, Philippe," Bishop Martin replied, and His Excellency nodded his head in agreement.

"Furthermore, you fear, Excellency, that the Church's reputation will be severely damaged if more and more adults start to come forward to tell their stories of how they were sexually abused as children by brothers or priests, and more clerics start appearing in civil courts as sex offenders."

"Yes, that is indeed my greatest fear, Philippe. We need these priests dealt with by the Church's tribunals where the Pontifical Secret protects everyone."

"And Edmund, you also mentioned that the Congregation for the Doctrine of the Faith is overwhelmed by administrative laicisation applications worldwide."

"That's correct, Philippe. Understandably, the Australian bishops prefer this approach if they lack knowledge of the trial process. It's certainly quicker and easier."

"So how will the Congregation cope if it starts to receive a growing number of laicisation applications or preliminary investigation reports, and you then have to instruct bishops on how to proceed if you require that a penal trial occur before a Tribunal? Not to mention the appeals or challenges to a verdict that may come later."

Bishop Martin sat staring at Bishop Gagnon for a moment before he replied.

"Well, yes, that's a good question, Philippe. The thing is, none of us anticipated that we would be dealing with such a high number of cases. It's taken us completely by surprise. And if more and more adult survivors start to come forward, then, well, I'm not sure how we will cope. Frankly, the administrative process is turning into an absolute nightmare."

"It also concerns me, Excellency, that there was no mention of child sexual abuse in my briefing from the Archbishop of Melbourne. What does that imply? Is he unaware of the issue? It stands to reason that if it's happening elsewhere, it's probably happening in Victoria, in Melbourne. This leaves me in an extremely invidious position and could have implications for the proposed course in canon law."

"I'm so sorry, Philippe, but we felt it necessary to prepare you for what you might find when you get to Australia," His Excellency stated. "We need to have someone there who can keep us informed of what's happening on the ground, someone we can trust."

"I see. There's another alarming aspect, and that's the effect that such abuse might have on a child. How much do we know about that, Edmund?"

Bishop Martin sighed, "At this stage, I know very little, I'm afraid," he said, removing his glasses and wiping them with a handkerchief.

"Well, that's something else I'll have to follow up on, although getting such information will be extremely challenging."

"Tread very carefully, Philippe," His Excellency stated. "The reputation of the Church must be protected. Scandal must be avoided at all costs."

***

Bishop Gagnon sat back and tried to relax as his Qantas Boeing 747 took off from Heathrow Airport. He was grateful that he would have time over the next twenty hours to reflect on the information he had received three weeks earlier from his briefing at the Bar della Pace. The thought of sexual abuse being perpetrated against a child sickened him, and he was finding it hard to come to terms with the fact that such horrendous practices had been taking place for decades in Australia.

Thank God I'll be taking my leave in Bali before reporting back to Rome. I'll need all my strength before facing the fallout from being the bearer of bad news if His Excellency and Edmund are right and more stories of current and historical abuse continue to emerge.

His thoughts were interrupted by a Flight Attendant saying, "Can I offer you a drink, Your Excellency? We'll be serving lunch in about half an hour."

"Yes, thank you, a glass of red wine."

Sitting back, he sipped his wine whilst gazing out of the small, oval window. He had spent the last three hours pouring over reports and papers and welcomed the break. Seeing the ocean below, his thoughts turned back to Bali, and then a sudden memory flashed into his mind of himself sitting on his surfboard, feeling the undulating waves lifting and lowering him as he lazily paddled his legs following a surfing lesson from his father.

He recalled his father shouting from the beach, *"Well done, Philippe. Come on in now; your mother wants us for lunch."*

Philippe was seven years old when Louis, his father, and his mother Avril first took him to Bali in 1948. His French father, who had been raised in America, and his French mother first met in Bali when Louis went there to surf in 1940, and Avril was there with her parents. Her anthropologist father was there to study the ancient Subak water-irrigation system used for a thousand years for rice farming in Bali.

When Avril and her parents returned to France, Louis followed. Under the gathering shadow of war, an engagement and marriage quickly followed. The young couple managed to flee France when Germany invaded and made their way to America. Initially, they stayed with Louis' parents in New York before moving to live in Los Angeles.

On their return to Bali with their young son in 1948, Louis purchased some land and built a surfing shack. As the family returned over the years, 'The Shack' was transformed into a beautiful house of bricks and natural stone with teak floors, bamboo poles and a towering, thatched roof. Philippe had inherited the house upon his father's death and ensured it was maintained despite his infrequent visits.

When Philippe was about to turn thirteen, his parents had taken him to Bali to celebrate his birthday. It would be his last visit before he entered Our Lady Queen of the Angels Minor Seminary in Los Angeles in September 1954. Over the next six years, they returned a couple of times, and then in July 1960, the family returned to Bali to celebrate his nineteenth birthday. This holiday was a final opportunity for them to be together before Philippe entered St John's Major Seminary.

***

As His Excellency continued to gaze out of the window, memories surfaced of his last birthday holiday with both his parents and the other memories that were forever buried except when he visited Bali, and it was impossible to escape them.

Why now? Could it be all the talk about sexual abuse, or maybe the wine and seeing the ocean below? He wasn't sure, but here they were, vivid as ever, washing over him.

***

She had been sitting on the beach under an umbrella and had waved to him to come over, his mother's new friend Rosemarie.

"Were you going to walk right past me without saying hello?" she had asked, scanning him with her ocean blue eyes, her right, beautifully arched eyebrow raised to underscore the question.

He remembered feeling embarrassed at being caught out. He *had* wanted to avoid her, primarily because he found her incredibly attractive. He guessed she was in her mid-to-late thirties, slightly younger than his mother, and at ease in her skin. According to his mother, she had a string of ardent admirers, which he didn't doubt. She was petite with long, shapely legs that he pretended not to notice, smooth olive skin smelling faintly of coconut oil, her dark mid-length hair twisted up and casually clasped, tiny tendrils escaping; he imagined them kissing her face and caressing her neck.

"Come and sit next to me, Philippe," she said, patting the sand beside her.

"Your mother tells me that you're going to be a priest, which I think is a terrible waste. How on earth did you make such a decision?"

He recalled how he had completely misread the lightness of the moment and had replied in profound seriousness, "I just knew in my heart that my whole life, everything I would become, everything I would do, would be devoted to working for the Lord."

His response silenced Rosemarie until she finally said, "And when did you have this revelation that this was your path in life, Philippe?"

"When I was ten years old, my grandfather told me stories of priests in the resistance in France and how they'd saved hundreds of Jews from being deported and sent to concentration camps. My grandparents hid a Jewish couple in their home before the Church helped them to escape."

"So, they were your heroes."

"Yes."

"And you're a secret rebel, given that I happen to know that officially, the Catholic Church supported the Vichy government!"

"Well, yes, I suppose I am. But priests like Father Glasberg dared to face that evil and do what they believed was the right thing."

"But you don't have to become a priest to do the right thing, Philippe, to make a difference. You could become a lawyer, a teacher, or even a politician."

"I know. But you don't understand. I don't want to build a career or work for something like a political party. I want to work for the Lord in whatever way he chooses."

"Oh my Philippe, you're so serious. So, what about sex? Have you thought about how you'll deal with celibacy? You're a very handsome young man, and when you become a priest, I can assure you this will become a big problem for you. Women, young and old, will find you very attractive and will flirt with you outrageously."

He remembered how the sudden shift in conversation had caught him completely off guard, and he'd felt himself blushing profusely, at which point she stood up abruptly.

"Philippe," she said, and before he could reply, "follow me," as she headed towards her bungalow.

Not knowing what else to do, he obeyed her instructions.

***

As soon as they were inside, she turned to him and said, "You don't have to be a virgin before you're ordained and take the vow of celibacy, do you?"

"Well, umm, it's part of our ongoing formation to resist temptation," he stammered.

"But if you're not, it can't prevent you from becoming a priest if you decide to go through with it, can it?"

"Umm, no, I don't think so. But we have to be of 'good morals', and maybe we would have to say something to the Rector. I don't know because I've never thought about it happening to me. I'm not sure, but I think we also have to make a 'Canonical Confession' before ordination."

"What happens then?"

"I suppose they'd have to decide if you were still worthy to become a priest. I think it would be more serious if the sin happened after entering a Major Seminary."

"That's settled then. I'm sure *you* will be the ideal candidate once you enter the Seminary Philippe, and they'll be only too happy to have you unless, of course, you decide to leave. How many seminarians end up leaving before ordination?"

"Umm, I think it's about two-thirds."

"There you are then; you may be one of the two-thirds. Now come with me, Philippe," she said as she took his hand and led him into her bedroom.

Starring out of the window, he could still recall the sense of unreality that had enveloped him. His emotions were in turmoil, a mixture of fear, anxiety and, most distressing of all, arousal, which he felt powerless to control.

***

She sat down on her bed and pulled him down next to her.

"Now listen, Philippe," she said, "we're in the midst of a sexual revolution. Because of the Pill, men and women can now enjoy sex outside of marriage without the worry of unwanted pregnancies. You need to understand that the belief that sex is only permitted within marriage and that it's primarily for the sake of having children is being challenged by the men and women of today. Sex, Philippe, is also about pleasure, intimacy, and love, not just about reproduction."

He could still remember the shock he felt as he listened to her. Nobody had ever talked to him before in such an open way about sex, let alone a woman. He knew nothing about the so-called sexual revolution, and what was this Pill?

Rosemarie then proceeded to tell Philippe that, in her view, it was utterly absurd to expect a young man to agree to remain celibate when he had no idea what he was giving up.

"By the way, Philippe, you're not gay, are you?"

"No, I'm not. We're warned about 'special friendships'. There's a rule that we don't go on walks or to the movies in pairs."

"And why is that?"

"I think because of the fear that male friendships are dangerous and could become what is called a 'particular friendship' that could slide into something sexual. It does happen, or I've suspected something's going on. But no one talks about it, *ever*. It's the 'Don't ask, don't tell' rule. But I'm not interested in all that."

"I see. And what do your teachers say about how to deal with feelings of sexual arousal?"

"We're told to say the Mass and the rosary every day, and the rest will take care of itself."

"And how is that working for you, Philippe?"

"Umm - " was all he could say as he rubbed his sweaty palms together.

"Well then, today *I* will be your instructor. I'm going to teach you how to make love and please a woman. Tomorrow, I leave the island, and you will never see me again. But I believe that one day you will thank me for this, Philippe. At the very least, it will make you compassionate towards those who are struggling with their sexual desires and identity."

And then he remembered how she had burst out laughing as she saw the look on his face.

"Oh Philippe," she said, "Don't look so terrified; God will not strike you dead! Now stand up."

And so it began...

***

First, she had told him to lift his arms, and she removed his T-shirt. Then she pulled off her top, exposing her small, firm breasts. Next, she dropped her shorts, revealing she wore no panties.

Philippe remembered standing utterly still, completely transfixed.

Then, in a swift movement, she pulled down his shorts and underpants, exposing his erection.

As he looked down in horror, she reached out and placed his hand on her breast before reaching down with her right hand to caress him and - he came immediately.

"Ah," she sighed and said, "That's to be expected. Don't be embarrassed, Philippe. Now, we'll take a shower together."

In the shower, she soaped him all over, then told him to do the same to her. As he soaped her breasts, his arousal recovered. She placed her hands on either side of his hips, pulling him towards her and then massaged him with her body, her hips moving in a slow, circular motion before she reached down and grasped him. He let out a groan, his arms spread out, his hands pressed hard against the sides of the shower as he came to a shuddering climax.

She smiled up at him. "There, now the real lesson can begin. After you've dried yourself off, come back to the bedroom. You'll learn to practice foreplay, increase your stamina and please your partner. A woman needs foreplay, Philippe, and you need to have this knowledge and skill in case you change your mind about becoming a priest."

"Foreplay?"

She laughed, "You'll see."

***

When he returned to the bedroom, Rosemarie was standing there naked except for a black lace bra.

Moving slowly towards him, she put her arms around his neck before kissing him gently. Then, taking his hand, she led him to the bed.

"Sit," she ordered, and then she straddled him and kissed him again, more urgently.

"Now slip the two straps off my shoulders, one at a time and slowly. And kiss each shoulder after you do it."

He followed her instructions, gently kissing the velvety smoothness of her skin.

"Now reach behind and undo my bra."

He remembered how he'd fumbled to unhook her bra, eventually getting it undone and tossing it aside.

His excitement was rising, and Rosemarie sat back and ordered him to take deep breaths.

"This time is to be savoured, Philippe; *this* is foreplay; take it slow," she whispered.

"That's better. Now cup each of my breasts in your hands and suck each of my nipples."

He did as he was told as she arched her back, closed her eyes and presented her breasts to him. She then grasped his hair, pulled his head back and kissed him passionately before jumping off him and getting onto the bed.

"Come, Philippe," she said, opening her arms and stretching her legs wide, "lay on top of me."

She then guided him as he slipped into her. She was warm and very wet. "Slowly, Philippe, try to hold off for a moment," she urged.

But she had asked too much, and he exploded into her. A second later, she came, her nails digging into his back as her body was engulfed in the throes of her orgasm, and she screamed out, "Oh *My God*, Philippe!"

Afterwards, they lay together, and she held him before murmuring, "Now you know what it's all about."

***

Rosemarie got up, kissed Philippe, went to the bathroom, returned, pulled on her shorts and T-shirt, and padded off to the kitchen. "Time for a lunch break," she said, "to be continued later." Philippe pulled on his clothes and followed her.

As Rosemarie prepared their lunch, she explained to Philippe how the Civil Rights Movement had inspired the Women's Rights Movement, which was also part of the second wave of feminism.

"The role of women in American society is changing, Philippe. There is a grassroots revolution called consciousness-raising. And now, women within the Church are challenging the Church's traditional interpretation of women's role as self-sacrificing and passive. They want to change the Church's hierarchical structure. Women of today want equal rights and equal opportunity."

"I know nothing of this."

"Well, I'm not surprised. That's why I'm telling you what's happening in the world. I dread to think what happens to men who leave the priesthood and go out into the real world and try to have a relationship with a woman.

"But enough talk Philippe. Finish your lunch. We only have a few hours left, and it's time for you to learn how to please a woman in bed."

***

His Excellency was so deeply engrossed in his thoughts that he had to be shaken on the arm by the person sitting next to him to tell the Flight Attendant which meal he would prefer for lunch.

"And a glass of red wine, please," His Excellency said.

As he sipped his wine, the memory of the overwhelming guilt he'd experienced after leaving Rosemarie came flooding back. The thought that he had separated himself from God through the sins he'd committed had made him feel physically ill.

He and his parents were also leaving the island the following day, and he prayed that they would not bump into Rosemarie at the airport.

When he arrived back at The Shack, he told his parents he was exhausted from his last day of surfing and wanted to get an early night before they left in the morning. In his room, he prostrated himself on the floor and prayed and prayed that God would forgive him for his terrible sins. It was not the sex that had traumatised him; it was the knowledge that in his heart of hearts, at that moment, he knew that he had wanted it, and he had enjoyed every second of it. *I have betrayed you, Lord, by giving way to temptation.*

***

Two days after the family returned to Los Angeles, Phillip's grandfather arrived from France.

At the first opportunity, Phillips said, "Can I speak to you privately, Grand-père?"

"Of course, my boy, I'm here to see you before you disappear into the Seminary again."

When they were alone, Philippe told his grandfather how he had gone with Rosemarie to her bungalow, and they had had sex.

"I have committed a terrible sin, Grand-père - several times - six times. How can God forgive me?"

"And did you plan to go with her to have sex, Philippe?"

"No, of course not. She told me to follow her to her bungalow, and I obeyed her. I didn't know what would happen, and then I didn't know how to escape the situation. But by then, Grand-père, I wanted it, I wanted it to happen."

Philippe sat with his head bowed, staring down at his tightly clasped hands.

"Oh, Philippe, you must not judge yourself so harshly. I assume this was the first time such an experience happened to you."

"Yes."

"So, for years, you've resisted temptation, presented to you here in the form of a young man's dream fantasy, to be seduced by a beautiful older woman.

"Well - "

"You're a healthy young man, Philippe, with all the human desires and frailties that come with that. Have you been to confession yet?"

"No."

"My advice, dear boy, is to keep it simple. You'll be asked how many times, of course. Be honest with your answer, but do *not* reveal any other details. Your confessor is there to help you share the experience that has made you feel far from God so God can help you get past it. Your confessor will hear your genuine sorrow and regret at not resisting temptation and your vow that it will never happen again."

"Yes, Grand-père, thank you."

"There is one other thing, Philippe. You have been given a gift. You have learnt the necessity of discernment. There will no doubt be other times in your life when you must decide whether or not you should practice *blind obedience* – choose wisely, my dear boy."

PART THREE

The Child Migrant

CHAPTER NINE

As Oliver walked over from the Ocean Beach Hotel and stood on the grass looking out at the vast expanse of the Indian Ocean, wisps of memory snagged his thoughts - *an arrival, suffocating heat, hope, crushing despair.*

Three tankers sat balanced on the horizon's edge, awaiting permission to proceed into Port Fremantle and unload their cargo. After glancing in their direction, Oliver shook his head to dislodge the intrusive thoughts and turned to walk back towards the hotel. He saw Jimmy walking towards the entrance. He noticed his limp and was caught entirely off guard when he felt a lump rise in his throat.

"Jimmy," he called out, raising his arm and waving.

Jimmy turned and waved back and stood waiting as Oliver walked towards him.

"Hey Jimmy, good to see you; glad you could make it," Oliver said, giving him a gentle slap on the arm.

"Been a while, Ollie."

The two men went inside OBH, sat, and ordered two beers.

"So, how's things, Ollie?"

"Good news, bad news, Jimmy. Pam left me last week; it's over."

"Jeez, I'm sorry, mate."

"Don't be. It's a bloody relief. Still getting the nightmares, Jimmy?"

"Yeah, wake up every morning in a cold sweat. You?"

"Yeah, same bloody nightmares, never go away. Couldn't talk to Pam about them. Didn't know where to start. Who would believe the horror, Jimmy? How do you explain how the landscape of your life became a scorched earth? In the end, she'd had enough. She's found someone else; don't blame her. What did I know about relationships anyway? I'm surprised we lasted as long as we did. Thank God we didn't have kids."

"I've never been able to hold down a relationship. They fucked us up, Ollie. It's the same for Mikey."

"Yeah?"

"Yeah. Mikey's marriage is on the rocks, too, and he's so bloody depressed. I'm really worried he's going to top 'imself."

"Shit, I didn't know. Did he ever find out what happened to Kitty? I'll never forget how the nuns dragged her and Mary through the door after we had that meal at the orphanage before being driven to Baile in that bloody cattle truck. None of us could have imagined that Michael and Johnny would be separated from Kitty and Mary once we got to Fremantle. The cruelty of it. The sound of their screams through the door still haunts me."

"He did mention once that he tried to find her but was stonewalled whenever he spoke to anyone. They all said there were no records and then fobbed him off to yet another agency that knew nothing. I didn't ask him again after that."

"I wonder what happened to Johnny and all the others who came out with us once they left Baile. I don't suppose you remember leaving Southampton, Jimmy."

"Nah, none of the details, just a constant sense of fear that something bad was about to happen."

"It beggars belief that the Catholic Church and all the other ones were allowed to ship kids as young as six and eight out of the country and send them to the other side of the world with nobody but a bloody carer to look after them. You wouldn't remember Jimmy, but when they were taking our fingerprints and filling out all their bloody forms before we disembarked, we had no official documents, no passports, no birth certificates, no nothing."

"Do you remember your mum Ollie?"

"The memory of her face has faded, Jimmy, and no photographs, of course, to remind me. But I remember she was kind and loving, and the two of us were very close. I was devastated when she got sick, and I had to go to the Catholic orphanage till she recovered. But the worst moment was when the priest came and told me she'd died. I think I just shut down emotionally after that."

"Don't know a damn thing about my family. Never told anything. But now that we're talking, I do remember being given a small suitcase with clothes in it and being told to look after it. Never saw it again once we got to Baile," Jimmy said.

"Yeah, they gave me one, too, and the clothes were really nice: a dress jumper, jersey, corduroy shorts, shoes, underwear and even pyjamas. They disappeared the minute we got there.

"And all the lies they told us, Jimmy, about what a wonderful life we'd have in Australia: riding to school on horseback, lots of good food, all utter bullshit. And then there was Billy, the fucking bully. It started the minute I got on board."

"Why did he have it in for you, Ollie?"

"No bloody idea. Maybe just because he could. He was four years older and so much bigger than me. There wasn't much of me in those days."

"I felt sick to my stomach when I heard he'd become a priest."

"Me too, Jimmy, and that brings me to something I want to talk to you about. I was driving through Victoria Park a couple of weeks ago, and bugger me if I didn't see Billy walking into the Church. He's back."

"No shit! After what, a couple of years?"

"Yep, there he was, large as life, larger in fact. Billy Boy has put on a fair bit of weight. Priestly life agrees with him, the fucking arsehole."

"Yeah, well, we all knew that's why he became a priest, altar boys on tap."

"Do you remember when we saw him down in the cowshed, and he had the kid who'd only been there a couple - "

Jimmy interrupted. "Yeah, I remember. One of the many images I can't get out of my head that still haunts me."

"And when he walked out, he *knew* we'd seen what happened, and he fucking grinned. He bloody knew that we couldn't do a goddamn thing about it, that we couldn't tell anyone because he had the protection of O'Leary and Nolan. That feeling of powerlessness, you've got nowhere to take it, and it burns you up inside."

Jimmy nodded.

"I want to get him, Jimmy. I want to see him rot in hell. I need to get some justice for what he and that ring of paedophiles at Baile did. The fucking Catholic Church is never going to give that to us. I've been thinking about how to do it for years, and I'd like your help, Jimmy."

"Count me in, Ollie."

"Great, that's great, Jimmy. So, how's it going living down in Freo?"

"Well, I was thinking of moving out. Too much drama going on, and I don't need it."

"Then why don't you come and live with me now that Pam's moved on?"

"Really?"

"Sure."

"I'd like that. Be moving up in the world, living in Cottesloe."

"Yeah, well, it's the one thing I've had going for me, Jimmy, an engineer's brain that's made me wealthy."

"It's the only good thing I know that came out of that hellhole, Ollie. Those Italian stonemasons telling Dom Salvatore about you and him recognising your talent."

"Yeah, I'm grateful for that. Dom Salvatore was a decent bloke and a brilliant architect. After he got me the apprenticeship with Miller's, I went on to Tech and got my building registration."

"Still find it hard to believe that those arseholes got away with having us boys working from dawn to dusk as navvies constructing the admin building. It scared me shitless running up and down those bloody rickety planks, carrying bricks and rocks in buckets, barefooted and with no safety harness. Forced labour, that's what it was. I heard Dom Salvatore complain about the conditions to Brother Nolan once, and the evil bastard shut him down immediately."

"Bloody *slave* labour if you ask me. How did they get away with it?"

"Same way they got away with everything, Jimmy. People thought the sun shone out of a brother's arse, and they had power and influence that gave them protection. The Catholic Church thought Brother Nolan was a fucking saint, sticking that massive statue of him out the front. We were labelled as lying little sods making up wicked stories about the good brothers.

"Don't know if I told you, Jimmy, but I went and complained to the police after I left. They told me to 'piss off and stop telling lies', or they'd lock me up. Bastards."

"Jesus. We didn't stand a chance. When would you like me to move in, Ollie?"

"Just as soon as you can, Jimmy. The sooner, the better. Do you think Mikey would like to get involved? Might lift his spirits, the thought of getting our revenge on Father William Carson."

"Yeah, I think he just might," Jimmy said, a smile slowly seeping into the contours of his weary face. "I'll let him know we want to have a chinwag."

***

Oliver came out onto the verandah and put the tray with three mugs of coffee on the table. "Back in a tic," he said. "Just going to get the Tim Tams."

"Okay, mother!" Jimmy grinned at Michael, and they both went back to smoking their cigarettes in silence as they gazed out towards the Indian Ocean.

Turning to Jimmy, Michael said, "How's the leg, Jimmy?"

"Not the best, Mikey, not the best."

"Thought Brother Nolan was going to break both your legs that time before Ollie caused a ruckus and distracted him."

"Yeah, the cruel bastard punished Ollie for it, though. Wouldn't have survived that hellhole without Ollie having my back."

Oliver returned with the biscuits and finally sat down.

"How are you keeping Ollie? Jimmy tells me we're in the same boat."

"Yeah, Mikey, Pam finally left me. It's a relief to be honest."

"Same here; no surprise when Joan called it quits. Jimmy tells me Billy's back at his old parish."

"Yeah, Mikey, that's why I wanted us to get together. Of course, it's up to you whether or not you wish to join Jimmy and me, but basically, we want to make sure that Billy pays for what he did and is still doing.

"I want him to be exposed as a paedophile and in a very public way. I want it to reflect on the Church and all those fucking paedophiles at Baile. If we can somehow implicate Father O'Leary too, well, that would be a real bonus."

"Shit, Ollie, how are you going to do that? And how do you know that he's still doing it?"

"I happen to know that the reason he was moved away from Victoria Park for a couple of years was because a mother had made a complaint against him."

"Jesus, that son of a bitch."

"I've been thinking about this for a long time, Mikey. The thing is, there's no way he won't do it again, abuse some other kid. I'm keeping him under surveillance and have to figure out a way to expose him that doesn't end up with the usual cover-up by the bastard Catholic hierarchy."

"Yeah," Jimmy said.

"The Catholic Church has made these bloody arseholes untouchable. Look at Father O'Leary; he was part of the paedophile ring at Baile, coming down and staying from Geraldton. And Brother Nolan, he was one of the most sadistic, cruel bastards ever put on this earth.

"How many of us did they destroy Mikey? How often did people come to check up on the conditions at Baile? Every goddamn year or so, that's what. Came, went, wrote their bloody reports and fuck all happened. Were they all blind? It makes my blood boil just talking about it now."

"That's true, Ollie. I remember when two blokes and a woman came to visit the year after we got there. I remember them because it was a big deal that they came from England."

"Yeah, I remember that," Jimmy said.

"One minute in our crap shirts and shorts, no underwear or shoes. Then suddenly, all these good clothes and shoes appeared out of nowhere, and we had to get all dressed up. Ordered to be on our best behaviour, remember?" Mikey said.

"Yeah, I remember," Jimmy said. "They were the clothes they took off us the first night we arrived. Couldn't even remember how to tie shoelaces. Just a bloody performance for the visitors."

"Yeah, and then the whole performance again for some Australian blokes two years later."

"There was an article in one of the newspapers about a year after they changed the name of the place to Nolan College in 1966," Oliver said. "Did you see it? It was full of complaints of physical and sexual abuse experienced by former boys at Baile. Letters to the editor were full the following week. Nothing happened. Never heard that the Church took any action against the bastards."

"Yeah, I saw it," Michael said. "Just made me feel sick to my stomach, reading about what I'd lived through. Brought back terrible memories of the floggings after being told to 'drop your trousers' in front of everybody - the humiliation. And the way they spoke to us, Ollie, from that first day we arrived, calling us 'dirty, illegitimate sons of whores.' And the sexual abuse, it stripped me forever of my faith and ability to trust. They didn't save our souls; they *stole* them."

"We all deserve a bloody medal for surviving such horrors. What do you think, Mikey, want to join Jimmy and me in exposing the bastards for what they are?"

"Yeah, I'm in Ollie. What's the next step?"

"I'll let you know as soon as I know," Oliver said with a grin.

CHAPTER TEN

The journalist Peter Anderson had no idea that he was about to receive a telephone call from someone named Oliver Roff and that it would be one of the most critical calls of his entire career.

On the morning of that fateful call, Peter had been sitting back, taking in the hectic, noisy scene around him at the newspaper. Some people were yelling at each other; others were smoking as they pounded on their typewriters. A copy-taker was listening intently to the words coming down the phone line from a reporter, probably in a telephone booth somewhere. It was chaotic, and he loved it.

Peter had taken a step towards his journalism career in 1970 when he commenced the third year of his arts degree at the University of Western Australia. He joined The Vox student guild publication and always endeavoured to tell both sides of any story. This was second nature to Peter, who had grown up listening to his lawyer father and social worker mother vigorously debate the pros and cons of legislation, government policy, and work practices, not to mention what career their son should choose.

Following his graduation, Peter's parents rewarded him with a trip to the UK and Europe. His father said, "You've worked hard to achieve top marks, Pete. Go and visit your cousin James in England and then spend the next twelve months travelling through Europe. Enjoy this unique time in your life when you are still free of responsibilities and commitments."

There was a slight detour from the plan when Peter met a French girl on his way over to France and spent a month with her in Paris. He'd never been so grateful for having taken French as a major at university. He left for Italy when her Navy boyfriend came home on leave.

On his return to WA in 1972, he applied for a cadetship with The West Australian. After completing his probation period, he was offered a traineeship. Now, in his third year at the newspaper, he was getting wide, practical experience in reporting work. He aimed to become a top 'investigative journo', and his secret dream was to be recognised as a Walkley Award recipient for outstanding journalism.

Peter was about to get up and leave the room when the telephone on the desk rang.

"Hello, Pete Anderson."

"Hi Pete, my name's Oliver. I've seen some of your articles, and I think you might be interested in a story I have about a paedophile priest here in Perth."

Peter grabbed a biro and pad. "Hi Oliver, thanks for the call. How do you know about this priest?"

"Well, that's a long story in itself, Pete. He was on the same ship when I came to Australia in 1953. We were just kids. I was eight, and he was twelve. We both ended up at the Baile Trade & Farm School. That's actually where it all began."

"Where what began, Oliver?"

"It's where he started sexually abusing other kids. He went on to become a priest, and he's still doing it, abusing kids."

"How do you know - " Peter started to say.

"Look, Pete, why don't you come to my place, and I'll tell you the full story? I'm in Cottesloe. And please call me Ollie."

"Okay, Ollie. What's your address and phone number? I'll ring before I leave here."

***

"Nice place you have," Peter said, accepting the mug of coffee Oliver handed to him.

"Thanks; it was much tidier before my wife moved out. Let's go out onto the verandah."

"Mind if I take notes?"

"Sure, go ahead."

"So, you said on the phone that you arrived here with your family in 1953."

"No, didn't come with my family, Pete. We were a bunch of Catholic orphan kids from the UK sent to Australia as child migrants."

"You're saying you were sent out here alone as children. How is that possible?"

"Because we were all orphans, Pete. When my mum got sick, I was sent to a Catholic Children's Home. It was supposed to be just until she got better. But she didn't; she died. The priest told me that the Church would take care of me and that they would send me to Australia. Next thing I know, I'm on the *SS New Australia* coming here. Didn't have a clue where Australia was."

"That's unbelievable. Did the priest tell you what had happened, why she died so suddenly?"

"No, nothing. I was devastated by the news. We were so close, Pete. She was a wonderful, caring woman, my mum."

"I'm so sorry, Ollie. So, who looked after you on the trip?"

"We had a Carer. We called him Big Eddy. He was okay. Would've been in his late twenties, maybe. Kept us in order."

"Jesus, and what happened when you got here?"

"They grilled us with questions and filled in endless forms, no birth certificate or anything. Wasn't until I was older that I realised how odd that was. Still haven't got one. They told me I was one of the boys whose birth certificates were supposed to be sent out from the UK, but they never turned up. They said I'd have to write and get a copy from someplace in London."

"That's extraordinary. Do you have *any* records, Ollie? Who was responsible for sending you here?"

"No records, Pete. We were told we were orphans who nobody wanted and to be grateful the Church was taking care of us. 'Taking care of us', that's a bloody joke."

"What happened when you got off the ship?"

"They took us to a girl's orphanage where we had a meal. Then the girls were forced to stay behind with the nuns, and we boys were shoved onto a cattle truck and driven to Baile. It was devastating for the boys who had sisters."

"Good God, Pete! So, the Catholic Church was involved in this. But there had to be government involvement, too. You can't just pick kids up off the street and ship them to a new country without the British and Australian governments knowing."

"Well, that's true, Pete, because when we were kids, we used to have officials come to visit every couple of years or so. One lot came from the UK. We had to dress in clothes we never wore except for the visits and pretend we were having a great life with the brothers. They must have written reports, but nothing ever changed."

"Were you the first lot of boys sent to Baile from the UK?"

"God, no! By the time we got there, child migrants had been building the place for years. They'd constructed school buildings, dormitories, and kitchens, hacking at the ground with picks and shovels, mixing concrete by hand in the blazing heat and never received any wages. Too busy building the place to have time for proper schooling ourselves. Old boys told us how officials would come and visit, but once they left, the brothers returned to what they were doing before.

"What happened when you arrived at Baile?"

"They took away all our clothes, gave us a pair of shorts and allocated each of us a filthy, old, urine-stained mattress on the verandah to sleep on. Didn't even give us a bloody meal. The next day, we started working like slaves from dawn to dusk, building the administration building. It was exhausting, back-breaking work, but you had to cope or cop a flogging. The physical abuse was horrendous, Pete. Their favourite weapon was the strap or the cane. The strap consisted of four pieces of leather stitched together and a metal weight. They'd lash your hand with it, and it would become swollen and black and blue for several days afterwards.

"I got one hell of a hiding with the strap one day from Brother Nolan, the sadistic bastard. He made me drop my shorts in front of everyone and bend over so he could lash my bare buttocks. All because I wanted to distract him from laying into Jimmy with his fists and strap for raiding the vineyard for grapes the night before."

"Jesus," Peter said.

"And we were always hungry, Pete. Our food was disgusting. It was often burnt, mouldy or not cooked properly. The porridge was lumpy and often contained mouse droppings. When we were given fruit, it was partly rotten or well past its 'use by' date and might have maggots. The orchard and vineyard were out of bounds for us boys. The pigs got better fruit and vegetables than we did, and sometimes, we'd manage to steal some of it. The brothers ate like kings right in front of us."

Peter was so shocked by what he heard that he forgot to take notes and just stared at Oliver as the story unfolded.

"When we arrived, there were twelve brothers and one priest. Five of the brothers and the priest were paedophiles. We called them the 'Baile Buggers'. And that's where it all started with Billy, the priest I telephoned you about."

"How do you mean?"

"Well, Billy was a big kid and a bully right from when we were on the ship coming out together. He fitted right in at Baile because there was a culture of bullying there. Billy was a mean bastard to the little kids, always picking on them. That's probably why the brothers and Father O'Leary liked him.

"He became one of the pets. Most of the brothers had their little group of them, and they used to show kindness to them. Those of us who weren't in an exclusive group were treated with cold detachment, brutality, and humiliation. And you had to be careful who you talked to because *squealers* reported everything they heard to the brothers, hoping to gain favours such as extra food or less physical punishment."

"So there was nobody you could turn to for support."

"Nope. The boys who had a brother patron, like Billy, were given jurisdiction over groups of younger boys for chores and working parties. When Billy was older, he started taking some younger kids down to the cow shed. One time, Jimmy and me, another boy who came out from the UK with us, crept up to the shed and looked through the window. We could see what he was doing and hear the kid crying.

"It was awful, and we had no way of stopping it. We tried telling one of the brothers who we thought we could trust. But he accused us of telling terrible, filthy lies and said we should be ashamed of ourselves. We never did that again. But we knew he was still doing it."

"This is unbelievable, an absolute horror story."

"It doesn't end there, Pete. Billy's patron recruited him. He became a priest and ended up at Victoria Park. Then he suddenly disappeared for two years before recently turning up again. I hired a private detective to find out why he left. He discovered that a mother had complained to the Bishop that Father William had been 'interfering' with her son, an altar boy at the Victoria Park Church."

"Jesus, Ollie, what you're telling me defies belief. There are two separate stories here. First, I'm going to search when I get back to the newspaper because there must have been articles about child migrants arriving by ship in Western Australia from the UK in 1953. It had to be newsworthy at the time. Maybe there are articles about previous arrivals.

"I'll speak to my editor and tell him I want to follow up on this child migration. It's just unbelievable that kids could be shipped out to Australia, deported, and then left in a place where they're abused and there's no supervision, no accountability. Where was the duty of care? There must have been government policies involved. And this whole thing about you not having any documentation. That's just not right. There have to be files and records somewhere."

"I had no idea where to start looking. The brothers brushed me off when I asked about them. They said files and records would be everywhere, and I'd have to track them down myself. I'll need my birth certificate to get an Australian passport. I'm not even an Australian citizen! You're just left feeling like you've no fucking identity."

"What do you mean you're not an Australian citizen?"

"You'd think it would be automatic citizenship, seeing as we were brought here as children, wouldn't you, Pete? But no, I'm just a resident. I have to apply for naturalisation and then *pay* to become an Australian citizen. And it's bloody hard filling in the forms when you don't have the information required. It's going to be a nightmare trying to get a passport."

"Well, I'm going to help you with that, Ollie. It just so happens that I'm off to London next year for my cousin's engagement. Then I'll work in London at The Daily Mail for four months.

"If it's okay with you, during that time, I'll do a search for your birth certificate, order a copy and send it to you. There'll be an address on it, and even though it'll be an old one, I can still try to track down people, relatives, or neighbours, for example. There may be someone who knew your mum or even you before you went to the Children's Home. I'll also get a copy of your mother's death certificate and try and find out where she's buried for you."

"That's brilliant. Thanks, Pete, thanks a lot."

"And I'll research how you could have been sent here alone. By the way, what was the name of the Children's Home you were sent to?"

"Nazareth Children's Home in Romsey."

"And what was your mother's name?"

"Enid, Enid Roff."

"Thanks. Now, if you can write a letter permitting me to access your records, I'll visit the Children's Home and see if they'll give me any information. Don't hold out much hope, though, because of privacy restrictions. Also, given the circumstances, they may not want anybody to see the files. Let's hope they haven't lost or destroyed them.

"But back to the priest. I'm finding it hard to get my head around it, Ollie. Going from sexually abusing little kids to still abusing kids as an adult, as a priest. It's horrific."

"Yeah, it is, and most people don't want to believe it, besmirching the good name of the brothers and wonderful priests and all that. Nothing has happened since Baile was closed down. Not a damn thing. All those paedophile brothers and the priest got away with it. Zero consequences for ruining the lives of hundreds of innocent boys."

"I'm so sorry, Ollie. How do you want to go about this story?"

"I want to see Father William Carson, Billy, punished and everybody to know what they did, Pete, but I'm still not sure how to go about it. The Church sent him away after the last incident, and they could even send him overseas if we exposed him. That's another favourite strategy of theirs.

"I'll try to come up with a plan by the time you get back from London. Right now, I just wanted to know if you'd be interested in helping to expose the evil bastards. I had no idea you'd be offering to help me get hold of my documents. I'm so grateful."

"No worries. So, we have two major scandals here. I'll do everything possible to discover how you could have been put on that ship. My being in London will help with that. And when I get back, I'd like to interview other men who went to Baile. I'd also like to visit Baile if any brothers are still there. See if any of them would be willing to talk to me. What do you think?"

"I know at least two men you can interview, Pete and I'm sure there are more who'd be happy to speak to you. Jimmy is staying with me but he's out right now. The brothers will be much older, of course. But they'll still be living there, in the magnificent accommodation we built for them. Can't imagine where else they'd go.

"As to whether or not any of them would be willing to speak to you, well, it's hard to say. I have my doubts, but you never know. Maybe one or two have developed a conscience or want to present their side of the story."

"Good. So I'll be in touch before I leave for London. Don't forget to write that letter for me to take to the Children's Home. Once I'm in London, I'll track down your birth certificate, and I'll telephone you once I've got the details."

"Can't thank you enough, mate. The best thing I ever did was get up the nerve to call you at the newspaper."

"So glad you did, Ollie."

***

Peter got into his car and sat there, his thoughts swirling around.

How is this possible? Was the question he kept asking himself as he shook his head. *How the hell is this possible? Jesus, those poor, bloody kids.*

Peter finally started the car and headed back to the newspaper. Once there, he made a beeline for the editor's office, rapping on the glass partition before barging in uninvited.

"Boss," he said, "you're not going to believe this - "

PART FOUR

THE LIE

CHAPTER ELEVEN

"Oh My God, you're finally here," Veronica said, throwing her arms around Tiana and giving her a massive hug. "Come in; let me help you with your suitcases."

"Thanks, Vron. It's great to be back in London. Wow, I love what you've done with the flat."

"So happy you finally made it. It must have been hard leaving your mother. How is she coping?"

"Remarkably well. She seems to be really on top of things."

"How did she feel about you coming to London?"

"All for it. Thank God we had that wonderful experience together in Florida. It completely changed our relationship. I don't know how we would have coped if we hadn't been supporting each other through it all. She's been amazing."

"And how are you feeling? Do you miss him terribly?" Veronica asked, looking intently at her friend.

"It's so hard, Vron. It's an ache that won't go away," Tiana said, her eyes welling up. "Christmas was tough; we all missed him so. Thank God for the family. But I'm hoping being here with you will help me come to terms with my life as it is now, without him."

"Brilliant, it's time to move forward. I'm going to introduce you to the London scene, and we're going to enjoy our freedom. No more Sister Agnes, and if that doesn't call for a celebration, I don't know what does."

Tiana laughed. "Okay, I'm ready, willing and able."

"And what about the Will? Are you worth a fortune now?"

"Well, let's say a 'small fortune'. Maman and I have put big business decisions on hold for a year while we come to terms with our new reality. Maman will be attending board meetings and keeping an eye on things. But I'm not about to splurge, except for a new wardrobe."

Well, we're in the right place for that," Victoria said. "We can start with King's Road and Carnaby Street. This evening, I thought we'd have dinner at The Pig's Ear. It's literally up the road, and we can walk there. It's very cosy, and the food is fab."

"Sounds perfect."

"And tomorrow, we can hit King's Road first and shop till we drop!"

"Now you're talking," laughed Tiana. "Do you mind if I make a quick telephone call to tell maman I've arrived in one piece?"

"Sure, go ahead. Whilst you do that and settle yourself in, I'll pop out for a few grocery essentials and a bottle of wine. Won't be long."

Tiana made a quick call to her mother before getting out the number for Vatican City. She couldn't believe her luck in having the flat to herself so soon, allowing her to make the private call she'd longed to make for weeks. She felt bad not telling Veronica, but she knew she would disapprove.

***

"Pronto, Vaticano," the voice said.

"Hello, please may I speak to Bishop Gagnon," Tiana said.

"What department, please?"

Tiana hesitated...

"Em, I'm not sure."

"Congregation, Institute?"

"I'm sorry, I don't know."

"Un momento. One moment, please..."

After a lengthy pause, the voice returned.

"Sorry for the delay. Bishop Gagnon is overseas."

"Overseas! Where overseas?" Tiana said, completely taken aback by the news.

"I'm sorry, I don't have that information. Is there someone else you could speak to?"

Tiana racked her brain, trying to think clearly. Suddenly, she remembered Archbishop Armand's name and the papers her mother had signed for him.

"Em, yes, Archbishop Armand."

"One moment, please..."

Tiana sat on the floor, clutching the telephone in a state of anxiety. She had waited so long to hear his voice, and now this.

Calm down and think, she told herself.

"Armand."

"Oh, Your Excellency, thank you for taking my call. It's Tiana Manning. I'm ringing on behalf of my mother. She wants to confirm that you received the documents that required her signature. She couldn't sign them before Bishop Gagnon left Paris, but she mailed them a few days later."

"Yes, Mademoiselle, Bishop Gagnon informed me that he had dropped them off to Madame Manning, and I have since received them."

"Oh, excellent, my mother will be relieved to hear that. We also wanted to thank Bishop Gagnon for his support when my father was suddenly rushed to hospital."

"He did mention that he arrived at a fortuitous time, Mademoiselle. My deepest condolences for your loss."

"Thank you, Excellency."

"Unfortunately, you've missed him; the Bishop has gone to Australia."

"Australia - Oh," Tiana said, feeling her stomach lurch.

"Yes."

"Will he be gone for long?" Tiana asked as she squeezed her eyes shut, praying he would say it was a temporary visit.

"I really can't say Mademoiselle. Perhaps Madame Manning could write to him care of the Catholic Archdiocese of Melbourne."

"Oh yes, I'll pass that on to my mother," Tiana replied. I appreciate your help, Your Excellency."

"My pleasure. Please pass on my thanks to your mother for her ongoing support for our charities. Au revoir Mademoiselle."

His Excellency put down the receiver. *Interesting,* he thought.

At the other end, Tiana put down her receiver and wanted to scream with frustration.

"First Rome and now Australia. It's just not fair! I won't be beaten, I won't," she swore to herself.

Despite being so shaken by the news that The Bishop was now on the other side of the world, Tiana made every effort to keep the conversation light when Victoria returned. She was in no fit state to deal with any probing questions.

"So, what's the plan for tomorrow, Vron?" Tiana said, keeping her tone upbeat.

"Well, Kings Road first, then maybe Carnaby Street if we don't find what we want, then lunch. Afterwards, I'd love to drop by James J. Fox. I want to pick up a box of cigars. You can give me some lessons, and we can practice and start lighting up when we're out. It's going to be so much fun."

"Sounds like a plan," Tiana said, pleased to have something else to occupy her thoughts. "We should start with a box of Romeo y Julieta."

***

The following morning, they were up bright and early, downed tea and toast and then set off for the King's Road.

It didn't take long for them to find a boutique they liked, and they both disappeared into the changing rooms with an armful of clothes.

"What do you think of this Vron?" Tiana said, emerging from the changing room in a brown velvet miniskirt and crocheted top.

"Love it. I think I'll get myself another miniskirt, too."

"I also need a maxi skirt and a couple more tops. I love the bohemian look," Tiana said, starting to enjoy herself.

"You know what else is really in," Veronica said, "the Diane Von Furstenberg silk jersey wrap dress in gorgeous prints. They have them at Harrods. Let's get one each tomorrow. Perfect for going to lunch at La Famiglia and watching celebrities. It's another terrific restaurant just near the flat."

"I knew you'd be up on all the 'in' places," Tiana said, grateful for Veronica's enthusiasm.

"But of course! Speaking of which, we have a date tomorrow night at the Windsor Castle Pub in Notting Hill. Do you remember Jenny Ward from school?"

"Sure."

"Well, I bumped into her the other day, and she invited me, and you, of course, to join her and her fiancé James for drinks. He's Australian, and his cousin is here from Australia for their upcoming engagement party. Jenny's a lot of fun; it'll be great."

"Australia," Tiana said. "I've wondered what Australia is like."

"Since when?" Veronica asked, laughing at Tiana.

"Since now," Tiana said, laughing in return.

***

Soon after arriving in London, Peter was invited to The Daily Mail for an informal visit before starting work there after his cousin's engagement. He hit it off with one of the journalists and wanted to get to know him better.

"Do you mind if my mate Andy comes this evening, James?" Peter said. "Andy gave me the guided tour at the newspaper yesterday and introduced me to a few other journos. He seems like a good bloke, and I'd like to show my appreciation by inviting him to join us."

"Perfect," James said, "because Jenny's invited two old school friends to come."

"Hope they're as much fun as Jenny."

"I haven't met them, but Jenny says they're both pretty smart, going up to Oxford Uni next year. Tiana's father died the morning of their graduation day, terribly sad. Victoria's family is super wealthy, but Tiana's wealth is another level altogether. She's half French, and she speaks Spanish, too. You'd better be on your toes, Pete."

"I think I'm in love already," Peter said.

***

Tiana decided to wear her new miniskirt for the evening, and Victoria went for leather. She wore her Harley Davidson black 'T' shirt with her new hip-hugging leather pants and her favourite leather high-heeled black ankle boots. Over the top, she wore her leather studded biker jacket. She pulled her long, curly red hair into a ponytail, wore twisted gold hoop earrings and completed the look with black winged eyeliner, mascara, and cherry-red glossy lipstick.

"What do you think?" she asked.

"Wow, biker chic, very cool and sexy!" Tiana said, grinning.

Tiana teamed her new velvet brown miniskirt with a cream V-necked mohair sweater. Her tiny waist was cinched with a tooled etched leather belt and silver buckle. She complimented the miniskirt with her over-the-knee brown suede leather boots. A diamond heart pendant, a birthday gift from her Aunt Vivienne, hung from the delicate rose gold chain around her neck. Over the top, she wore her full-length, cream Mongolian sheep fur coat. Her thick, wavy, ebony hair fell loosely to her shoulders, and she completed the look with smoky eye makeup and pink lipstick.

"What do you think?" she asked.

"Wow, French chic, very cool and sexy," laughed Veronica.

"Ha," Tiana said.

They decided to go to the pub an hour early, order drinks, take in the atmosphere, and allow themselves time to light up and practice smoking their cigars before the others arrived.

"That is the most beautiful lighter," Victoria said.

"I know; papa had exquisite taste."

***

Peter and Andy had also decided to arrive early at the pub.

They ordered their drinks and looking in the mirror behind the bar; Peter saw Tiana and Veronica sitting at a table behind them.

"Don't turn around, Andy," Peter said. "Look in the mirror. There are two stunning women behind us, and would you believe they're smoking cigars."

"Bloody hell, now that's sophistication. Any chance they're the ones we're meeting with your cousin?"

"I don't know. But if they are, I'm indebted to Jenny for life."

"What should we do?" asked Andy. "It could be awkward if we start talking to them, and then it turns out we're meeting two other women."

"Let's just pretend we're journalists and sit within hearing distance and see if we can pick up any clues," Peter said.

"Idiot! But that's a good idea."

The two men picked up their drinks, strolled casually to a table behind the two women, and proceeded to eavesdrop. This was not an easy task since the noise grew louder as the pub became increasingly crowded.

***

Tiana and Victoria had noticed the two men and watched them walk past. Sensing they might be nearby, Tiana spoke to Victoria in French.

"Do you think that could be them?" Tiana said.

"I certainly hope so. Which one do you like, the tall one or the blond one?"

"The blond one. He's got to be the Australian with that tan."

"Cool," Victoria said. "I like the tall, dark and handsome one."

Just then, Jenny and Michael arrived. They waved to Tiana and Victoria and then waved to Peter and Andy. The four turned to look at each other and broke the awkward pause by bursting into laughter.

"We were wondering if one of you was the cousin from Australia," Tiana said.

"Yes, I'm the tanned, blond Australian one, and my tall, dark, and handsome friend is Andy. He's English!"

"Oh, mon dieu, you speak French," Tiana said, her cheeks turning pink.

"Yes," laughed Peter. "I thought I'd better confess sooner rather than later."

"Well, I'm glad you've all hit it off," Jenny said. "Let's get a larger table and order drinks and hot chips."

The rest of the evening was a roaring success. Victoria found she and Andy had a friend in common and had similar tastes in films, books, and sports. Tiana got over her embarrassment and decided she liked Peter. He was relaxed, funny and very attentive. Jenny was delighted that she had invited Victoria and Tiana and that the evening had gone so well.

"Well done, darling," James said. Should we invite them to the engagement party?"

"Oh yes, we definitely should. They all get on so well, and it's great for Pete to have new friends whilst working in London."

***

Peter invited Tiana and Victoria to join him and Andy the following evening.

"Come and see what it's like in a crazy newspaper haunt," he said.

"Pete is getting into the swing of working at The Daily Mail by first hanging out at The Harrow, our local pub," Andy said, grinning at Peter.

"We'd love to," Victoria said.

"Yes," Tiana said. "I want to know more about what it takes to be a journalist sleuth who listens to other people's private conversations."

"Touché," Peter said. "See, I told you I spoke French!"

***

The following evening, Peter was the first to arrive at The Harrow, which was already starting to get crowded. He stood in the main bar and ordered two beers whilst waiting for Andy to arrive.

"Over here," he shouted, waving to Andy as he walked through the door.

"Saw the headlines, Kingsmill massacre, terrible business," Peter said.

"Yeah, the Provos. Ten Protestant men were shot dead with bloody machine guns, and only one survivor."

"Will it never end? Looks like things are looking bleak on the economic front, too."

"Yes, you've picked a bad time to be here, Pete, what with high inflation and currency depreciation. Currency crisis, here we come. On a slightly less 'doom and gloom' note, there's a scandal brewing. The goss is that Princess Margaret and Lord Snowdon are heading for a divorce."

"Don't imagine the Queen will be happy about that."

"No, Her Majesty will not be amused."

"Incidentally, There's something I've been wanting to talk to you about, Andy. Shortly before leaving Perth, I had the most remarkable interview with a man who said he'd been shipped out to Australia in the 1950s as a British Child Migrant. He was eight years old and all alone, apart from the fifteen other orphan kids shipped out with him. They had one carer to look after them, some young bloke in his twenties."

"Child migrants?" Andy said.

"Yes, this deportation had been going on for years. I told my editor about it, and he wants me to follow up now I'm in the UK. The story gets worse, Andy. Ollie, the man I spoke to, told me horrendous stories of how the kids were sent to a Catholic institution where they were physically and sexually abused. Nothing was done about it. He said there was even a team that came from the UK to check up on them one year, but nothing came of it; nothing changed. The abuse continued."

"Jesus, that's terrible. I've never heard of child migrants. There had to be government policies and agreements between the UK and Australian governments.

"Well, that's exactly what I said to Ollie."

"And Church involvement, too."

"Yes, and I don't anticipate the Catholic Church being receptive to my enquiries. I think that will be one of the most challenging parts of the investigation."

"Hmm, this is just the kind of story our editor would be interested in. Ask your editor to call him Pete. I'll set up a meeting with Harry's secretary, so you're ready to go once you're on board. A good place for you to start would be the Home Office and probably the Australian immigration officials at Australia House here in London."

"Fantastic, thanks, Andy. But there's even more to the story. There's a priest..."

"Hang on, Pete, I've just seen the girls arrive."

Andy stood up and waved to Veronica and Tiana.

Peter wasn't surprised to see heads turn as the two women approached them. The combination of Veronica's flamboyant style and Tiana's elegant sophistication was arresting.

Peter stood and moved forward to greet them.

"Wonderful to see you again," he said. "What can I get you both to drink?"

***

After the four moved upstairs to the smaller saloon bar, Peter asked, "So what are you both planning to do now you're on sabbatical from your studies for a year?"

"Have fun," Veronica replied. "I don't intend to open a book for the next twelve months."

"I'm with her," Tiana said. "What will you do, Pete, until you start at the newspaper? Would you like to have a guided tour of London?"

"Well, we were just discussing that," Peter said. "Have either of you ever heard of British Child Migrants?"

"Child migrants, no," Tiana said.

"Well, I interviewed a man before I left Perth who said he was shipped from Southampton to Fremantle, Australia in 1953 as an eight-year-old orphan. There were fifteen other orphan children, and when they arrived, the boys were placed in a Perth Catholic institution on a farm property way out in the countryside. Whilst there, they were physically and sexually abused."

"Oh My God," Veronica said.

"Sent to Australia and then sexually abused in a Catholic institution. How is that possible?" Tiana asked.

"That's exactly my question," Peter said. So, until I start at The Daily Mail, I'm looking into it. Andy and I are hoping to persuade the editor of The Mail to get involved. My editor in Perth is already on board. I think this could become a big story.

"I've also promised Ollie, that's the man I interviewed, that I'll follow up on getting a copy of his birth certificate and also a copy of his mother's death certificate. They weren't even given their basic documentation when they left the institution as young adults."

Tiana and Veronica looked at each other.

"Oh my goodness, we can handle that part of the research," Tiana said.

"Yes," Veronica said. "We know how to do that. We did a whole family history project at school, and part of that was researching our family trees. We all went to St Catherine's House, here in London, to search our family records."

"You have to get there really early," Tiana said. "People start to queue up to get in, and the public search room gets hot and crowded. That's because so many people are searching for their family histories now, and there's no fresh air or air-conditioning in the room. By lunchtime, it gets so busy it's like Piccadilly Circus. At least it's not a school holiday right now. That's when it's the worst."

"Well, yet another reason I'm indebted to Jenny for inviting you both for drinks last night," Peter said. "That would be fantastic if you could both handle that. But are you sure the conditions sound awful?"

"Yes, I'm so happy we can do something to help Ollie," Tiana said.

"Me too," Veronica said, sounding equally enthusiastic. "Even if I must take back what I said about not opening a book. You can't imagine how large and cumbersome the volumes are there."

"Okay, let's make it official. I'm engaging you both as my two Assistant Sleuths on this case," Peter said.

They all laughed.

"So when do your Assistant Sleuths commence their duties?" Andrew asked.

Peter looked at Tiana and Veronica.

"We'll start on Monday," Veronica said. "Give us the details, Pete."

*****

When Tiana and Veronica arrived at St Catherine's House on Monday morning, they found themselves number twelve in the queue. They were all prepared with their thermos of tea and packet of Digestive biscuits.

Once inside, they headed to the public search room.

"Where shall we start?" Veronica said.

"Let's start with his mother's death certificate. Pete said Ollie sailed for Australia in January 1953, shortly after he was told his mother had died. So we should start with December 1952, just in case, then January 1953."

"Right, let's find the 'R's' in the Deaths Registers."

Two hours later, after repeatedly checking the entries and after the inclusion of November 1952, no record was found of the death of Enid Roff.

"What the hell," Veronica said.

"I don't understand Vron. How could Ollie be sent away as an orphan if his mother hadn't died when they said she had?"

"Well, there's only one answer. They bloody lied to him, didn't they."

"But why? Why would a priest deliberately lie to a child about his mother's death?"

"I don't know. I can't think of any reason to justify that," Veronica said.

"And if his mother didn't die, then she must have recovered from her illness. So what did they tell her when she wanted her son back? Oh, Vron, this is just too awful."

"We have to do more research," Veronica said.

"Okay. Let's go to Births and search the register for Ollie's birth."

An hour later, they had found it.

"Well, the only additional information this gives us is the address where Ollie was born. It's a shame there's no mention of the father," Tiana said.

"Not much help. Well, let's go and order a copy of Ollie's birth certificate to be sent to us, and then we can go and have lunch. We'll come back afterwards," Veronica said.

***

"Gosh, it's good to sit down," Tiana said, slumping into her chair. "So tiring standing up all the time looking through those huge volumes."

"So where do we go from here?" Veronica said as she washed her ham and cheese sandwich down with a cup of hot tea.

"Well, we've gone through Births and Deaths, leaving us with Marriages. Suppose Enid got married later after Ollie left the UK."

"Of course, that's a brilliant idea, Assistant Sleuth. But that could cover a lot of years."

"Yes. But she's alive somewhere, Vron, and we must find her for Ollie and her, too."

"Okay, so Ollie was born in 1945. Let's say she was seventeen then. That means in 1953, she was twenty-five when Ollie left. Let's say she married somewhere between twenty-six and forty. That's fourteen years, which makes it 1954 to 1968."

"Well, if we say she was seventeen in 1945, she would be forty-eight or forty-nine now. I think it's more likely she was older when she had Ollie. She could be in her early fifties now."

"I remember from our project that a marriage certificate would give us her age as well as her address, not to mention the name, age, and address of the groom. And if she moved in with the groom after they were married, who knows, they could still be in the same house."

"Oh, Vron, fingers crossed. Hurry up and finish your other sandwich. We need to get back there."

***

Once back at St Catherine's House, they spent the next two hours searching the volumes for 1954 and 1955 in the Marriage Registers, but without success.

"Okay, let's call it a day, and we'll come back first thing tomorrow and keep going," Veronica said.

"Alright. I'll telephone Pete and invite him and Andy to come for dinner tomorrow evening at The Pig's Ear. I'll tell him we'll give them our report then. I hope to goodness that we have some news to give, apart from ordering a copy of Ollie's birth certificate and not being able to find his mother's death certificate."

Veronica nodded her approval. "Good thinking. All I want this evening is a glass of wine, early supper and bed. This sleuthing is hard work. It's given me eye strain reading all those entries."

"Second that," Tiana said with a weary smile. "My back aches, and I've got sore arms from lugging those heavy volumes."

"I'll set my alarm for six-thirty," Veronica said. "We need to try and get as near to the front of that darn queue as possible."

CHAPTER TWELVE

Veronica and Tiana were fifth in line outside St Catherine's House when the doors opened the following day. Once inside, they began searching Marriages for 1956, and barely an hour later, there she was, Enid Roff. She was born on the third of February 1927 and married Jack Sinclair, who was born on the sixteenth of December 1918

"Oh My God, it's her," Veronica shouted.

People turned to look and then smiled, understanding completely how an entry could generate such excitement.

"Holy cow," Tiana said. "We've found her. Her home address is the same as on Ollie's birth certificate. According to her birthdate here, she must have had Ollie when she was eighteen, so we were only a year out. It says she was a waitress at the time of the wedding, which probably doesn't help. But Jack was a firefighter, and that gives us a great lead, plus the two witnesses plus Jack's home address from when they got married. They could still be there, Vron."

"Fingers crossed. Pete will be so happy we found Enid but gobsmacked that Ollie isn't an orphan."

"I know, and to think his mother's been alive all this time. Ollie will be devastated when Pete tells him. All those missed years together. It makes me feel sick."

"Me too. And I've just had another thought," Veronica said. "Suppose they had children, and Ollie now has siblings he didn't know existed either."

"Oh my goodness, I bet you're right, Vron. We can search Births under Sinclair, Jack's surname. We should start in 1956 and search for, say, the next five years."

"You start the search, and I'll dash out and get us some sandwiches and refill the thermos so we can work right through lunchtime and the afternoon," Veronica said.

By three o'clock, Tiana and Veronica had discovered that Enid had given birth to a daughter, Susan, in 1957 and a son, John, in 1959.

"Oh my goodness, look, this is fantastic. The father's address on the two birth certificates is the same as Jack's address on the marriage certificate, and he was still a fireman when they were born. What are the chances they still live there, Vron?"

"Well, if not, the chances are great that we'll find someone who knows where they are now, given they lived so long in the area. Let's call it a day. We've searched up to 1961, and we need to order copies of Enid and Jack's marriage certificate and Susan and John's birth certificates."

"Right. Pete and Andy will be stunned when we tell them our results this evening."

***

When Peter and Andy arrived at The Pig's Ear, Tiana and Veronica were seated at a table.

The two men took their seats and looked at the two serious faces of the women sitting before them.

"Spill," Andy said.

Veronica nodded to Tiana to deliver their report.

"Well, we have good news, and we have bad news.

"The good news is that we found the record of Ollie's birth, and tomorrow, we should get a copy of his birth certificate.

"The bad news is that we could not find his mother's death certificate."

"Bloody hell, what does that mean?" Peter said.

"It means the priest lied to Ollie about his mother dying," Victoria said. "Go on, Tiana."

"But the exciting news is that we found Enid's marriage certificate. She got married to Jack Sinclair in 1956. That, of course, is three years after Ollie was sent to Australia as a supposed 'orphan'," Tiana said.

"Good God," Peter said, looking shocked. "Bloody hell."

Tiana reached out and covered Peter's hand with her own. "I know," she said. "It's beyond belief that Ollie could have been lied to like that. And what on earth did they say to Enid when she got better and went to the Catholic Home to get her son? It's just too awful to imagine how heartbreaking it must have been for her to hear that her son had been sent to Australia. Maybe they even lied about that, too."

Peter sat shaking his head. "I thought I'd heard the worst when Ollie told me his story, but this - this is beyond everything. It's positively evil. How could they? Now I wonder how many other kids sent to Australia with Ollie weren't orphans. Ollie said he found out after they arrived at Baile that they'd been sending 'orphan' children from the UK to Australia for years. But who were they? And how did *they* pull it off?"

"Exactly," Andrew said. "You're right, Pete; this story will be huge. We have to find out how the British and Australian governments and the Church were able to pull this scheme off. Makes me embarrassed to be a Catholic, although I doubt if it was just the Catholic Church."

Peter got up and gave Tiana and Veronica each a kiss on the cheek before sitting down again.

"Thank you both for doing such a brilliant job," he said. "First-class."

"Hear, hear!" Andrew said. "I think they deserve a promotion."

"Absolutely, I hereby promote you both from Assistant to Senior Sleuths!"

They all laughed and started to relax after the stress of the revelations.

"Let's order drinks and dinner on me this time, and then we can decide where to go from here," Tiana said.

"Good, I'm starving," Veronica said. "And since this is now a project, we should name it, like 'Operation Ollie'."

"Perfect," Peter said. "Or 'OO4' for short since there are now four of us sleuths!"

"Oh, this is so good," Veronica said. "I see a new career beckoning."

"Well, after we've eaten, let's go back to the flat and make a plan," Tiana said. Nods of agreement all around.

***

After the short walk back to the flat, Tiana organised drinks whilst Veronica put on the coffee.

"Lovely flat," Andy said, following Veronica into the kitchen.

"Thanks. My parents hardly ever use it now, so it's virtually mine. It's a perfect base, being so central, especially now. We can make this our research headquarters."

"Great, but are you sure you both want to take time out of your break to help Pete with this?"

"Are you kidding? It's the most exciting thing that's ever happened to us."

"Okay."

"Come on, you two," Tiana shouted from the sitting room, "let's get started."

"Coming," Veronica and Andy called out together.

***

"So the first issue we must address is contacting Enid. The second issue is telling Ollie his mother is alive and that he has two siblings, a half-sister and a half-brother. Thirdly, we need to find out how this whole child migration scheme was possible. I mean, who consented to sending the children to Australia?" Peter said.

"Well, Vron and I will track down Enid and Jack's current address. If we're lucky, they'll still be at the same address entered by Jack on the marriage certificate and the two children's birth certificates. Jack was a firefighter then, so that's another great lead we can follow up on."

"Okay, great, and I'm going to telephone an expert for advice on how to tell Enid her son is alive and living in Australia. It's way outside my comfort zone and expertise, and I can't stuff it up. The expert is my mum. She's retired now, but she was a social worker for twenty-five-odd years, and she'll know exactly how to go about it. She'll also be able to help me decide how to tell Ollie. Shit, it's going to be such a shock for them both."

"And I'll contact a couple of my friends in parliament, Pete and see what suggestions they have about researching relevant policies."

"Thanks, Andy. I'll also follow up on your suggestion to visit Australia House. Surely, they'll have some records. And I want to visit the Catholic Home Ollie was sent to when his mother got sick. I want to know if they have any records. Not that I'm expecting them to be happy about an Australian journo rocking up on their doorstep to check on their past shady practices."

"Okay, so let's meet back here next Friday evening, which gives us a week to gather more information," Tiana said. "By that time, we'll have all the certificates we ordered. Come for dinner."

"Perfect," Peter said.

"So who's for a Brandy?" Victoria asked.

***

The following day, Veronica and Tiana decided the quickest way to check if Jack still lived at the same address was to ring directory enquiries.

"I can't believe we didn't think of this before," Veronica said. "Let's ring the operator and ask for Jack's telephone number and see if the address checks out."

"Brilliant, do it now."

Veronica dialled one hundred and asked the operator for the number for a Jack P. Sinclair in Portsmouth.

After a short pause, the operator returned and said, "There are two entries for that name with that initial."

"Oh, two entries. Well, the address for the person I'm looking for is 17 Whitecliffe Avenue, Portsmouth. Yes, you have one with that address. That's fantastic. What's the number, please? Thank you so much, operator."

"Holy moly, we've done it. It's the same address, so we've found Enid. What shall we do next?" Veronica said.

"I'm not sure. Do you think we should go down to Portsmouth on Monday and check the address out?"

"Well, we can't do more than just look at the outside. We can't approach anyone. We can check out the neighbourhood and the local Catholic Church to get a feel for the place."

"Speaking of the local Church, we could also see if there are Baptism records for Susan and John Sinclair," Tiana said.

"That's a great idea. Let's telephone the Portsmouth Diocese and find the closest Catholic Church to Whitecliffe Avenue. We could then get the train to Portsmouth, go straight to the Church, and check out the neighbourhood from there."

"Right, I'll ring the diocese first, then the station to check out the timetables for Portsmouth. We should also make an appointment with the priest when we know the name of the Church and ask him to do a preliminary search for Susan and John's baptism records," Tiana said.

After Tiana learnt that the Church nearest to Whitecliffe Avenue was St Joseph's and then discovered that the fast trains to Portsmouth from Waterloo Station left in the evening, she suggested that they catch the train from Victoria Station on a Tuesday morning.

"It'll take longer stopping at more stations, but if we leave at eleven, we'll arrive by one o'clock. We can grab lunch somewhere and head to St Joseph's Church to meet the priest. I'll ring and make our appointment at the Church for later in the afternoon. Going on Tuesday will also give the priest more time to search the records.

"After we've been to the Church, we'll see how far it is to walk to Whitecliffe Avenue. I'll take my camera to get a photograph to send to Ollie. After that, we'll get a taxi back to Portsmouth, have dinner and get the late evening train back to London. Mission accomplished."

"Great plan," Victoria said. "We're bloody good at this, even if I say so myself!"

***

On arrival in Portsmouth, Tiana and Veronica had just over two hours before their three-thirty appointment at St Joseph's. They decided to visit the old part of town and the harbour, where they had lunch at The Wellington before getting a taxi to St Joseph's for their appointment with Father Ross.

"Let's hope this was the family's Church, and we gave Father Ross enough details to find the baptism entries if they exist," Veronica said.

They walked into the Church and were greeted by a smiling priest.

"Welcome," Father Ross said. "I have good news for you. Both Susan and John Sinclair are recorded in our baptism register. Their baptisms were performed by Father Dolan, the parish priest who was here before me."

"Oh, that's great news. Do you mind if I take some notes?" Tiana asked.

"Not at all. Follow me; I've got the page open in the Baptismal Register where Susan's baptism is recorded."

After Tiana wrote down the details, Veronica said, "Can you tell us how to get to Whitecliffe Avenue, Father."

"Oh, so you're new to the area. Well, it's just down the road. Turn right when you leave the Church, and it's the third road on your right off Tangier."

"Do the family still come to Church here, Father?" Tiana asked.

"Enid Sinclair used to come at Easter with the children when they were younger but comes mostly by herself now. Susan and John come with her at Christmas sometimes, but I've only met her husband once when he came to pick them up."

"Oh, I see," Tiana said, glancing at Victoria.

"Thank you again, Father," Victoria said. "You have a lovely Church."

After they left the Church, they were relieved to see a telephone box on the next corner.

"Thank goodness," Tiana said. We can come back and ring from there for a taxi to take us back to Portsmouth Harbour. Let's return to The Wellington until it's time to catch the evening train to London."

"Good idea. Ah, here we are, Whitecliffe Avenue. It's another street of terrace houses. It was a good idea to bring your camera, Tiana. Seeing it in a photograph will be another bit of proof for Ollie that his family exists."

"Rather strange that Jack never goes to Church with the family, don't you think Vron?"

"I know, I thought that too."

"Oh, here we are, number seventeen. Quick, take the photograph now, Tiana, whilst there's nobody around."

Their mission completed, they headed back to the telephone box.

"We're building up quite a lot of real evidence," Tiana said as they walked briskly up Whitecliffe Avenue. "What with the certificates from St Catherine's, confirmation of the baptism records from St Joseph's and now the actual house where his family live. Pete will be pleased with our contribution to '004'."

**

While his two Senior Sleuths travelled to Portsmouth, Peter had been on the telephone with his mother, Jean, in Australia. After checking up on his parents' news and updating his mother on all the engagement plans, he said, "You remember I told you about Oliver and my promise to get a copy of his birth certificate whilst I'm here in London?"

"Yes, I remember, such a tragic story. How did you go?"

"Well, the story gets worse. I have two friends helping me, and they went to St Catherine's House here in London to do a search for Ollie's birth certificate and his mother's death certificate, and you won't believe what they found out. Ollie's mother didn't die, which means that when he was sent to Australia, he was not an orphan. Three years after he left the UK, his mother married, and she has a daughter and son from her marriage."

"Good God," Jean said. "That's horrendous, Pete. All this is so hard to fathom."

"I know. Ollie told me that the older boys at Baile said boys from the UK had been coming there for years, so I suspect there could be other children who weren't orphans when they were sent out to Australia. It beggars belief.

"The thing is, Mum, I'm not sure how I should approach his mother, Enid and how on earth I should tell Ollie that his mother has been alive all these years. What should I do? What should I say?"

"Hmm, I'll have to give that some thought, darling. Give me a day or so."

"Okay, Mum, thanks, but that's not all. I spoke to my Editor after my interview with Ollie, and he agrees with me that there's an important story here. So, whilst I'm in the UK, I'll be looking into how it was even possible for Ollie to be exported as a child migrant from Britain to Australia. There's the possibility that my Editor here at The Daily Mail might also be interested in running the story, especially after I tell him that they lied to Ollie about him being an orphan when they packed him off to Australia."

"I had a feeling this was where it was leading," Jean said. "It's an incredible story, Pete."

"It is Mum. So, I'm assuming Enid returned to the Catholic Home to get Ollie when she recovered from her illness. The question is, what explanation did they give her for the fact that her son was no longer there? So, fingers crossed, she'll be willing to speak to me and have contact with Ollie."

"Well, leave it with me, Pete. I'll also speak to dad. He's bored stiff in retirement, and I'm sure he'll jump at the chance to look into the legality of the whole thing at this end."

"That's great, Mum; dad would be perfect for that research. I'll ring you in a few days once I've learned more. Love you lots, bye."

***

The following morning, Peter rang the Home Office and was told to go to the newly opened office at Kew in Richmond upon Thames, where all their archives about the principal policies and actions of the UK central government and English and Welsh Governments were now being stored.

On his arrival, Peter was stunned by the sophistication of the filing system. The officials couldn't have been more helpful, and he spent the next three days going back and pouring over documents and gathering information to share with team OO4 and his mother.

After three days of solid reading, Peter decided to get an early night and telephone his mother at seven o'clock on Thursday morning. As a child, he had spent many afternoons sitting in the University of Western Australia library doing homework whilst his mother searched the shelves for books for her research and lecture material. He couldn't wait to tell her about the Kew Archives in London.

***

Fortified by a strong cup of coffee, Peter rang his mother the following day, and after the small talk, he said, "I've just spent the last three days in the most modern archive in the world. The equipment includes a computerised document ordering system and mechanical handling of records. The records are placed in buckets that go up and down and pop out on the appropriate floors; it's amazing! The officials were helpful, and the place had a scholarly atmosphere that reminded me of UWA, and I thought of you, Mum; you'd love it."

"Lucky you, it sounds impressive."

"That was the good part. It was all looking really positive until I found out about the 1958 and 1967 Public Records Acts. Long story short, in 1958, records were closed for inspection for fifty years. Then, in 1967, that was reduced to thirty years. However, some are closed for longer, even seventy-five or one hundred years, because of security, sensitivity of information and so forth. That meant I had Buckley's chance to read anything about the deportation schemes in the 1950s. It will be a challenge researching anything beyond 1946, possibly 1947.

"What I did find out is that when post-war immigration was resumed, emigration was carried out under the old procedures based on the Custody of Children Act 1891, which implied the right in the voluntary agencies to, and I quote, 'dispose of children apparently abandoned'."

"That sounds positively archaic."

"I know. I think it's likely that the Act would have been updated or changed over the next year or so. Then I discovered that the legislative basis for British *funding* of the child migration schemes goes back to 1922 and the Empire Settlement Act, which was subject to renewal every fifteen years. It was extended in 1937 and presumably ongoing after that. It was this Act that enabled the British Government to enter into a partnership with the Australian Government in an Assisted Passage Scheme for adult and family migration. A small amount of the funds was channelled to non-government organisations like the Catholic Church to assist their child migration schemes by subsidising the fares and maintenance of the children.

"Since Ollie was sent to Australia by the Catholic Church in 1953, it must have been under this funded scheme that the voluntary agencies were encouraged and given financial backing. Can you believe it? In other words, the financial support of the British Government made the child migration schemes possible."

"I can believe it, Pete. But how much of it was actually spent on the children, and how much of it went into the coffers of the Catholic Church? That's the important question."

"Good point, Mum. They had what they called 'Sending Agencies' who were responsible for the admin of the schemes. From what I can gather, the key one for the admin of Catholic child migration at this end was the Catholic Child Welfare Council for England and Wales.

"This central hub of diocesan child rescue administrators processed the child migration applications. The Catholic Church, the Church of England, the Methodist Church, and other leading British charities had all been involved in child migration prior to the Second World War. Bloody hell, mum! Then there were the 'Receiving Agencies'. I'm hoping you can follow up on that aspect regarding Perth."

"That's horrendous, Pete. It makes it sound like they're sending and receiving packages. But are you focusing on the Catholic Church? Otherwise, you could get bogged down researching a whole lot of information not relevant to Ollie's case."

"Yes, Mum, I'm only interested in information relevant to Ollie, Western Australia, and the Catholic Church. Something else I learnt is that the official definition of a child migrant refers to poor, abandoned, often illegitimate children between the ages of five and thirteen from orphanages, institutions, and workhouses in the United Kingdom.

"The practice was to document illegitimate children as orphans as that was thought to have less stigma for the child. The argument was that this would give them a fresh start in life in a new country. However, Ollie told me that the brothers used to call the boys terrible names for being illegitimate. So, our suspicion that more children like Ollie are not orphans could be correct. The question is, how many of them are there?"

"That question has terrible implications, Pete."

"I know, Mum. So many of them could have mothers and family members they know nothing about."

"And mothers who have children alive whose whereabouts they know nothing about," Jean said.

"Exactly, Mum."

"So we should discuss how you will approach telling Enid and Ollie about each other. You must tell Enid first, Pete. But you have to be discreet because she may not have told her husband about Ollie, and she would then need to decide how to deal with that aspect. Secondly, she may be a mother who wants to keep the door closed on that part of her life and doesn't want to have anything to do with Ollie. It's tragic, but it does happen."

"Well, Ollie said Enid was a wonderful mother, and it was obvious that he loved her, so I think it more likely that she would want to meet him than not.

Whether or not she's said anything about Ollie to her husband, Jack, is another matter entirely. We'll have to wait and see. So how should I approach her Mum?"

"I suggest you write her a letter first. Be upfront and tell her you're a journalist from Australia who was approached by a British migrant who wanted to tell you his story, but don't mention his name. Say he told you that when he was an eight-year-old boy, he was sent to a Catholic Home when his mother became very ill. After he was told his mother had died, he went to live in Australia. By the way, what was Ollie's address on the birth certificate, Pete?"

"It was a house in a village called Embley near Romsey. That's the town where the Catholic Home was that Ollie was sent to when Enid got sick."

"Okay, so you say you discovered he was born in the village of Embley. They'll have Electoral Rolls or Registers over there, so you say that after checking the roll, you think there is a possibility that she lived there at the same time as the boy, which would be the late forties or early fifties. You're wondering whether she might know of anyone who could give the man any information about his relatives.

"Say you would greatly appreciate it if she could write to you or telephone you if she believes that she might be able to help. In this way, you're giving enough clues, but you're not saying she is the mother. Enid can then decide whether or not she wants to contact you. Hopefully, she won't start to wonder how you got her current address. We'll deal with how to approach Ollie once we know Enid's response."

"That's brilliant, mum, thanks. I'll write the letter today, and fingers crossed that Tiana and Victoria have confirmed her current address. If all goes well, we could hear from her in a few days."

"I do hope so, Pete, for Enid and Ollie's sake. So I spoke to dad, and the terrible saga piqued his interest. He wants to help by examining how such a scheme was set up here in Australia."

"Great Mum. Tell him that from what I can see, the UK child migration programmes to Australia operated through a bureaucratic maze of government admin systems. At this end, there were the three bodies within the UK Government, the Home Office, the Commonwealth Relations Office, and the UK

High Commission in Canberra, which mediated contact between the national governments. Then there's the Australian High Commission and Australian immigration officials at Australia House in London. I'm going to visit Australia House later this morning.

"At your end, there's the Australian Commonwealth Government, then the State Government Immigration and Child Welfare Departments, not to mention all the numerous voluntary organisations involved in sending and receiving children. No wonder the welfare of the children fell through the cracks with all these competing departments and interests. It's a wonder they could keep track of anything, let alone what was happening to individual kids. What a bloody nightmare."

"Good heavens, well, this is just what your father needs to get his brain firing and keep him occupied."

"He'll probably need to go to Canberra, Mum."

"That's not a problem. We'll go together. It'll be a nice trip anyway as it's been years since we last visited there. I've also been speaking to Rosemary Stanton. She was one of my social work students, and she's in the Department for Community Welfare here in WA. It used to be the Child Welfare Department up until 1972, from 1927 to 1972, if I recall correctly. It was administered by the Child Welfare Act 1947. Rosemary was shocked by what I told her and said she'll look into it to see if she can find any reference to child migration within the department."

"Well, you've certainly got everything happening over there, Mum. My team here will be impressed."

"So who's in your team?"

"Well, there's Andy. He's a journo with The Daily Mail, and we've become good mates since he gave me an informal guided tour of the newspaper. It was Andy who suggested I start my research with the Home Office and the one who said I should approach Harry, the Editor here at The Daily Mail, to see if he would be interested in running the story in conjunction with The West Australian. I've got a meeting set up with Harry once I'm officially on board the newspaper after James and Jenny's engagement party.

"Then there's Tiana and Victoria, the two women that Andy and I met when we had an evening at the pub with Jenny and James soon after I arrived here. They both went to school with Jenny. It just so happened that they were the full bottle on doing searches at St Catherine's House, so they offered to help. They were the two friends I mentioned before who discovered that Enid was still alive.

"At the moment, they're tracking down her address, which we hope will be the same as the one on her marriage certificate. If so, then she's living in Portsmouth, which is only about two hours away. We're all getting together at Victoria's flat tomorrow evening, where we'll update each other on our progress during the week. It's great having their help. We all get on so well together."

"It sounds like you've settled in there, Pete. Keep me in the loop. Dad and I will keep digging this end, and I'll let you know as soon as we have anything that might be useful."

"Okay, thanks, Mum. Love you. Bye."

CHAPTER THIRTEEN

The minute Peter finished his conversation with his mother, he wrote the letter to Enid, incorporating all of Jean's suggestions whilst they were still fresh in his mind. He explained that he was staying with his cousin whilst in London and gave Enid James' home phone number and address. He placed the letter in an unsealed envelope as he planned to read it to the team on Friday evening. Then, hopefully, he would be able to address it and send it on its way via a London post box. After completing the task, he decided to treat himself to breakfast at his corner café and then visit Australia House on the Strand.

***

Entering through the revolving doors of Australia House onto the ground floor, Peter was immediately struck by its grandeur and elegance. *Hmm, the word Imperial comes to mind.* Moving through to the visitor's lounge, he was surprised at the number of people sitting and milling about. He approached the woman at the enquiries counter.

"Good morning," he said. "My name is Peter Anderson, and I'm a journalist visiting from Western Australia. I want to speak to someone about a story I'm doing on British immigration to Australia since the end of World War II. It's for my home newspaper in Perth, The West Australian."

"I see. Well, Mr Anderson, the best person for you to speak to would be our Chief Migration Officer, Mr Thomson. I'll see if he's available."

Taking a seat in one of the comfortable green leather chairs, Peter felt utterly justified in using his ruse to access the information he wanted. After all, there was an element of truth to it, as his research was being done for The West Australian on immigration.

After fifteen minutes, Mr Thomson emerged from one of the doors. With a warm smile and firm handshake, he introduced himself.

"Good morning, Mr Anderson; I'm told you're interested in our immigration history with Australia since the end of World War II."

Rising and taking Mr Thomson's hand, Peter said, "Good of you to see me, Mr Thomson, and please call me Pete."

"Come with me then, Pete and let's see how I can help. What brings you to the UK?"

"Well, I'm here for my cousin's engagement. I'll also spend four months working at The Daily Mail before returning to The West Australian in Perth. My editor thought that whilst I'm over here, it would be a good opportunity for me to do a story on immigration."

"Well, that's wonderful; please take a seat," Mr Thomson said as they entered his office. Peter looked around the walls, which were full of immigration posters. One of the posters said, 'There's a man's job for you - In Australia'. It showed an image of a muscly, bronzed, young blond man wearing a slouch hat, T-shirt, track pants and sandals. Another poster showed a couple running hand in hand out of the surf with the text 'See you in Australia'.

"Wow," Peter said. "What a collection."

Mr Thomson smiled. "It's a visual history of what we do here. I don't know how much you know about Australia House and the Office of the High Commissioner, but the promotion of immigration, trade, and commerce has always been part of our core business. You say you're interested in immigration since we started again after the war."

"Yes, that's right."

"Well, from 1945 to the beginning of this decade, most Britons travelled to Australia under the 'Ten Pound Pom' assisted passage scheme, over one million. The scheme was co-funded by the British and Australian Governments. The High Commission handled most applications, overseeing the process from initial enquiry to formal interview and medical examination."

"Good heavens, that must have kept everyone very busy," Peter said, taking notes.

"Indeed, they had to hire more staff, extending opening hours to eight at night on three nights a week to keep up with the demand. When Sir Thomas White was High Commissioner in 1951, it was all happening here at Australia House. They had lectures, lunchtime recitals and vocal competitions. The surge of visitors during this period wasn't just those going one way either. It was boosted by young Australians taking advantage of cheap fares on migrant ships returning from Australia."

"When did you start working here, if you don't mind me asking?"

"I came here in 1964 when Sir Alexander Downer became the High Commissioner. We still had record numbers of emigrants to Australia, and staffing at the High Commission peaked at the beginning of this decade in 1971."

"Is the assisted passage scheme still running?"

"Oh yes, but in 1973, we had to increase the amount for an assisted passage from ten pounds to seventy-five pounds. Despite that, we still have huge numbers of Brits seeking a new life overseas."

"And what about migration to Western Australia?"

"Western Australia was a very popular destination in the 1960s and also now in the 1970s because of the significant discoveries of nickel, petroleum, bauxite, and alumina. The discovery of these resources has resulted in more jobs, making Western Australia an attractive destination for skilled migrant workers.

"Of course, in the 1920s, it was a different story when assisted migration was organised to develop farmland throughout the Wheatbelt and Southwest of Western Australia and strengthen British cultural identity in Australia."

"Is that when juvenile and child migrants were first sent to WA?"

"In the 1920s? Yes, that's correct, although youth migration formed a very modest percentage of the overall migrant intake. The youth were fifteen to nineteen years old, male and female, from ordinary family backgrounds, and they made their own decisions to migrate. Australia needed farm labourers and domestic servants, so youth immigrants were ideal.

"The Big Brother Movement, which sponsored lads fifteen years and older from disadvantaged backgrounds, was part of that before and after the war. We have photographs of groups of them after the war who came to Australia House to meet up before heading off to their ship."

"And what about child migration after World War II?"

"You mean young, unaccompanied minors?"

"Yes, my editor said he thought quite a few children came to WA during the forties and fifties, so I'm assuming that was part of a child migration scheme."

"Well, 1945 was when Prime Minister Ben Chifley first created the Department of Immigration and when Arthur Calwell, the new Minister for Immigration, promoted the notion of 'populate or perish'. Child and youth migration was a small part of that overall growth plan.

"But child migration didn't start up again until 1947. You should try to get hold of Calwell's book, which supported the child migration plan as part of the national response to the serious demographic challenges facing Australia. Our Chief Migration Officer was involved in the early stages, trying to determine how such a child migration scheme could be implemented."

"And what did they come up with?"

"Supporting the work of approved voluntary migration organisations."

"Did the High Commission continue to be involved?"

"Only insofar as medical interviews and final selections were undertaken here before our immigration officials accepted the children. That's after the children had been selected while under the care of a local authority here in the UK and had received the specific approval of the Secretary of State."

"I see. So you would hold the records of the children who were sent."

"Not anymore; all those records have been sent to Canberra."

"Was there any follow-up between the UK High Commissioner in Canberra and the High Commissioner here on how the scheme worked?"

"That I can't tell you, but I highly doubt it. If you want more details on how the scheme worked, I suggest you visit the Home Office, the Department of Immigration and Ethnic Affairs, and State Government Departments in Australia when you return. And I dare say you'll find articles and photographs of 'war orphans' in your newspaper. There was a lot of publicity in the press about their departures at this end and their arrivals at your end."

Peter put his notepad and biro in his pocket and rose and shook Mr Thomson by the hand. "I can't thank you enough, Sir, for taking the time to provide me with such an excellent overview of immigration to Australia. My editor will be delighted."

***

Tiana and Veronica were busy in the kitchen when Peter and Andrew arrived early Friday evening.

"Mmm, something smells delicious," Andrew said.

"We decided to do a lamb roast," Veronica replied, kissing him on the cheek.

"We wanted to make you feel at home, Pete," Tiana said. "Pour yourselves a wine; we'll be dishing up in about fifteen minutes. Will you carve Pete?"

"Definitely, every self-respecting Aussie knows how to carve a lamb roast!"

Dinner was on the table thirty minutes later, and they raised their glasses in a toast to 'Operation Ollie'.

"Okay, who's going first?" Andrew said.

"We will, you start Vron," Tiana said

"So, due to our superior sleuthing skills, we got Jack and Enid's current address."

"Bloody hell," Peter said.

"And then we went down to Portsmouth and interviewed the priest at the local Catholic Church, where we learnt that both John and Susan were baptised there. Enid still goes to the Church on special occasions, like Christmas, but interestingly, the current priest has only met Jack once," Veronica said.

"You two are amazing," Andrew said.

"Thanks, Andy. We thought you'd be impressed. So after leaving the Church, we walked to Enid and Jack's house, and Tiana took a photograph to send to Ollie."

"Bloody brilliant! I can't thank you both enough because I've written a letter to Enid, which I've brought with me, and now we can post it tonight."

"Oh my God, that's so exciting," Tiana said. "Go on then, read it to us.".

"First, I have to give all credit to my mum. I've had a couple of telephone conversations with her, and she advised me exactly how I should approach the whole loaded situation and made suggestions on what I should say," Peter said.

He then took out the letter and read it whilst everyone listened intently.

"That's so well done, Pete," Tiana said. "Your mother is so wise to say be upfront about being a journalist. Do you really think Enid will want to be in contact with Ollie?"

"Yes, I do; he spoke about her with so much love."

"And that's so clever using Ollie's Birth Certificate and the Electoral Registers as explanations about how you knew she lived in Embley," Veronica said.

"Oh my goodness, I can't wait to see what happens when she gets the letter Pete. I wonder if she'll telephone you," Tiana said.

"Frankly, the thought terrifies me. I'm so worried I'll say the wrong thing and stuff things up."

"No, you won't," Andrew said.

"We have faith in you," Tiana added.

"Any thoughts yet on how you're going to tell Ollie?"

"Not yet, Vron; mum said to wait until we see how Enid responds first."

"Well, we just have to be patient," Andrew said. "So, how did you go, Pete, with the Home Office and Australia House?"

"I ended up spending three days amongst the archives in the Home Office's new facility in Kew. It's fantastic, by the way. I learnt that because of the 1967 Public Records Act, I had no chance of reading anything beyond 1946 about the deportation scheme. However, I did learn that the legislative basis for the scheme's funding on the British side comes from the 1922 Empire Settlement Act.

"Now we need to find out how the scheme was funded at the Australian end as both Governments jointly funded it. There were also what they called Sending Agencies from this end and Receiving Agencies in Australia. My dad is going to check up on the Catholic Receiving ones. He's a retired lawyer and wants to get involved.

"One other important thing I found out is that the practice was to document illegitimate children as 'orphans' to avoid them being stigmatised. So it looks like there might be a whole lot more kids sent out who weren't, in fact, orphans and may, like Ollie, have had mothers or other family members come looking for them, only to be told God knows what story."

"Jesus, this story gets worse and worse," Andrew said.

"Yesterday I went to Australia House. I spoke with the Chief Migration Officer, a likeable bloke and the full bottle on migration. He's been at Australia House since 1964. I got the interview because I told him I was doing a story on immigration for my editor at The West Australian in Perth.

"What blew me away was learning that child migration was no secret, especially after the war. It was even mentioned in a book by the first Australian immigration officer in 1945. However, I did get a strong sense that Mr Thomson was less keen to talk about that aspect of the scheme, wanting to focus more on youth migrants. When pressed, he told me that the children were interviewed, had medical examinations, and were accepted for migration by the migration officers at Australia House.

"I asked about the records, but he said they were sent to Canberra. Once I asked if there was any follow-up about how the scheme worked, he referred me to the Home Office and the relevant government departments in Australia. I think he was getting a bit suspicious, so I ended the interview. I got the feeling the High Commission was more involved than he was letting on.

"I've already told mum that they'll need to go to Canberra, and mum is going to find out what she can about the former Child Welfare Department's involvement in WA. I also want to learn about the Catholic Church's Receiving Agencies. Dad will be looking into that aspect."

"Wow, Pete, you've done heaps," Tiana said. "How brilliant that you have your mother and father working on it in Australia."

"I know, and I told mum about our team here, too. She was very impressed."

"Well, I feel embarrassed that I haven't contributed anything so far," Andrew said. "But I do have a lead, which, given what you've just said, Pete, could be helpful. I caught up with an old friend from Uni the other day called Phillip Hastings. Phil's a social worker. During our conversation, I mentioned in passing that a friend of mine, a fellow journalist, was researching child migration. I wasn't expecting him to know anything about it, but it turns out that his father was in Parliament in the late 1930s as the Member for Elmet. That was when they were debating the Empire Settlement Bill.

"Years later, he told Phil how he was vehemently opposed to child migration, and that was the main reason why he voted against the Bill. He even helped break up the migration of young children to Canada when he was a member of the Overseas Settlement Committee. He was extremely upset when they passed the Bill to include child migration. Phil thinks he might be able to dig up his father's copy of the second reading of the Bill. How random is that?"

"That's incredible, Andy. He must have had powerful feelings on the issue. What a legend. I'd love to see his argument," Peter said.

"I'll let you know as soon as Phil gets back to me."

"Well, we've all been so absorbed in the conversation that we've completely forgotten about pudding," Tiana said. "Who's for apple pie?"

"Sounds wonderful," Peter said. "I'll clear whilst you serve."

Following apple pie and over a glass of brandy, everybody agreed that the team had collectively done an excellent job.

"Now all we have to do is be patient and wait for Enid to respond to the letter," Victoria said.

"What will you do, Pete, if she agrees to meet up," Tiana asked.

"I'm not sure until I speak with her or get a written response. She'll have to take the lead on that one."

"Promise you'll let us know when you hear from her."

"Absolutely, Vron, I won't be able to get here quick enough."

"But what if she doesn't reply?" Tiana said.

The question hung in the air.

***

That night, Tiana lay awake thinking about Enid. *Does she think about Ollie and wonder where he is and how he's doing? I wonder how The Bishop is and how he's doing. Is he happy, or does he miss Rome? How am I going to get myself to Melbourne without raising suspicion? All the talk about Australia is making me miss him even more.*

CHAPTER FOURTEEN

The telephone rang late Tuesday afternoon, and James picked up.

"Hello, James speaking."

The male voice at the other end sounded hesitant.

"Good afternoon, Em; I wanted to speak to Peter Anderson."

"Yes, sure, that's my cousin. Hold on, please, I'll get him."

James dashed down the hall to the sitting room.

"Pete, come quickly. I think it's the telephone call you've been waiting for, but it's a man."

Peter couldn't get to the phone fast enough, tripping on a rug as he raced up the hall.

"Hello, Pete Anderson here."

"Oh, hello Pete. My name's Jack. I'm Enid's husband. You wrote to her about a boy sent to Australia.

"Yes, that's right," Peter said, holding his breath.

"Well - " There was a lengthy pause before Jack said, "She thinks it could be her son. Could you come down to Southampton to see her - see us - speak to her?"

"I most certainly could," Peter said. "When would you like me to come? I'm free any time."

"Could you come tomorrow?"

"Yes, absolutely. What time?"

"Say eleven."

"Perfect. Would it be okay if I brought someone who's been helping me with my research since I've been in London?"

"Yes, of course; see you tomorrow. Thanks, Pete."

***

Peter rang Veronica and Tiana and told them he'd heard from Jack and was coming over with Andrew. They both arrived at the flat an hour later.

"Sorry for getting over here so late," Peter said.

"Don't be ridiculous, Pete; we'd have killed you if you hadn't come over," Veronica said. "So tell us word for word what Jack said."

Peter repeated the conversation, including asking Jack if he could bring someone with him.

"Well, now we know that Jack knows about Ollie, although we can't be sure when she told him, now or before," Tiana said.

"Exactly. But it's a huge relief that he knows because it means one less complication for Enid and us."

"So, what's the plan, Pete?" Andrew said. "Would you like me to drive you down to Portsmouth?"

"That would be brilliant, Andy. Would you come in with me, Tiana? And would that be okay with you, Vron?"

"Love to," Tiana said.

"No problem," Veronica said. "After we drop you both off, Andy and I could go back to Portsmouth Harbour and hang out at The Wellington, and you could ring us there when you want us to pick you up."

"Great plan, thanks," Peter said.

***

The next day, they drove to Portsmouth, where Andrew and Veronica dropped Peter and Tiana off at 17 Whitecliffe Avenue.

Peter rang the front doorbell, and Jack opened the door.

"Come in, come in," he said, a welcoming smile on his weather-beaten face. He shook hands with them both, and Peter took to him immediately. Jack was about six foot two and looked extremely fit for his age. He had a 'no nonsense' haircut and wore a well-worn bomber jacket over jeans and a T-shirt.

I could see him as a fireman, Peter thought, *just the person you'd want to turn up in an emergency.*

"Please go through," Jack said. "Enid's in the kitchen. We thought it would be cosier and more relaxed there."

Tiana and Peter walked through to the kitchen and saw Enid standing by the kettle, busying herself, putting out mugs on the bench top. She turned around, and Peter instantly saw the strain on her face. Jack walked over and put his arm around her, emphasising how petite she was. She was dressed in a brown, long-sleeved jumper worn with a brown patchwork skirt and black boots. She had a short, pageboy haircut, fastened back on one side with a tortoiseshell hair clip. Peter could see the likeness with Oliver. They had the same grey-blue eyes, small nose, and mouth. Oliver was slightly built like his mother, but he was muscular and strong from his years of labouring at Baile.

"Hello," Enid said so softly that Peter could hardly hear her.

"Hello, Enid," Peter said. "I'm so pleased to meet you."

"And I'm Tiana," Tiana said, stepping forward and shaking Enid's hand.

Then, barely above a whisper, Enid said, "Is it my boy, is he my Oliver?"

The minute she said, "Oliver", Enid erased any doubt that she was Oliver's mother, and Peter said, "Yes, we believe so."

A terrible wail filled the room.

Peter and Tiana stood frozen, watching in horror as Enid collapsed against Jack, who managed to get her into one of the kitchen chairs.

Fuck, I shouldn't have been so blunt. Fuck, fuck!

"Oh, how *could* they?" Enid cried, looking desperately up at Jack. "How *could* they? Oh my boy, my boy."

"Oh, luv," Jack said, looking helplessly at his wife.

Then, turning to Peter and Tiana, he said, "Tell us, please tell us what you know."

Peter and Tiana sat down opposite Enid and Jack at the kitchen table.

"First," Peter said, "I'd like to tell you how impressed I was by your son when I met him, Enid. He contacted me at the newspaper, and when I interviewed him in his home, it became clear to me how courageous he'd been whilst growing up in such difficult circumstances. He's a very successful builder now. You'd be proud of him. I like him a lot."

Enid stared at Peter, wide-eyed, hanging on to his every word.

"We couldn't believe it when you wrote that Oliver was told that Enid had died, and how did he end up in Australia?" Jack asked. "Did the family who adopted him take him there?"

"Well, no. You see when the priest told Ollie that you had died, Enid, they said the Church was going to take care of him and send him to Australia for a better life. So since then, he's believed that he's an orphan."

Enid gasped, her hand covering her mouth as she shook her head from side to side.

"He left the UK in January 1953 on the *SS New Australia*."

"Is there nothing they haven't lied about," Jack exclaimed, his hand balling into a fist.

"When Enid first told me about Oliver, I told her the Church couldn't put a child up for adoption without her signing any papers. We went back to the Children's Home in Romsey, and they told us there was nothing they could do. They said Enid had signed some papers when they first took Oliver away to the orphanage. They took advantage of her when she was so ill, the bastards.

"They refused to give us any more information. I was so bloody angry, and we felt utterly helpless. I couldn't go inside a Church after that, except for the kids' baptisms, and I only did that for Enid's sake."

"I'm so sorry, Enid," Peter said.

"How are you luv?" Jack said, turning back to Enid. "We knew this would be tough, but you're so strong."

Enid gave Jack a weak smile, then, turning to Peter, she said, "Is he married? Do I have grandchildren?"

"Ollie is separated, and no, no children."

Tiana stood up, wanting to do something to disrupt the sadness that now enveloped them all. "Let me make us all a cup of tea," she said.

Jack nodded. "Thanks," he said. "I think we could all do with one."

Enid suddenly started talking. "They told me my Oliver had been adopted by a wonderful family who could give him everything I couldn't," she said, looking at Peter. "I thought I'd die when they told me that. The shock. They said nothing about Australia."

"I can't begin to imagine what it must have been like for you," Peter said.

"I've never stopped thinking about him, wondering what his life was like and whether he was happy," Enid said. "Every day I've prayed that one day I would see him again."

"It's true," Jack said. "Every birthday, she's mourned for him. They broke her heart."

Tiana put the milk and sugar on the table and poured tea into a mug for Enid. "Ollie wants to get a passport," Tiana said, "but he didn't have any documentation. Pete offered to get him a copy of his birth certificate when he came to London and also a copy of your death certificate, Enid. And it was only when Veronica and I couldn't find any record of your death certificate that we realised something was terribly wrong. Then we searched Marriages, and we found you both."

"Ah, so that's how you found out where we lived," Jack said. "We did wonder about that."

"Yes, then we confirmed it through the telephone directory."

"So you knew all along that Enid was Oliver's mother?"

"Yes, but we had to be very careful what we said in the letter," Peter said, "in case Enid had chosen not to say anything to you, Jack, or didn't want to pursue the matter further. And, of course, we never mentioned Ollie's name. So when you said, 'my Oliver', it confirmed everything."

"You handled it very well," Jack said. "Can't tell you how grateful we are."

"Well, I stuffed up telling you so bluntly that it was Ollie," Peter said. "I'm so sorry, Enid."

Enid gave Peter a soft smile. "No, you didn't luv. I was desperate to know the truth. It couldn't have been easy coming here to give us such news."

"So what happened to him then?" Jack asked.

"He was sent to the Baile Farm & Trade School, a Catholic institution run by the St Isidore Brothers about sixty miles north of Perth in Western Australia."

"An institution. Oh, my poor boy."

"So, where would you like to go from here?" Peter asked, desperately wanting to avoid having to answer any questions about Oliver's life at Baile.

"I want to contact him as soon as possible, of course," Enid said.

"How do you think we should go about it?" Jack asked Peter.

"Well, I've thought about it," Peter said. "Maybe the best way would be for you to write him a letter, Enid and send photographs. And when you've posted it, I could ring Ollie and explain what's happened, tell him your letter is on the way, and that will give him time to absorb the news. What do you think?"

Enid and Jack looked at each other and nodded. "Yes, we think that's a good way to go about it," Enid said, her voice sounding stronger now. "And then I'm going to see my boy in Australia!"

That made everybody smile. "Oh my," Enid said, "I forgot about the cake. Let's all have another cuppa."

***

Peter and Tiana walked into the bar in The Wellington, surprising Andrew and Veronica.

"We thought you were going to ring us to come and get you," Veronica said.

"I know, but Jack insisted on driving us here," Peter said.

"So, how was it? Did it go okay?" Andrew asked, scanning the faces of Peter and Tiana.

"Couldn't have been a better outcome, in the end. But I completely stuffed things up initially by telling Enid too abruptly that Ollie was her son, confirming her worst nightmare," Peter said.

"Don't be so hard on yourself, Pete. She did ask you point blank. Her reaction was horrifying, though. It reminded me..." Tiana stopped talking. "Sorry," she said. Peter reached over and squeezed her hand.

"Enid told us that when she first returned to get Ollie, they told her he'd gone to a wonderful family that would give him a better life than she could provide. Can you believe it? Didn't say anything about sending him off to Australia," Peter said.

"Jack is wonderfully supportive and adores Enid. He was furious about how they'd treated her when she told him about Ollie. They both returned to the Home, wanting to find out what had happened to him. But the Sisters refused to tell them anything, saying he had a new life now."

"This is testing my faith," Andrew said. "The whole bloody lot of them should rot in hell. I don't understand how they could do this to people."

"Just what I'm wondering," Veronica said.

"So where do we go from here, Pete?" Tiana asked.

"Well, after Enid writes to Ollie, and once the letter's on its way, I'll telephone Ollie and tell him about Enid and that he can expect her letter."

"Bloody hell, don't envy you that one," Andrew said.

"I'll try and be more tactful this time around," Peter said. "I should probably get my mum to give me a script."

***

It was a week before Peter got the call from Jack telling him that Enid had written and posted the letter to Oliver.

In the meantime, Peter had rung Jean and told her how bad he felt about his initial handling of the situation with Enid and Jack.

Jean said the same thing as Tiana.

"Don't beat up on yourself, darling. These types of situations are impossibly hard to navigate. And it all turned out wonderfully in the end. It was a brilliant outcome for Ollie that probably wouldn't have happened without you, Tiana, and Veronica. What could be better than finding a loving mother and supportive stepfather? You've done well."

"Thanks, Mum."

"Just take it slowly when you tell Ollie; it will be such a shock for him. I know it's a bit cliché, but start with something like, 'There's something I have to tell you, Ollie, that's going to be a big shock.' Something along those lines."

"Okay, yes. Fingers crossed, I'll do a better job this time."

***

Peter could feel his anxiety rising as he waited for Oliver to pick up the ringing telephone.

"Hello, Oliver here."

"Ollie, good to hear your voice."

"Pete, this is a surprise. How's the trip going?"

"Great, thanks, Ollie. Now I have some news. I've sent you a certified copy of your birth certificate."

"Bloody brilliant! Thanks, Pete. I'll reimburse you when you get back."

"No worries. Now, there's something else I have to tell you, Ollie, that will be a big shock."

"What do you mean, Pete?"

"Are you sitting down?"

"Bloody hell, Pete, get on with it!"

"Well - Err, you know how I said I'd also get you a copy of your mum's death certificate?"

"Yes."

"Em, well, there wasn't one."

"What do you mean 'there wasn't one'?"

"She hadn't died, Ollie. She's still alive. The priest, the Church, they all lied to you."

There was a lengthy pause before Oliver said, "Jesus, okay, I'm sitting down now."

Another lengthy pause, then, "Bloody hell, Pete, is this true?"

"Yes, Ollie. She's written you a letter, which you should get soon."

"But how, Pete, how is this possible? Why didn't she come to get me?"

"She did, Pete, but they'd already put you on the ship to Australia. They told her you had gone to live with a family who'd give you a better life. They didn't even tell her you'd been sent to Australia. She assumed the family was in the UK. She was heartbroken."

"Oh my God, I feel sick."

"I'm so sorry, Ollie."

"I can't stop shaking Pete."

"It's the shock, Ollie."

"All those years, Pete, all those years of misery, and she was *alive* all that time? Oh, my God, I could *kill* them."

"I know Ollie."

"How on earth did you find her?"

Peter explained how Tiana and Veronica had become involved and had gone to St Catherine's House, where they discovered that Enid, his mother, wasn't dead.

"They couldn't find her death certificate, so then they checked Marriages and discovered that she'd married three years after you left the UK. Then they tracked down Enid and her husband Jack's home address.

"Then I wrote a letter to Enid, and Jack telephoned us a few days later and invited us to go down and see them."

"God, Pete, how can I ever repay you? If it weren't for you, I'd never have bloody known. Those *bastards*."

"Well, the important thing is you know now. Your mother is a beautiful woman, Ollie. She never forgot you and prayed she'd see you again one day. Jack is a great bloke, adores your mum, and is fully supportive. He hates the Catholic

Church for what they've done to you both. And you also have a half-sister and brother."

"Oh my God, really? This is all so overwhelming, Pete."

"Understandable, Ollie. Will you be Okay? Is Jimmy there?"

"Yes, Jimmy's here. He'll be shocked. Could it be the same for him, Pete? Jesus! This might have opened the most gigantic can of worms. It'll take me a while to get my head around it all."

"Well, take care of yourself, Ollie. We can't have anything happening to you now, or your mother would never forgive me!"

"Oh Pete, *'my* mother'. I'd better go before I start blubbering.

CHAPTER FIFTEEN

All four members of Operation Ollie barely had time to draw breath before launching into the next week, which was packed with activity. James and Jenny's Engagement Party was held the weekend after Peter and Tiana visited Enid and Jack. Peter started working at The Daily Mail the following Monday. On Wednesday, Veronica and Tiana went down south to spend a few days with Veronica's parents before celebrating her mother, Suzanne's fortieth birthday on the weekend.

The Friday after Tiana and Veronica returned to London, Peter telephoned them in the morning. He said Ollie had received Enid's letter, and he couldn't wait to bring them both up to speed.

"Can you meet me and Andy at The Harrow later this afternoon, and I'll tell you all about it?"

"You're on; see you five thirtyish," Veronica said.

***

Once they were all settled in the saloon bar with their drinks, Peter said, "So Enid's letter finally arrived, and Ollie told me that reading it was the most beautiful experience of his life. He even admitted to crying whilst reading it for the first time. He then re-read it all again before finally handing it over to Jimmy. He said Jimmy cried too."

"Oh my," Tiana said. "Well done, Enid."

"Yes, Enid told him everything that happened when she went back to the Children's Home to get him after being hospitalised with double pneumonia, including all the lies that they told her. She also told him how understanding Jack was when he learnt she'd had a son before they met and that he insisted they go back and try to find out where Ollie had gone. Jack wrote a few pages, and even Susan and John wrote something."

"No wonder he cried," Veronica said.

"Then there were all the photographs, including a few of him when he was a baby and young boy. He said it made him feel sick thinking about how the innocent boy in the photographs was utterly destroyed by the lies and brutality he suffered at the hands of the Church and the brothers. His biggest challenge now is what to tell his mother. He thinks the harsh reality would be too shattering for her.

"But when all this comes out, she's going to learn the truth anyway," Andrew said. "Better that she hears it from him first."

"That's exactly what I told him, Andy. It'll be tough for him to keep things from her once she's staying with him, especially with Jimmy being there too. But now she's found him again, I think she'll be strong enough to face anything, plus she's got Jack for support."

"Bloody hell, now I'm wondering how many more men and women might come forward to question whether or not they have mothers who are still alive," Andrew said.

"My thoughts exactly, and I've already had this conversation with mum and Ollie. As I explained before, it's the fact that illegitimate kids were documented as orphans that makes the situation so complicated and messy.

"In Ollie's case, he was illegitimate but not an orphan. He was deliberately *lied to* and told he was an orphan because his mother had died. Some kids weren't told point blank that they were orphans but were *documented* as such, and so they grew up simply believing it, and it may or may not have been true.

Jimmy's is a case in point. And then, of course, there are genuine orphans. What a complete, bloody mess. No wonder the Catholic Church wants to make it as hard as possible for people to get hold of their records.

"Now Ollie and Jimmy are wondering if Jimmy's mother is also alive or if he has other living relatives he doesn't know about. Honestly, I don't know what we'll do if many more people come forward after learning about Ollie's story. When I first interviewed him, I had no idea it would turn out like this. His story was horrendous from the beginning, but now it just keeps getting worse with each passing day."

"It will be a massive story, Pete, involving the Catholic Church and two governments. I think we can anticipate a huge amount of resistance. No wonder our editor was keen to get involved."

"And to think we started with just one birth certificate, one missing death certificate and one marriage certificate," Veronica said.

"Yes, and what's starting to worry me, Pete, is that, unlike us three, you're not Catholic and may not understand just how powerful the Catholic Church is," Tiana said, looking anxiously at Peter.

"Don't worry, I'm getting the picture alright."

"Okay, well, we're getting off track; let's get back to Enid and Ollie. When are they going to meet?" Tiana said.

"Well, Enid wants to fly to Perth as soon as possible to meet Ollie, and, of course, she wants him to come to the UK to meet the family. She's flying out alone because Jack still works; he's in admin now, and John is still at school, but she's terrified of flying."

"Well, that's not a problem; we'll go with her," Tiana said, completely off the cuff.

"What!" Veronica and Peter said in unison, both looking shocked.

"You and me, Vron. We'll fly over with Enid, meet Ollie, and see Australia." They all stared at Tiana.

"Well," Veronica said, "It's usually me that makes the impromptu decisions. But yes, that's a great idea; I'm in."

"I'm stunned," Peter said. "I can't believe you'd go this far to help Enid and Ollie. It will certainly make all the difference to Enid to have you both with her. Are you sure?"

"Absolutely, I'm loving the idea," Tiana said. "We'll also get to meet your mother and father, Pete."

"I'll telephone Enid tomorrow and give her the good news; she'll be astounded. I think it would be best if you both liaise directly with her. By now, Enid and Ollie will have spoken by telephone, so she'll keep him up-to-date on all the arrangements."

"Do you think Enid will have a passport already?" Veronica asked.

"Good point, Vron, possibly not. So that could mean a ten-week delay before you fly out. I'm guessing you have yours."

"Of course."

"Hopefully, it won't take Enid that long to get hers," Tiana said. "Maye, she'll also be able to help Ollie get his passport sorted. He's got his birth certificate now, but Enid may have other ID records, such as vaccination cards or school reports. Possibly, they could help."

"Good thinking, Tiana, mention all that to Enid. So my contract at The Daily Mail is for four months, which means I'll be flying back to Perth the first week of June. Let's say it does take Enid ten weeks to get her passport; that means you'd be leaving about the second week of May. If she spends, say, three weeks with Ollie, then that's roughly about when I'll be returning to Perth. Could you possibly wait until then, or is that asking too much? You'll be staying with my parents, of course."

"Of course, we'll wait," Tiana said. "But check with your mother first, Pete. We can just as easily stay in a hotel. We also want to see parts of Australia whilst we're there."

Peter laughed. "I don't think you realise just how big Australia is. At least we could show you some of the diversity of Western Australia."

"So, is Melbourne far from Perth?"

"Good lord, Tiana, it's on the other side of the country! You'd have to fly there."

"Oh, I didn't realise," Tiana said. "Well, I'm sure there's lots to see in Western Australia."

"Yes, there is lots to see. Western Australia is about the same size as Western Europe and covers the entire western third of the country," Peter said, sounding somewhat miffed.

"Oh dear, my ignorance has offended you," Tiana said. "I'm sorry, Pete. Clearly, I haven't a clue about Australia."

"That's okay; I guess my cultural cringe is showing," Peter laughed.

"Well, now that we've overcome the awkward moment, let's have another round of drinks," Andrew said.

When Peter and Andrew left to get the drinks, Veronica turned to Tiana and said, "What's this sudden thing you've got for Australia and what's with Melbourne?"

"What do you mean?" Tiana said. "Aren't you keen to see some of the country and meet Ollie? As for Melbourne, it's the only other place I've heard of in Australia."

"Hmm, you seemed overly interested in Australia as soon as I mentioned that Pete and his cousin were from there," Veronica said, her voice sounding suspicious.

"Oh, rubbish; I just think it would be a great place to visit, and I want to meet Ollie. You're making something out of nothing, Vron."

Veronica stared at Tiana, her eyes narrowing. "Well, I still think something is going on that you're not telling me about. I..."

But just then, the two men returned, and she dropped the subject.

Tiana felt she'd dodged a bullet and prayed that she wouldn't get the third degree when they got home. *I'll have to watch what I say from here on.*

Her idea to accompany Enid had been spontaneous and genuine, as was her enthusiasm for meeting Ollie. But despite all the excitement and distraction of finding and meeting Enid and Jack, her longing to see The Bishop kept getting stronger. The sudden glimmer of hope that she'd found a way to get to Australia without people knowing she had additional motives, except for Veronica's suspicions, filled her with excitement. But now there was the additional challenge of distance.

Just my luck that Melbourne is hundreds of miles away from Perth. Now, I'll have to come up with another excuse to fly over there. This is so frustrating.

***

Enid and Jack were amazed and relieved to hear that Tiana and Veronica had offered to fly out with Enid. They invited them both to come down to Portsmouth so they could thank them in person.

"If you come down on the train, Jack will come and collect you both from the station," Enid told Tiana.

The following Monday, they took the train to Portsmouth and spent the afternoon with Enid and Jack. They also met Susan and John, who were so excited about finding out they had a big brother in Australia. It was clear that they were a very close and loving family who couldn't wait to make Oliver feel a part of it again.

Enid showed Tiana all the documents she'd kept from Oliver's first eight years, and Tiana helped her put together the ones they thought would be the most relevant for his passport application.

Enid and Veronica hit it off straight away, and Veronica helped Enid go through her wardrobe and decide what she should pack for the trip.

"Pete says it will be Autumn when we get there, but for us, it will probably feel like Summer."

"Sounds wonderful," Enid said.

They finished off the day with Jack and Enid taking Tiana and Veronica to dinner at The Wellington before they caught the train back to London.

"It just makes me so sad, Vron," Tiana said once they were alone on the train, "to think that this could have been Ollie's life. I don't know how anyone could get over having the life they were meant to have stolen by lies and deceit. I wonder how Ollie will cope with it."

"I don't know. But thank God his family is so wonderful. Imagine if he'd found out about them and they didn't want to know him or if his mother had died before he could meet her."

"Oh my God, Vron, that's too awful for words. What if there *are* many more people like Ollie, and that's what it's like for them when they find out that they're not orphans or they can't track down their families? It just doesn't bear thinking about."

"I know, and now I'm worried about what will happen once Ollie's story gets out."

"Me too. Pete hasn't told us the details of what happened to Ollie, but clearly it was horrendous. What do you think the Church will do?"

"Deny, deny, deny," Veronica said. Given what they've done, what else could you expect?"

***

In the end, it was weeks before Enid got her passport, which gave Tiana and Victoria plenty of time to visit their respective families and tell them about the upcoming trip to Australia. Veronica spent a few days with her parents, and Tiana flew to Paris for a week with her mother. She gave Adelia a brief overview of meeting Peter and Andrew, learning about Oliver and discovering that his mother hadn't died.

"Vron and I became quite the sleuths, Maman; we were very good at it," she said. "The hardest part was when Pete and I met Enid and Jack, her husband, and Pete confirmed that it was her son Oliver who had been sent to Australia. It was a terrible shock for her."

"I can only imagine," Adelia said. "That poor woman."

Adelia took it in her stride when Tiana said she and Veronica would accompany Enid to Australia.

"Could we not pay for her ticket?" Adelia asked.

"Well, since it's such a long flight, Vron and I discussed buying her a First-Class ticket to travel together. But then we thought it would be too over the top and might make her and Jack feel awkward. So we'll travel economy with her going to Australia. Enid will probably be flying back before us, so Vron and I will book first-class tickets home when we have a date."

"Very thoughtful, darling; your father would have been proud of you."

"So, how is everything going? Any problems on the business front?"

"No darling, everything is running like clockwork, just as we expected."

"Do we have any business interests in Australia, in Perth or Melbourne, for example?"

"Well, funny you should mention it, but one of our directors, Monsieur Laurent, told me just the other day that the company has negotiated the distribution rights to sell the range of Arguello cigars in Australia. They have become our top seller in Europe, so he wants us to take them worldwide, starting with Melbourne and then Sydney."

"Good heavens! Well, maybe I could fly over to Melbourne while I'm there, check out the cigar merchants, and even introduce myself to the best one and open up the dialogue."

"Well, that's a wonderful idea, darling, if you're sure you'll have the time. What about Veronica? Will she go with you?"

"Em, I don't know, maybe."

"Well, in that case, you should meet with Hugo Moreau, our top sales manager, and discuss what he thinks your approach should be. He can also give you background material to read to prepare yourself and sales material to take with you, such as brochures, maybe some of our recent press releases, and Hugo's business card for follow-up contact. I'll organise business cards for you, too, and send them over before you leave."

"That's brilliant, Maman, a real added benefit to the trip. Please set up the meeting with Monsieur Moreau."

Ha, Melbourne, here I come! But what about Vron? She'll be even more suspicious if I don't ask her to accompany me. And it would be much more fun with her. I'll figure it out.

Ultimately, Tiana decided it would be better to tell Veronica about her proposed visit to Melbourne when she returned to London. *I'll need to tell her eventually, and the longer I leave it, the more suspicious she'll be.*

***

Tiana opened the discussion the first day she was back by showing Veronica the Chanel suit her mother had bought for her before she left Paris.

"Wow, it's beautiful, Tiana, so soft and super chic," Veronica said admiringly.

"Maman bought it for me to wear when I go to Melbourne on business, Tiana said. "It turns out that we have the distribution rights to sell the Arguello cigars in Australia, starting with Melbourne. So I'll fly there to check out the best cigar merchant and introduce the owner to our company and the Arguello brand."

"What a coincidence," Veronica said, staring hard at Tiana. "Just the place you were so interested in."

"Oh, come on, Vron, I didn't know this would happen. Anyway, I was hoping you'd come with me. We'll impress them all when we demonstrate that we *can* actually smoke cigars," Tiana said, her instincts telling her this was the best approach to take with Vron. This was confirmed when she saw the smile on Veronica's face.

"Okay, it sounds like fun. I'd better make sure I have the right outfit, too, since you'll be looking so elegant. Is there anything else we'll need?"

"Heaps! We have to look businesslike because cigar shops are so incredibly formal. It's just as well papa trained me in all the etiquette and then took me to James J. Fox, so I learned first-hand how to behave and not make a complete fool of myself by saying and doing the wrong thing. Some tobacconists can be such snobs.

"So I'll have my briefcase containing the promotional material our sales manager Hugo Moreau gave me to show to the owner, plus his business card for future contact.

"Then I'll have my travel humidor to keep the cigars at the right temperature after I make the initial purchase. I'll buy five Romeo y Julieta for us and an extra two for the single cigar cases we both have for our handbags. If you want to get a travel humidor for the trip, we can get twice as many cigars to carry us through."

"Okay, I'll do that."

"Then obviously your lighter, and don't forget your cutter."

"Just as well I went with you to James J. Fox, so I've got an idea of how it all works. This cigar caper is full on."

And that's only the half of it. Now, I'll have to find a way to escape to see The Bishop without setting off Vron's suspicions again.

Tiana decided to go to the cigar merchant before contacting The Bishop. This would give her a legitimate story to explain her sudden appearance in Melbourne.

And I'll tell him His Excellency Archbishop Armand told me he could be contacted in Melbourne.

***

Over the following weeks, Tiana and Victoria spent most Friday evenings meeting Peter and Andrew for drinks at The Harrow or getting together with Jenny and Michael at the Windsor Castle Pub. On Saturday evenings, the four often went to the cinema together, and on cold, wet Sunday evenings, more often than not, Veronica and Tiana would end up cooking a roast for them all at the flat.

In the second week of April, Andrew said, "The weather's so much better now; why don't we drive down to Portsmouth next Saturday and visit Enid and Jack? I'd love to meet them, and there may be an update on Enid's passport; it must be getting close now."

***

Enid and Jack were delighted to see them all but had no news on the passport front. Enid was in constant touch with Ollie by telephone, and they both felt frustrated at the delay.

"I hope it comes soon," Jack said. "I couldn't possibly tell you what my wife says about the HM Passport Office. I'm seeing a whole new side of her!"

Finally, after nine weeks, Enid's passport arrived, and Tiana booked her and Veronica's tickets to fly out with Enid on Friday, April 7.

***

Once the big day arrived, Peter and Andrew joined Jack, Susan, and John to see the three excited women off.

"I can imagine all the emotions Ollie is going to be experiencing waiting for you at Perth Airport," Peter said to Enid. "I gave him my parents' telephone number so he could arrange to meet them before you arrived. Mum and dad want to support him, especially on the big day when they're waiting for you to walk out of Arrivals."

"That's so thoughtful of you and your parents, Pete. Jack and I can't thank you enough for everything you've done for us."

"No worries, Enid."

Andrew looked miserable as he stepped forward to hug Veronica.

"I'm going to miss you, Vronie. I can't wait for you to come back."

Tiana was surprised to see that Veronica seemed close to tears. *Wow, this is getting serious. I need to pay attention.*

"Miss you too, baby," Veronica said, giving Andrew a kiss and the longest hug back. "I'll call you as soon as I can."

Tiana remembered how The Bishop had come striding towards her at Orly Airport. *Oh, if only he would be there to meet me at Perth Airport and take me in his arms.*

Peter walked up to Tiana, "I'm going to miss you too, Senior Sleuth," he said, reaching out and tucking her hair behind her left ear.

It was a small gesture but done so tenderly that it sent a shock wave through Tiana. *Oh, mon dieu, he's falling for me, and I didn't even notice. Merde – this is so bad.*

"Now feeling incredibly awkward, she said, "I'm so looking forward to meeting your parents, Pete. And - I'll call and let you know what happens when Ollie and Enid first meet. I bet we all end up in tears."

"Yeah," Peter said.

Tiana gave him a quick hug, "See you in Perth," she said before joining the long line waiting to board. Just before entering the tunnel to the aircraft, she turned to wave and saw the disappointment still written on his face.

CHAPTER SIXTEEN

O liver began to panic the minute he knew that Enid was flying to Perth to see him.

"Shit, Jimmy, we have to clean this place up," he said, looking around the lounge room. "I can't have mum coming with it looking like this."

Jimmy laughed, "She's not coming for weeks, Ollie; plenty of time to get organised."

"I'll get one of those cleaning services to come in and go right through the place the week before she arrives. And I'll buy new furniture for the third bedroom so it's all fresh for her."

"Are you sure you don't want me to move out, Ollie?"

"Don't be ridiculous, Jimmy. Anyway, I need you here for support."

Jimmy laughed again. "Jeez, you've got it bad, Ollie! You've got to stop panicking. She's going to be just as nervous as you."

"She's going to see how screwed up my life has been, Jimmy. I'm scared I'll be a huge disappointment to her."

"Bloody hell, Ollie, none of that was your fault. Look how successful you've been. You've built a career and bought this house in one of the top suburbs in Perth."

"Yes, but my personal life, Jimmy, my failed marriage, no kids..."

"Look, mate, she won't care about any of that. Just having you back will be enough for her if her letter and telephone calls are anything to go by."

"I hope you're right, Jimmy. I hope you're right."

***

Enid was experiencing emotions and sentiments identical to her son as their plane approached Perth. Looking back and forth from Tiana to Veronica, she said, "I'm so worried that I'm going to be a disappointment to Oliver."

"Oh, Enid, what could make you believe such a thing," Tiana said. "Ollie is going to think you are the most wonderful woman in the world."

"Exactly," Veronica said. "You never forgot him; you tried to find him, and now you've flown across the world to see him."

"And what's the bet that Ollie thinks the same thing, that *he* will disappoint you? And once you're together, you'll laugh at how silly you both were to think such a thing," Tiana said.

"Oh, I hadn't thought of it like that. Of course, I won't be disappointed in him. Goodness, I don't know what I'd have done without you girls coming with me. You've both been so kind. I'd have been such a mess without you here."

"Well, ever since we met Pete and Andy and then went to St Catherine's House looking for you and Ollie and then found you, it's like we've been on this amazing adventure," Veronica said. "And now we're about to see Australia. We're having a wonderful time, Enid."

Enid couldn't help laughing. "Well, that's a positive spin if ever I heard one."

Tiana saw the perfect moment to mention the trip to Melbourne and said, "And I'm getting the opportunity to expand our family business. I've been asked to go to Melbourne to source a top cigar merchant for our premium handmade Arguello cigars. Vron is coming with me."

"Well, I never," Enid said. "I didn't realise your family business was cigars."

"Well, it's a tiny but exclusive part of it," Tiana said.

"Goodness, but I don't suppose you smoke them yourself."

"Oh yes, I do; both Vron and I smoke," Tiana said, grinning at Veronica. "We'll show you when we get to Perth."

***

As the plane finally descended, all three women were affected by nerves as they anticipated Enid and Oliver's meeting. Enid took them both by the hand and clung on to them as the plane taxied to a stop.

It seemed to take forever to get through customs, but finally, the moment arrived, and the three walked through the Arrival doors.

***

The following day, Tiana telephoned Peter and described how she first saw Ollie standing beside his parents, Jean and William.

"It was easy to recognise him as he looked so like Enid. He seemed rooted to the spot, so your father had to give him a small nudge forward," she said, laughing at the memory.

"Then, as Ollie walked towards her, Enid started to walk faster and faster till she was running, and she threw herself into his arms. First, they just clung to each other, and then they both started crying, hugging each other as though they'd never let go. By then, Vron and I were also in tears, and so was your mother. Even your father looked teary-eyed.

"They finally drew apart, and Ollie kept saying, 'Oh mum, oh mum,' staring at her, while Enid stroked his cheek, saying, 'My boy,' her eyes never leaving his face. It was so incredibly touching, Pete.

"Finally, Ollie said, 'Come on, Mum, let's get your luggage; you must be exhausted. I'm taking you straight home.'

"So once we'd retrieved our luggage, Ollie and William went to get the cars, Enid left with Ollie, and Vron and I went home with your parents. Once we got there, we were all so excited that we ended up drinking Camomile Tea and talking for the next hour or so until we finally fell into bed at about two in the morning. I imagine the same thing happened with Enid and Ollie."

"I wish I could have been there," Peter said. "So when are you seeing Enid and Ollie again?"

"Your parents have invited them to dinner here tonight, together with Jimmy. They're so lovely, Pete. They can't do enough to make us all feel comfortable."

"That's my parents."

"Then tomorrow, Ollie has invited us all to go over to his place for lunch, and then in the evening, we'll have drinks and dinner at the Ocean Beach Hotel, which sounds lovely.

"Oh, by the way, I haven't told you yet, but I'm flying to Melbourne to check out the cigar merchants there. We distribute Arguello premium cigars in Western Europe, and now one of our company directors wants to take the brand worldwide. He's negotiated the distribution licence for Australia. He's singled out Melbourne as the city to explore first. My coming here seemed like the ideal opportunity to take it further and make a connection."

"Wow, quite the businesswoman."

"Well, I was sixteen when papa first started training me in this aspect of our family business, so I'm excited about becoming more involved now. Vron's coming with me."

"Right, so will you both go there before I return?"

"Well, Enid will only be here for three weeks till the twenty-eighth. We don't want to leave before then, especially since Ollie has a big project. It meant that he could only take off the first week of her visit. Of course, they have the evenings and weekends together, but Vron and I want to spend time with her and Jimmy during the daytime over the following two weeks. Your parents have a few things planned for us, too."

"I see."

"So we're flying to Melbourne on the twenty-ninth, the day after Enid flies out. When do you get back here?"

"I fly out of Heathrow on Friday, June seventh."

"Oh, we'll be back by then."

"Okay. Well, I think you'll like Melbourne. I prefer it to Sydney. It's far larger and more sophisticated than Perth. Thanks to the Italian immigrants, Melbourne has an amazing coffee culture. Lygon Street in Carlton is the place to go. It's also a real 'foodie' city with heaps of fantastic restaurants, and I imagine there are lots of cigar connoisseurs. I hope you find your ideal merchant."

"Thanks, Pete, see you back here then," Tiana said, deliberately keeping her tone light and casual.

***

Both Tiana and Veronica thoroughly enjoyed their time in Perth. Veronica later described it to Andrew: "It's a large town rather than a city, where the pace is slow, and the lifestyle is incredibly relaxed."

Jean and William's house was on The Esplanade in Mount Pleasant. It over-looked the Swan River, and Tiana and Veronica got into the habit of jogging halfway around the river before breakfast. On some evenings, they'd walk down to the Raffles Hotel with Jean and William, listen to the music, and have a few drinks before Oliver, Enid, and Jimmy joined them for dinner.

***

Enid was stunned when she saw Oliver's house in Cottesloe. Later, she told Jean, "I can't believe my son owns such a large house in such a posh area. We have a tiny terrace house in Portsmouth."

"I'm sure Oliver won't be the least bit concerned with the size of your house, Enid," Jean replied. "It's the people living there that he'll be focused on."

"Yes, of course, silly of me to worry about such unimportant things. You know, Jean, once Oliver and Jimmy sat down with me and talked about what it was like for them both growing up in the institution, it was all I could do not to break down.

"I'm sure they didn't tell me the half of it, but the way they were forced to work on the buildings, the physical punishment, the terrible food, and no proper schooling, I just don't understand it. How could the brothers be so cruel, and how could the Church let it happen year after year? They must have known about it.

"I don't think I'll ever be able to forgive them for what they did to my boy and our family and all the other boys."

"Oh, they knew, alright," Jean said.

***

In the second week, when Oliver returned to work, Jean and William decided it was the ideal opportunity to show their visitors more of Perth. On Monday, they took a river cruise from Perth to Fremantle, where they had lunch at the Sail & Anchor Hotel. Afterwards, before catching the train back to Perth, they wandered around the Fremantle Markets, which had been restored the year before in 1975.

The following day, the weather was perfect, so they took the ferry to Rottnest Island, just nineteen kilometres offshore from Perth.

"We locals call it Rotto," William said as they headed to the island. "It used to be an Aboriginal penal colony, but the prison closed in 1904. Jean and I have spent many wonderful holidays there camping, swimming, and fishing. It's very informal, and there are no cars, so be prepared to cycle around the island."

"What are quokkas?" Veronica asked. "I heard someone mention them."

"They're little furry macropods about the size of a cat that live on the island," Jean said. "They hop and bounce around like Kangaroos, but they can also climb trees. They're so cute and look as if they're smiling, but don't get too close. Unfortunately, you probably won't see them today as they're nocturnal; you'll have to make do with picture postcards."

After their Rotto trip, Enid felt like a day at home. So Tiana and Veronica decided to take the opportunity to go to Perth and purchase their tickets to Melbourne. Tiana bought two first-class tickets so they could sleep more comfortably on the TAA night flight, and she booked a chauffeur to pick them up from the airport and take them to the hotel.

Tiana asked for the name of the top hotel in Melbourne. "Oh, that would be The Southern Cross Hotel," the booking agent said. "It's where all the celebrities stay. Would you require two single or double rooms?"

"No suites?"

"I'm afraid not."

"A double room then," Tiana said, "We'll need it for three days." Then, smiling at Veronica, she said, "All in the name of impression management, Vron."

Veronica rolled her eyes.

***

On the final week of her stay, Enid just wanted to be at home in Cottesloe.

"It's so beautiful here," she said. "I love walking on the beach and then going over to have a coffee at the Ocean Beach Hotel and look out over the ocean. I'm going to miss this beautiful place when I go home."

In the afternoons, Veronica and Tiana joined Enid and Jimmy in a game of cards or monopoly and in the evening, Enid cooked dinner. She cooked traditional English food that Oliver remembered from his childhood.

"I used to have dreams about your roast beef and Yorkshire pud and rhubarb and apple crumble, Mum," he said. "This is absolute heaven."

The last day of Enid's visit was very emotional. They all went out to dinner, and Enid told them they had given her the best three weeks of her life.

"I'll never forget you all and how wonderful you've been to me," she said. "I'll be seeing you girls soon, and my boy will be coming for Christmas, but he's also promised me another visit with the whole family when we can all come out together. I can't wait to come back."

"When are you coming over, Ollie?" Tiana asked.

"I'm taking a six-week holiday," Oliver said. "So I'll come over two weeks before Christmas, and then I'll have another month afterwards with the family."

"That's great. London is wonderful at Christmas time, and that will allow us to see you too," Veronica said.

Oliver and Enid wanted just the two of them to go to the airport when Enid left. So they all said their tearful goodbyes at the restaurant, with Tiana and Veronica promising to visit Enid as soon as they returned to the UK.

***

Tiana and Veronica flew out of Perth the following evening. The chauffeur picked them up from the airport, and they were amazed at the size of Melbourne as they drove through the city to their hotel.

"Pete told me it was larger than Perth," Tiana said. "But I hadn't expected it to be like this. It really is a city."

"Oh my goodness, look, they've got trams," Victoria said. "We'll have to take a ride on one of them."

Once they'd checked into the hotel and got to their room, they decided to take showers and get dressed in their more formal outfits before having breakfast downstairs.

Veronica decided to team her green and black silk von Furstenberg wrap dress with a dark green velvet jacket and black court shoes instead of the ankle boots she would typically wear with the outfit.

"The receptionist said there can be three seasons in one day here in Melbourne, so that should have me covered for any changes."

"Perfect, and I'll wear a silk shirt with my suit in case it does get warmer later. Dressed like this, we won't need to change if we go somewhere nice for dinner."

"Let's go downstairs and have a big breakfast before we head out," Veronica said. "I'm starving."

"Yes, and after breakfast, I must speak to the Concierge. Given that the wealthiest people are guests here, he will know where to send us to purchase premium, handmade cigars."

"Smart thinking. I have a good feeling about this project of yours."

"Hold that thought," Tiana said.

***

After breakfast, Tiana and Veronica headed for the hotel entrance, where Tiana approached the concierge. Seeing his nametag, she asked if he spoke French.

"Mais Oui, Mademoiselle, how can I be of service," Claude replied.

A very animated conversation in French followed, in which Tiana learnt that Claude had worked at the hotel since its opening in 1962 and had been there when the Beatles came in 1964. He had an Australian wife and two sons, nine and twelve.

He said that if they wanted to eat fabulous French food in an informal atmosphere, they should go to Mietta in Fitzroy, where there was a brilliant French chef, but they would need to take a bottle of wine. And if the Mademoiselles wanted to go upmarket, he recommended Florentino's for superb Italian food. For coffee in Lygon Street, he suggested Tamani. And whilst there was a tobacconist in the hotel, Claude said that the best place to buy handmade cigars was at the Alejandro Cigar Merchants in Elizabeth Street.

After Claude had summoned the taxi to take them to Alejandro's, he and Tiana parted like old friends.

***

"Well, you certainly have your mother's gift for charming people into bending over backwards to help you," Victoria said once they were in the taxi. "I'm impressed."

"That's thanks to maman's training and those endless Monday Afternoon Teas," Tiana said. "But now I value what I was given."

"I must say you look very professional dressed in your Chanel tweed suit with your Dupont briefcase; so very French!"

Tiana laughed. "Well, if the owner isn't there this morning, I'll leave my card, and we can make an appointment to go back and see him later."

"You have a business card?"

" Yes," Tiana said, grinning at the surprised look on Veronica's face. "It was maman's suggestion. She had them printed and sent to me, along with Monsieur Hugo's cards."

"Well, I can't wait to see you turn your charm on the tobacconist and the owner if they're not one and the same. I bet they've never had someone like you walk in the door before."

Tiana grinned, "Fingers crossed, I don't stuff up."

PART FIVE

THE TIMING

CHAPTER SEVENTEEN

As they walked into Melbourne's premier tobacconist, Veronica whispered to Tiana, "It's nothing like James J. Fox, obviously, but not bad."

"Good morning," Tiana said to one of the attendants standing behind a counter. "May I speak to the tobacconist?"

It was not unusual for male customers to be *accompanied* by younger women. But elegant young women like Tiana and Victoria, alone - this was a first.

The attendant buzzed under the counter, and Mr Henderson emerged. Tipping his head, the attendant silently nodded toward the two women looking at one of the humidor cabinets.

"Ladies, how may I assist you?" Mr Henderson said smoothly. "My name is Henderson, and I am the manager here at Alejandro's."

"Good morning, Mr Henderson," Tiana said. "My name is Tiana Manning, and this is my friend Victoria Pemberton. We've just arrived in Melbourne, and we would like to purchase our favourite cigar, the Romeo y Julieta."

"Certainly, Miss Manning, please follow me."

Mr Henderson led the way to one of the humidor cabinets, and Tiana and Victoria stepped forward to look closely at the cigars, looking for cracks, blemishes, or dry specks.

Everything seemed in order, so Tiana turned to Mr Henderson and said, "May I open the cabinet, Mr Henderson?"

"But, of course, Miss Manning."

Tiana opened the humidor, removed a cigar, and quickly closed the door. She then checked for smoothness when she rolled the cigar before giving it a gentle squeeze to check it was spongy to the touch and held its shape when she pressed her fingers to it. Finally, she took a whiff to make sure it had a rich aroma.

Turning to Mr Henderson, she smiled and nodded her approval.

"Excellent, Mr Henderson, we'll take 12 cigars. Thank you."

Smiling in return, Mr Henderson said, "Are there any other cigars you would care to sample ladies."

"Yes," Veronica said. "I'd like to try something different, but also mild to medium, as I'm still developing my palate. What about you, Tiana?"

"Yes, I'd like to try something new too, although I do like the cedar and spice-tasting notes of Romeo y Julieta."

"Then I suggest the Cuesta-Rey No.95, one of our top-selling premium cigars. It's named after the bottles of Chanel No.5 that Stanford Newman of the Newman Cigar Company often purchased for his wife," Mr Henderson said, smiling at Tiana.

"The cigar is a Lonsdale vitola with a 42-ring gauge that will feel smooth and elegant in your hand. It has a sweet coffee bean flavour with nutty undertones and doesn't require much ignition. After pulling some cold air through the cigar, you may pick up some cedar and spices like coriander. I think you will enjoy this cigar. Would you both care to try one?"

"Absolutely," Veronica said. "It sounds wonderful. But first I need a new cutter. I could have sworn I had mine with me, but I must have left it somewhere on the other side of the country.

"Do you prefer single or double Miss Pemberton?"

"A double, please, Mr Henderson,"

"Very well, I'll bring you a selection with the Cuesta-Rey cigars," Mr Henderson said, leading them to the smoking room.

On his return, Victoria selected her cutter, and she and Tiana chose their respective cigars. Mr Henderson then left them to their smoking enjoyment.

Over the next hour, two elderly gentlemen entered the smoking room at different times, and Tiana and Victoria found it difficult not to laugh when they saw the shocked looks on the faces of both men when they saw the two young women sitting there smoking. Mr Henderson smiled when he saw his two regular customers enter the smoking room.

Tiana couldn't resist saying "Bon jour" to each of them to see their startled reaction.

"You are wicked," Veronica whispered, making a supreme effort not to giggle.

***

After emerging from the Smoking Room, both Tiana and Veronica thanked Mr Henderson for his excellent recommendation.

"We've decided to change our order to six Romeo y Julieta and six of the Cuesta-Rey. Thank you, Mr Henderson," Tiana said.

"Very well, Miss Manning, and is there anything else I can help you with?"

"Yes, I was wondering who owns this tobacconist?"

"Mr Alejandro's family opened this tobacconist in 1884, and Mr Raúl Alejandro is the current owner."

"I see. And have you heard of the Arguello brand of cigars, Mr Henderson?"

"No, I have not. Would you happen to know where the cigars are rolled?"

"Tampa, in Florida, and the tobacco comes from the Dominican Republic. My father fell in love with the cigar in 1972. In 1973, when I was sixteen, he took me to meet the Arguello family, and we went to their factory in Ybor City in Tampa, where I saw exactly how the cigars were made. It was handy being able to speak Spanish. The whole experience was amazing."

Mr Henderson looked impressed and said, "And is your father involved in the cigar business, Miss Manning?"

"Insofar as he wanted to be a distributor for the Arguello brand so he could add them to the list of premium hand-rolled cigars we sell on our cruise line and at our resorts. And now we have the distribution rights to sell them in Australia, and we are looking for a select number of cigar merchants to carry the Arguello brand."

Mr Henderson looked genuinely surprised.

"Well Miss Manning..."

"Please call me Tiana."

"And please call me Victoria."

"Well, Miss Tiana and Miss Victoria, Mr Alejandro is not here right now. But he will be back this afternoon if you would care to return, say three o'clock."

"That sounds perfect, Mr Henderson. Here is my card."

"Am I correct in assuming from your accent that you are French Miss Tiana?"

"Half French and half English, Mr Henderson."

***

When Mr Henderson went home that evening, he told his wife about the two young women who had visited the tobacconist that day. "You could have knocked me over with a feather," he said. "Here was this young woman, eighteen or nineteen at the most, clearly extremely wealthy, and she casually mentions she's looking for business and speaks Spanish!"

***

"Holy Moly, Tiana, you were amazing. I'd love to be a fly on the wall when Mr Henderson tells his boss about you," Veronica said the minute they left the shop.

"Thanks Vron. And what a bonus that I'll be able to speak to Mr Alejandro in Spanish. That should impress him."

"This is turning out to be enormous fun," Veronica said.

"Well, we have to be back at three, so there's no time for a lengthy lunch now. Let's follow Mr Henderson's advice on where to go for a sandwich and cup of tea before we have to get back. I'm excited about meeting Mr Alejandro and seeing if I can pull it off and get him interested in selling Arguello cigars."

Tiana and Victoria went to The Hopetoun Tea Rooms in the Block Arcade, which turned out to be surprisingly elegant, having just been renovated in the Victorian style.

"Wow," Victoria said, "If you're going to get a sandwich, you might as well do it in style. And look at those cakes, or should I say gateaux! Well done, Mr Henderson."

***

Returning to Alejandro's after lunch, both women were excited.

"I wonder what he's like," Tiana said.

As they walked through the door, they saw Mr Henderson talking animatedly to an elegant gentleman, and Tiana guessed correctly that it was Mr Alejandro. Tiana estimated that he was in his late fifties from how his dark, thick, wavy hair had turned silver at the temples. He was tall, about six foot, she thought, and was clean-shaven. He was dressed in a beautifully tailored navy blue suit, a white shirt with a dark blue tie with tiny white dots and in his breast pocket, a white handkerchief with a delicate, dark blue border. The outfit was completed with black patent leather shoes, gold cufflinks, a gold watch and a gold signet ring. Tiana's expert eye quickly took in every detail.

The two men turned as the women entered the door, and Mr Henderson made the introductions.

"Mademoiselle Tiana, what a pleasure to meet you," Mr Alejandro said, stepping forward to shake her hand."

"Señor Alejandro," Tiana said.

"And Miss Victoria,"

"How do you do Mr Alejandro."

"Mr Henderson has been telling me about your visit this morning."

"I hope his report was favourable," Tiana said with a smile.

"To say he was 'impressed' would be a grave understatement," Mr Alejandro replied, smiling in return. "Please come into my office."

The office was as elegant as Mr Alejandro. On the right-hand side of the room, there was a beautiful solid Spanish walnut desk with carved drawers, doors, and sides, as well as brass handles and locks. To the left of the room, there were four comfortable aged leather club armchairs with brass stud detailing. They were set around a large solid wood coffee table upon which sat four crystal glass cigar ashtrays. On the walls, there was a sketch of the shop when it first opened in 1884 and framed photos of members of the Alejandro family throughout the generations.

"What a beautiful office you have," Tiana said. "It reminds me of my papa's study, my favourite room in the apartment."

"Was that in Paris, Mademoiselle?"

"Yes, I grew up in Paris and went to boarding school in London, where Vron and I first met. Now we live together in London. Do you know Paris Señor?"

"Oh yes, I've visited Paris several times. It's one of my favourite cities in the world. I also like London very much. Henderson tells me that you also speak Spanish, Mademoiselle."

"Yes, from the time I was born, I had a Spanish nanny. She taught me words, and then, when I was older, I used to listen to her talking with her Spanish friends. I was fluent by the time I was eleven."

"And you, Miss Victoria, do you speak Spanish?"

"No, Mr Alejandro, my language abilities are limited to English and French."

"So, what brings you both to the other side of the world?"

"Well, initially, Vron and I were coming to Australia to visit Perth. Then, when I told my mother about our upcoming trip, she mentioned that our family business had secured the Australian distribution rights for the Arguello brand of premium handmade cigars, to be commenced in the two cities of Melbourne and Sydney. So since I was coming to Australia, it seemed foolish not to fly over to Melbourne to see if there was a premier cigar merchant who would be interested in the Arguello brand."

"I see. And what can you tell me about the Arguello brand Mademoiselle Tiana."

Speaking in Spanish, Tiana told Mr Alejandro how the Arguello company had been founded in Ybor City in Tampa in 1924 by twenty-three-year-old Carlos Arguello, a Spanish immigrant. She explained that his son Juan had taken control of the operations when Carlos retired at sixty-eight. She also told him about her visit to Florida and the factory in Ybor City and how her father had been teaching her about the distribution side of the business.

"Papa and Señor Juan Arguello became good friends, and papa became an Eastern Europe distributor for the brand. The cigars became the top sellers on our cruise line and in our resorts. So now we want to take the brand worldwide, starting in Australia.

"My papa died last year. Otherwise, I'm sure he would have loved to visit Australia himself. But if you met Señor Juan Arguello, you would also like him. Cigars are his passion, of course, and he is very charming."

"Mademoiselle, I'm so sorry to hear of your tragic loss. My deepest condolences."

"Thank you, Señor," Tiana said, pausing for a moment.

Then, continuing, she said, "I've brought some of our sales material, brochures and press releases with me if you're interested. I can also give you a breakdown of our sales last year."

"Well, Mademoiselle, I have to say this is one of the most fascinating sales presentations I've ever received. Your knowledge of the cigar business at such a young age is impressive. I would very much like to take this further. How would you suggest that we proceed?"

"Well, Señor, I have the business card of our top sales manager, Monsieur Hugo Moreau, who will be delighted to answer any of your questions and personally manage your account should you wish to proceed. He will also arrange for a box of cigars to be shipped to you immediately. Also, if you would like, I will personally contact Señor Juan Arguello and tell him of your interest in the brand."

"You are well prepared, Mademoiselle. I shall contact Monsieur Moreau. I will also give you my private telephone number so you can give it to Señor Arguello when you speak to him. I am deeply interested in the history of the cigars we sell here and would enjoy speaking with him."

"Certainly Señor, I'm sure he will be delighted to share his knowledge of all the Arguello cigars with someone who appreciates the artistry required to produce a premium hand-rolled cigar."

"Well said Mademoiselle. And please give the sales material and other documents you mentioned to Mr Henderson.

"So now that our business is completed, how long are you staying in Melbourne, and what are your plans for dinner tonight?"

"Well, we have no plans for dinner, and we are staying two more days."

"In that case, I'll ring my wife and tell her I'm bringing home two young ladies for drinks, and I'll book a table for four for dinner at Florentino's, one of our premier restaurants for Italian food."

"That's so kind of you; thank you so much," Tiana said. "We've been told that Florentino's is a wonderful restaurant."

"Really, by whom?"

"The Concierge at our hotel," Veronica said, laughing. "He's French too, and he and Tiana became best friends."

"Ah, you must be talking about Claude," Mr Alejandro said. "He knows everything. Did he send you to us?"

"He did," Tiana said.

"Good man, I'll have to thank him."

***

Tiana had expected Mr Alejandro's wife to be older, so she was surprised when they were greeted at the door by a younger woman who appeared to be in her late thirties. She would learn later that Margaret was Raúl's second wife. His first wife Maria, whom he had loved deeply, had died of cancer. Margaret had been one of the nurses caring for Maria. She and Raúl had started dating a year after his wife's death, and they were married soon after.

"It was one of the things I loved most about Raúl," she said, "the way he was so devoted to Maria."

Whereas Raúl's first wife was Spanish, Margaret, or Maggie as she was called, was Australian. She was tall, five foot eight inches, and a natural blond, her hair falling straight to her shoulders. She had a very slim build and looked stunning in a midnight blue, long-sleeved velvet jumpsuit that made her look taller. It soon became apparent that Maggie loved fashion as much as Tiana and Veronica. She recognised immediately that Tiana was wearing a Chanel suit and later told Tiana that she thought it was 'exquisite'.

She said, "I've made Raúl promise to take me with him on his next visit to Paris."

"Well, you must let us know when you're coming," Tiana said. "Maman will organise a showing for you at Chanel."

By now, everyone was on first-name terms, and Raúl said, "Good heavens, Tiana, I'm not so sure it was a good idea inviting you two here; you could be a terrible influence on my wife!"

Victoria asked Maggie the name of the designer of her jumpsuit, which was exactly her style.

"It's by one of our top Australian designers, Carla Zampatti. Why don't we go shopping tomorrow, and I'll take you around to our top boutiques here in Melbourne, where you can see what our designers have to offer," Maggie said. "We tend to prefer a more relaxed style here in Australia."

Tiana jumped at the opportunity to take time out to contact The Bishop and said, "I'd love to come for the morning, but then I need to go back to the hotel and start taking care of some business."

"Well, Veronica and I can do some sightseeing in the afternoon, and then why don't you both come to us for dinner? I have some friends who would love to meet you, and here we can all relax. Raúl can show you how good he is on the barbecue," Maggie said, smiling at her husband.

"That sounds wonderful," Tiana said.

"Well, now that we've all been organised, let's head off for dinner," Raúl said.

***

The Italian food at Florentino's was superb, and their table of four grew to eight as two other couples came over to say 'hello' and then decided to join them. It was clear that Maggie and Raúl were a popular couple in Melbourne's social set.

At one point in the conversation, Raúl told the other diners how impressed he had been by Tiana's knowledge of cigars.

"I'm curious as to whose idea it was for you to visit the Arguello family and the factory when you were only sixteen. Was it you or your father?" he said.

Seeing the amused look exchanged between Tiana and Victoria, he said, "Ah-ha, I see there's a story here. Do tell us."

Tiana then told them all how she'd seen the picture of Lady Scott-Fernsby in Tatler at the dentist and how the story had evolved from there. She told them about her visit to Florida and how Isabella Arguello had taught her how to cut and light a cigar and how to use her eyes, fingers, and nose to judge a cigar's quality.

When she got to the part about her mother being invited to be in the advertisement for the launch of a new Arguello cigar and described what her mother wore, everyone at the table was sitting in rapt attention, wholly mesmerised by Tiana and her story.

When she had finished, Raúl said, "Tiana, nobody will ever be able to top that story. Please tell Señor Juan Arguello that my wife and I will visit Florida next year on our way to Europe. We would be delighted if he would permit us to visit the factory to see his cigars being made."

"Florida *and* Europe next year!" Maggie said to Raúl. "Tiana, you're a miracle worker. I've been begging him to take me overseas for two years."

Raúl smiled at his excited wife. "Well, Tiana painted such a vivid picture that I want to meet Juan and Isabella Arguello myself. Knowing the families personally and meeting the men and women who produce the final product all add immeasurably to the enjoyment of smoking a handmade cigar. Speaking of which, gentlemen, ladies, who would care for a smoke?"

***

Once Raúl and Maggie had dropped them back at the hotel, Victoria looked at Tiana and said, "Oh my God, you had them all eating out of your hands. You were incredible."

"I must admit that once I started telling them how everything happened, it did sound pretty amazing," Tiana said. "I can't wait to tell maman about it all. I think she'll like Raúl and Maggie, and we must go to Paris when they come over and return their hospitality."

"I like Maggie too. I'm looking forward to tomorrow."

"Well, I'll come shopping in the morning, and then I'll come back here for lunch and ring maman later in the afternoon. I also want to speak directly with Monsieur Hugo and brief him so he's fully prepared for when he hears from Raúl. I'll ask him for Señor Arguello's telephone number to speak directly with him before we leave Melbourne. Papa always said business is all about who you know, and he was right, of course."

***

Lying in bed and unable to sleep, Tiana didn't know whether she was still hyped up after the success of the afternoon and evening or because she was finally going to see The Bishop.

I won't telephone; I'll go straight to the Cardinal Knox Centre and take it from there. Someone is bound to know where he is.

***

Jumping into a taxi after leaving Veronica and Maggie, Tiana headed to the information centre next to St Patrick's Cathedral to enquire where she could find The Bishop.

At the enquiry counter, she said, "I've just arrived in Melbourne, and I'm trying to contact Bishop Gagnon."

"Do you know what parish he's in?"

"No, sorry. He came to Melbourne in January this year from the Vatican."

"Would you take a seat, please? I'll have to make some enquiries."

After a twenty-minute wait, Tiana was finally signalled to return to the enquiry counter.

"We have been able to track down where you might be able to find Bishop Gagnon. It seems that he is connected to St Thomas Theological College, which is next door to St John's College Seminary. I suggest you make further enquiries at the Theological College's office."

"I see. Is that far from here?"

"Only about twenty kilometres; it's just near the University."

***

Tiana caught a taxi to St Thomas Theological College and walked quickly into the building, down the hall and into what seemed to be a lounge area. She wasn't sure where to go until a student showed her the way to the office.

"Hello," Tiana said. "I'm hoping you can help me. I'm looking for Bishop Gagnon. I was told he might be here at the College."

"Oh yes, the Bishop was here. But he left yesterday to go on leave."

When she heard the news, Tiana just stared at the poor woman before finally repeating, "On leave."

"Yes. Then I believe he will be going to Rome."

Staring at the woman for several more seconds, Tiana eventually managed to say, "Do you have any idea where he is taking his leave?"

"Oh yes, we were all telling him how we were filled with envy that he was going to Bali."

"Bali," Tiana repeated, never having heard of the place.

"Yes, it's one of the Indonesian islands. It's a beautiful place to visit. It's a long way from here, of course, but not that far from Perth.

"Are you feeling alright?" the woman said. "Would you like to sit down?"

"I'm fine, thank you. I'm just a little disappointed that I missed the Bishop. When is he expected back here?"

"We're not entirely sure, but we're hoping mid-July."

"I see. Would you mind ordering me a taxi to take me back to the Southern Cross Hotel in the city?"

"Certainly, and I'll make you a cup of tea whilst you wait."

"You're very kind, thank you."

***

Back at the hotel, Tiana gave Claude a quick wave before walking through the foyer to the Club Grill, where she ordered a glass of red wine and a medium-rare steak.

Sipping her wine, she thought, *This is just too cruel. I'd be closer to him if I'd stayed in Perth. How on earth am I going to come up with an excuse to go to Bali, and how would I find him on a whole damn island? This has all been for nothing. Just as well, the business side of things went so well; otherwise, I'd shoot myself right now.*

She could feel her eyes smarting with tears and ordered another glass of wine. And then, as she remembered what the woman in the office had said, she had a tiny glimmer of hope.

Why didn't I think of it before? I'll catch him in Rome before he returns to Melbourne. I will not give up. I must see him again. I have to tell him how I feel about him.

CHAPTER EIGHTEEN

Tiana went to her hotel room and made two planned telephone calls. The thought of seeing The Bishop in Rome lifted her spirits. First, she called her mother, and the response boosted her mood even higher.

"You are your father's daughter," Adelia said. "I couldn't be prouder of you. To open up a new market is an outstanding achievement, even for someone with far more experience than you, my darling. Monsieur Laurent and Monsieur Hugo and, of course, Señor Arguello will be so impressed."

"Thank you, Maman. It was papa's training that made it possible for me to carry it off. Everyone loved hearing about our experiences in Tampa, especially your photo shoot. Having Vron to talk to and back me up made all the difference. She and Maggie hit it off. They're off sightseeing together right now. Maggie loved my Chanel suit, by the way. We must lay out the red carpet when Raúl and Maggie come to Europe next year."

"Bien sûr, we'll organise an itinerary of places to visit when you return. We'll give them a visit to remember. As soon as you give me the dates, I'll book a showing at Chanel to get the ball rolling."

Tiana laughed. "I'll let Maggie know, Maman, she'll be so excited.

"I'm going to telephone Monsieur Hugo next and brief him on the call he'll receive from Raúl. Vron and I fly out of Melbourne tomorrow evening, so I'll call you once we're back in Perth."

***

When Veronica arrived, Tiana had just finished her call to Monsieur Hugo. A porter followed her, carrying three large boxes and four carrier bags. Veronica promptly collapsed into a chair.

"Oh my goodness, Tiana, Maggie and I had the best time shopping this afternoon."

"I can see that! What happened to sightseeing?"

"No time for that. Wait till you see what I bought you."

Just then, the telephone rang, and Tiana picked up.

"Hi Andy, so good to hear your voice - Yes, hold on, Vron's right here."

Veronica jumped up and grabbed the telephone. "Hello baby, how are you?"

For the next few minutes, there was complete silence at Veronica's end until she suddenly screamed and shouted, "Yes, yes, absolutely yes. Oh my God, I love you, baby." She looked at Tiana, grinning from ear to ear.

She continued to listen to Andrew on the other end of the telephone before saying, "What, you're bringing it to the airport? Oh My God, you crazy man."

There was more silence before Veronica said, "Okay, I'll wait to speak to mummy and daddy until after I've spoken to you when we get back to Perth. We fly out tomorrow evening - Yes, I'll tell Tiana right now; I love you baby, bye-bye."

When Veronica put the telephone down, Tiana said, "Did Andy just propose to you?"

"Yes, yes he did, Oh my God, I can't believe it, I'm so excited."

"Wow, congratulations. I didn't realise things had become *that* serious."

"I know; I think it's because of the trip. The separation has made us realise how much we want to be together. I miss him so much, Tiana. He's going down to speak to my parents this weekend. Oh my God, I can't believe it. I'm 'unofficially engaged'. He said he would meet me at the airport with the ring!"

"Holy cow, what a romantic; on bended knee at Heathrow airport. That'll be a story to tell your children and grandchildren."

They laughed and hugged before Tiana said, "This calls for champagne. I couldn't be happier for you, Vron; Andy is a great guy. I bet Pete will have heaps to tell us about what happened before Andy telephoned you to propose. Do you want to tell Raúl and Maggie at the evening barbecue?"

"Oh my goodness, Tiana, I can hardly think straight. Yes, let's tell them. They'll get to meet him when they come over next year."

"What about your parents?"

"I'll have to wait until Andy has spoken to them. I'll ring them once we're back in Perth."

"Well, I have another telephone call to make to Señor Arguello. Monsieur Hugo gave me his private number, and then we must get dressed for the barbecue."

"Right, I'll shower while you order the champagne and make your call. I'm going to wear the new dress I bought today. Do have a look at the one I got for you, Tiana. I'll put the box on your bed. Maggie and I chose it together. Hope you like it."

***

Both Tiana and Veronica were exhausted when Raúl and Maggie took them to the airport the following evening. The celebrations at the barbecue following Veronica's announcement of her 'unofficial engagement' had gone well into the early hours. Tiana and Veronica only managed to make it to Tamani's in Lygon Street for a late brunch before returning to the hotel. Veronica bought another suitcase for all her new clothes, and Tiana bought gifts for Claude's wife and two sons. Raúl had already given Claude a sizeable tip as a token of appreciation for the part he had played.

At the airport, Maggie told Tiana and Veronica how much she'd loved meeting them both and couldn't wait to catch up again in Paris. "I'm going to miss my two new friends," she said.

"And I'll telephone Monsieur Moreau tomorrow afternoon," Raúl said. "This is just the start of what is going to be a very long and successful partnership."

***

Jean and William picked Tiana and Veronica up at Perth airport, and Veronica immediately started telling them how Tiana had turned into a phenomenal saleswoman.

"You should have heard her speaking to Raúl, Mr Alejandro, the owner of the Tobacconist, in Spanish. He looked so impressed, and by the end of our dinner as his guests at Florentino's, she had all eight people sitting at the table hanging on to her every word. She was incredible."

"Well, you were a massive help Vron. I'd have been so nervous if you hadn't been there supporting me. And we had so much fun, especially in the Smoking Room!"

They both laughed.

"You should have seen the shocked look on the faces of the two elderly customers when they came in and saw us both smoking our cigars," Veronica said.

"I'd like to have seen that," Jean said. "So does this mean you'll return to Australia on business, Tiana?"

"Well, next year, Vron and I go up to Oxford University and Raúl and Maggie are coming to Europe, so I'll see them then. I'm not sure what will happen after that. But you haven't heard Vron's big news. Tell them, Vron."

"Andy proposed on the telephone two days ago, and we're now unofficially engaged. I still can hardly believe it."

"My goodness, that's wonderful, Veronica, congratulations," Jean said.

"Well, you've both packed a lot of surprises into this trip," William said. "And Pete flies in the day after tomorrow. There's never a dull moment around here."

***

Peter was surprised that everyone had come to the airport to pick him up.

"Well, I hadn't expected this welcoming party," he said as William hugged him.

"I think the girls want to grill you about 'The Proposal'," William said.

"And here I was thinking it was because you missed me," Peter said, grinning at them all.

"I certainly missed you," Jean said, stepping forward to give him a big hug.

"Well, I can tell you, Vron, the past week or so has been pretty tough for me. I've listened endlessly to Andy trying to decide whether to wait until you returned or propose on the telephone. And then I had to listen to him going on and on about how wonderful you are…"

At this point, Veronica punched his arm and then hugged him.

"I'm going to tell Andy you said that," she said, laughing at Peter.

"Seriously though, he's nuts about you, Vron. He was so nervous before he picked up the telephone to call you that his hands shook."

"Aww, I can't wait to get back to him."

"After he's spoken to your parents, asking your father for permission and all that, I think he's hoping you'll be on a flight home sooner rather than later."

Veronica looked at Tiana, "Would you mind terribly if we left next week? That is unless you'd like to stay on for a bit."

"Let me think about it," Tiana said, aware Peter was staring at her.

***

The next day, Peter filled everybody in with his latest news after breakfast.

"So I managed to get down to the Nazareth Children's Home in Romsey before I left. That's where Ollie was sent when Enid got too sick to care for him. But just as I expected, they claimed they had no records relating to Ollie and categorically denied any knowledge of his being sent to Australia. They were unhelpful, dismissive, and completely lacking in compassion for his situation.'

"How awful for you," Jean said.

"We had better luck with Andy's friend Phil, who found his father's copy of the second reading of the Empire Settlement Bill in May 1922 and gave us a copy. The Bill intended to continue the 1922 Empire Settlement Act. It made for fascinating reading.

"In a nutshell, the British government was terrified that Hitler and Mussolini would start sending people to fill Australia's wide-open spaces or else hordes of Asians would overrun the country. Hence the maintenance of the White Australia Policy for the urgent redistribution of the white people of the Empire, to included children, adults or anybody considered to be suitable."

"Good summation, Pete."

"Thanks, Dad. It was clear from what I read that Phil's dad, the Member for Elmet, was one of the few who voiced his dissent against child migration in the debates. He stated he did not want to encourage the 'shovelling of little children overseas' who would be left to the mercies of people at the other end.

"He pointed out that women's organisations in Britain were dead against it, and in his opinion, child migration was a 'detestable and inhuman suggestion'. What a hero. Of course, as we now know, his worst fears would be realised after the Bill was approved and passed into law as the Empire Settlement Act of 1922. The Imperial, Commonwealth and State Governments then encouraged British residents to migrate to Australia to settle on the land and boost the labour force with good British stock."

"Pity there weren't more who backed him," William said.

"Exactly. I did a bit more digging and found out that by the early 1940s, childcare specialists in Britain had been lobbying heavily, and far more emphasis was placed on children's psychological needs. The large nineteenth-century 'barrack' institutions where children slept in dormitories and ate in large groups were no longer considered acceptable.

"But that didn't stop the Catholic Church from using that model in Western Australia. It didn't stop Britain from continuing to allow child migration to

Australia. It didn't stop the voluntary societies involved in child migration from taking the payment of subsidies to help meet the costs of fares, outfits and the maintenance of the children who'd been sent overseas. And it didn't stop the brothers at Baile from pocketing the maintenance money and forcing the boys to work for free, erecting their bloody buildings."

"You're really passionate about this issue. It's good to see," William said.

"Yes, Dad, and if you could learn more about the Australian government's child migration legislation, that would be really helpful. We know already that child migration to Australia started up again in 1947, and Arthur Calwell, Australia's first Minister for Immigration, was all for child migration as part of the whole 'populate or perish' scenario."

"Mum and I must go to Canberra, but that's not a problem. We could go next week. We may likely run into the same issues you had regarding the files' open access period, so probably a couple of days will be enough for us to get the information we need."

"Great, Dad."

"And when we return, I'll research child migration here in WA. I'm so sorry, Pete, but I haven't had a chance to do anything before now. It's been pretty busy here over the last few weeks."

"No problem, Mum. I'm catching up with Ollie later today, and I'm hoping I'll be able to interview some of the brothers at Baile. I'm seeing my editor tomorrow to bring him up to speed on everything we've done so far."

"Any chance Vron and I could come to your meeting with Ollie?" Tiana said.

"I don't see why not, but I'll double-check."

***

After a brief call to Oliver, Peter told Tiana and Victoria they would meet at the Ocean Beach Hotel at five o'clock.

"Ollie said you're both welcome to come along, but to warn you that he has information to reveal about Billy, as in Father William Carson, that you'll find distressing. Do you still want to come?"

"Yes," they both said.

"Okay then. Jimmy will be there, too. Don't worry about dinner tonight, Mum; we'll eat at the hotel."

***

When they arrived, Oliver hugged Peter.

"So good to have you back here. Don't know how even to begin to thank you for everything you've done for mum and me."

"No worries, mate. I'm just so relieved it worked out and you were both reunited. We have these two women to thank for much of the legwork."

"Yes, I know. And they've been fantastic to mum," Oliver said, smiling at Tiana and Veronica. "She's looking forward to seeing you both when you return."

"And I've got something big to tell her. Andy and I are unofficially engaged, but please don't say anything. We'll both visit her and Jack and tell them ourselves."

"That's great news, Vron, congratulations. Mum will love that. I won't say a word."

"Thanks."

"Congratulations, Vron," Jimmy said, hugging Veronica.

"Thanks, Jimmy. How are you?"

"Good, thanks, Vron, but anxious about what we're about to discuss. It's not pretty."

"Let me get you three a drink before we get into it," Oliver said.

***

Once everyone was settled, Oliver brought Tiana and Victoria up to date.

"So Billy, who came out on the ship with Jimmy and me, sexually abused younger kids at Baile. After he left, he became a priest, ending up in Victoria

Park. Then he suddenly disappeared and reappeared two years later, which made me very suspicious.

"I employed a private detective, and he discovered that a mother had complained to the Bishop that Father William had been 'interfering' with her son. Her son was an altar boy at the Victoria Park Church."

"Hang on, you're saying the Church just moved him somewhere else and brought him back when everything had settled down, and nobody was the wiser about what had happened?"

"Exactly, Vron, that's standard practice. And they'd have found a way to silence the mother, too."

"See, that's the power of the Catholic Church right there, Pete," Tiana said. "And who will believe a priest could do such an evil thing? It's unimaginable. Until Pete told us some of your story, Ollie, I'd never, ever heard of a priest or brother having sex with a child."

"It's utterly despicable; that's what it is," Peter said. "On so many levels. And it's a bloody crime."

"And it gets worse," Jimmy said.

"So after finding that out, I knew Billy, Father Carson, would abuse again; he can't help himself. So I kept the private detective on and put Billy under surveillance.

"Nothing happened for weeks until well after mum left. But then we had a breakthrough. John, the private detective, was following Billy one night and saw him meet up with a couple of other men before they went into a building at the back of the main drag in Victoria Park. As John watched, two more men entered the building, so clearly it was a meeting.

"The next day, in the early morning hours, John went through Billy's rubbish bin, which he'd been doing periodically for weeks. This time, he was lucky. He found a discarded advertisement that had been torn out of the local newspaper.

"It was an Ad for a trip to Bali, and when John read it, he got suspicious. He said it read like an advertisement for a 'child sex tour', and he thought that's what the meeting might have been about.

"Bloody hell, Ollie," Peter said.

"I know. When he told me, I couldn't bloody believe it. I felt sick to my stomach, and so did John. Anyway, John asked if I wanted him to infiltrate the group and find out everything he could about how it was operating. Of course, I said, 'yes'.

"So he rang the telephone number in the advertisement and was invited to attend the next meeting. He said it was the worst undercover job he'd ever done. Just hearing how Billy and two other priests talked about how they'd get access to the young boys over in Bali and what they'd do to them made him want to throw up. It took everything he had to maintain his cover."

"Sickening," Peter murmured. "Poor bloke."

"He learnt that there's an Australian guy who's been living in Bali for about three years who set the whole thing up. He got to know the locals and set up an unofficial Children's Home or Orphanage, although many kids there aren't orphans. It's just that their parents are too poor to support them.

"He's a paedophile, of course, and the whole exercise has been done to provide kids for these child sex tours. He has advertisements in local papers all over Australia with a local telephone number for each State. They have bastards like Father William Carson go over and bring gifts and take the kids out with them when they do the tourist thing and buy them food and drinks and even bicycles sometimes for older kids. Then, they take them back to this guy's home or one of the three houses the guy owns where his 'guests' stay.

"Each tour member pays for the tour *and* makes a large donation to the Orphanage. It's just too sickening for words and beyond anything I'd expected, even from scum-of-the-earth Billy."

Tiana was shocked on two levels. First, she couldn't believe that there was something as horrific as a child sex tour and second, hearing the name of that place again, Bali.

Victoria looked pale. "I feel ill," she said. "And where the hell is Bali?"

"I'm so sorry, Vron. I did warn Pete that the information was going to be distressing. Bali is an Indonesian island less than four flying hours away from Perth."

"That's the most disgusting, cruel thing I've ever heard," Tiana said. "Those vulnerable children. And why Bali?"

"Well, John got chatting with the guy organising the tour for this group, and he asked him lots of questions. A worldwide market has emerged of priests who take holidays overseas to have sex, and it's now recognised as a distinctive group of tourists. Children are not always the targets; of course, it could be juveniles or adults. The man said he usually gets two to three priests in each of his tours who are looking for child sex."

"But I thought all priests were supposed to be celibate," Peter said.

"That's a big fat lie," Jimmy said. "Some people say at least fifty per cent of them are having sex, maybe even eighty per cent."

"Jesus, it's hard to comprehend such a level of hypocrisy. And it breaks my heart to think of this filth in Bali. The Balinese are such beautiful, gentle people, and the island is a tropical paradise," Peter said.

"Well, John was told that Thailand used to be popular until stories started appearing in the newspapers. Now, it's Vietnam because there's press censorship there, which helps to protect priests who become involved in scandals. They enjoy the discretion Asian countries offer and dress in plain clothes to remain inconspicuous. Bali has the advantage of being so close to Australia, especially Perth."

"We often heard rumours growing up Catholic of priests having affairs with women. I've always thought celibacy was the most ridiculous thing, anyway. They don't teach you anything about it in school, but I researched it. The Church didn't even ban marriage until the twelfth century, and even then, it wasn't enforced until the sixteenth century at the Council of Trent. So basically, it's just a tradition or a rule the Church created. But the idea of a priest taking a holiday to have sex with a child, who could even imagine such a horror," Tiana said.

"Well, that's the thing," Oliver said. "They all talk about it amongst themselves. It's an open secret. That was the case at Baile. But the laity haven't a clue. And if you suggest such a thing about a priest, then you're the one who'll be accused of telling terrible lies. I was."

Everyone sat in silence, absorbing what Oliver had said.

Finally, Peter said, "Each time I think I've heard the worst, there's something else. I feel like I'm sinking into a bottomless pit of evil. And what gets me is that these men presumably return to their Churches or wherever and carry on as if nothing has happened. I don't understand how they can do it."

"Me neither," Jimmy said.

"So what are we going to do about Billy?"

"We're going to do everything we can to stop him, Pete, and make sure he doesn't get away with what he's done."

"So what's the plan?" Peter asked.

"Well, John will fly to Bali as a tour member. I'll be flying over the day after, as Billy would recognise me. Once John knows where they'll all be staying, I'll book somewhere I'm not likely to run into them. I'm hoping you'll come over too, Pete."

"Of course I will," Peter said.

***

Tiana couldn't believe that Peter and Oliver were going to the one place in the world where she wanted to go. *Surely Bali couldn't be that big an island, and there'll be somebody who knows The Bishop. I must find a way to get them to take me with them.*

CHAPTER NINETEEN

"It's not just Billy, aka Father William Carson, who I want to see get punished for what he's done," Oliver explained. "I'm also determined to blow the lid off the scandal of child sexual abuse at Baile. I want the world to know about those brothers and Father O'Leary and what they've all done. And having you and The West on board, Pete, is a key part of the plan."

"Well, I'll also be tying in the scandal of the deportation of British kids to Australia and how you ended up at the archaic Catholic institution here in WA. Plus, we've got the editor of The Daily Mail on board, and I'm sure its readers in the UK will be very interested in the British child migrant aspect. I still need to fill you in, Ollie, on everything I learnt about the child migration schemes whilst I was in the UK."

"This is going to be huge," Veronica said.

"It scares me," Tiana said. "I'm worried about what the publicity might do to both of you."

"This is my job, Tiana, to expose this kind of power and corruption," Peter said.

"And I don't give a stuff. I can always sell my house here and return to living in the UK. I finally got my passport. I'll take you with me, Jimmy."

"So where do we go from here, Ollie?" Peter said.

"Well, we want to get as much evidence as possible about the tour and the men taking it. John will see how willing the men are to let him take photos of them all. They may be a bit cagey about it. He'll try to get at least one or two photographs of Billy with the orphan kids. Of course, we'll make sure the kids won't be recognised."

"And I'll be there as just another tourist, so it won't seem odd if I take photos of the orphanage," Peter said.

"That's great, Pete."

"We also have the newspaper advertisement evidence, and I'm sure the Perth tour operator will get a few telephone calls when the story hits the press. I'll ask John to find out where that bastard lives or if he has a job elsewhere," Oliver said.

"I also want to be in Bali just in case something goes wrong with the tour or if John gets caught up in trouble there. Then, when the tour flies out, I'll ask John to take a photo of Billy at the airport to prove he was in Bali."

"So, to have it all linked in, I'd like to go out to Baile to take photos and, if possible, interview some of the brothers," Peter said.

"Shit, I forgot to tell you Pete. Whilst you were away, Jimmy and I went out to see them at Baile. We told them we were doing a story about us being stolen from our families and shipped out to Australia and the sexual and physical abuse that went on at Baile for decades. They were not happy. Then, a week later, one of the brothers, Brother Daniel, rang me and said he and Brothers Bernard and Mathew would be willing to speak to you. We must have put the fear of God into them."

"Bloody hell, that's great. I'll telephone them tomorrow and schedule a date to go out there, hopefully next week. Will you drive out with me, Ollie, if you could bear to see them again?"

"Can't; I'm working on a project all next week."

"How about you, Jimmy? Want to come with me for the drive?"

"Sure. I'll drive out with you, but I don't want to be there when you interview them. If they start to lie or make excuses about what happened, I'd do my block. Wouldn't be able to stop myself."

"No, of course, I just meant for the company there and back."

"Sure, I'd enjoy that."

"So whilst you're off interviewing the men, Pete, I'd like to go with your parents to Canberra to help with the research," Tiana said. "And then, when we return, could I come with you two to Bali?"

Everyone stared at Tiana in amazement.

"Well, I hadn't thought of that," Oliver said. "What do you think Pete?"

"Goodness, are you sure, Tiana?"

"Well, I'd like to see it through before I leave. And maybe you'd both look more like bona fide tourists if I was there with you. What do you think, Pete?"

"Bali is beautiful; I'm sure you would love it. While we're focused on Billy, you could be a genuine tourist for a few days. Have a break before returning to the UK."

"Would you mind terribly, Vron, if I don't fly back with you?"

"Well, no, not if that's what you *really* want to do."

"Well, that's settled then. I'll book you a ticket," Oliver said.

***

Tiana was sure she'd made her request to join Olive and Peter in Bali sound plausible. *Hopefully, even Vron won't think I've got an ulterior reason for going there. Oh, mon dieu, I can't wait. Please let him still be there and let me find him.*

The following week, Veronica flew back to the UK. Jean, William, and Tiana flew to Canberra, and Peter and Jimmy drove North to Baile.

***

After driving through the massive iron gates on stone pillars, Peter stopped the car to take a photograph. They then went down an endless rough track through farmland and several stock gates. Peter stopped the car again when he saw fourteen man-sized stone monuments.

"Good lord Jimmy, what are they?"

"The Stations of the Cross. Us boys built them. The bloody cement burnt my knees and feet, even between my toes. The bastards gave us no protective clothing or boots. I remember my knuckles bled from hauling those stones into place. They forced us boys to do men's jobs."

"Jesus, Jimmy."

"Yeah."

Peter took a photograph. "When we arrive, I'll give you the car keys, Jimmy, so you can get my camera out and take more photos whilst I do the interview."

"Okay."

They finally arrived at the central administration building, the front court-yard dominated by the bronze statue of Brother Nolan.

"We were forced to work on this building the day after we arrived," Jimmy said.

"Yeah, Ollie told me. How did they get away with it, Jimmy?"

"Nobody knew what was going on out here in the sticks. And if they did, they didn't talk about it."

"So no oversight and no accountability."

"Nope, not so far as protecting us kids was concerned anyway."

They parked the car and got out.

"No kids running around must be a holiday," Jimmy said.

"The place is now a fee-paying boarding school for Catholic graziers' sons. Thanks to the buildings we built for them, the Catholic Church is raking in more money. They even made some older boys stay on to work here for free when they should have been off working and getting paid."

"No paperwork or follow-up on the young men's ongoing welfare then," Oliver said.

"Nope, nobody cared. This place must be worth millions now, what with the buildings and upgrading of the land. The land was a gift to the Church, you know; nothing on it, though, just bare ground. Then, over the years, us boys worked like slaves to turn it into a capital asset for the bloody Church."

As they walked towards the building, a brother came through the front entrance to greet them.

"Hello, I'm Brother Daniel, welcome to Nolan College. Brother Bernard and Brother Mathew are waiting inside," he said, stepping forward to shake Peter by the hand.

Peter guessed that Brother Daniel was in his early seventies. He still had a firm grip and stood upright in his black robes. He had a head of thick white hair, but his blue eyes were pale, as though the light behind them had gradually faded.

"Back again, Jimmy."

"That's right, Brother."

"Please follow me. We thought we'd meet in one of the offices. It's pretty quiet at the moment whilst the boys are on holiday. Brother Mathew is bringing us some tea. Maybe you could go and help him bring it through Jimmy?"

"No problem. Then I'll go for a wander whilst you all do the interview."

Peter followed Brother Daniel through to the office where Brother Bernard was seated. He looked much older than Brother Daniel, and the look on his face appeared to express extreme displeasure. He nodded at Peter, then quickly looked away. Peter was relieved when Jimmy came in carrying a tray with five mugs of tea, milk, and sugar. Brother Mathew followed with a tray holding plates and slices of fruit cake.

After putting down the tray, Brother Mathew shook Peter by the hand. "Welcome," he said before busying himself, handing out the mugs and offering the fruit cake round. *He's nervous*, Peter thought, noticing the brother's hand tremble as he poured milk into his tea. *Or maybe it's because of his age or some affliction.* Brother Mathew looked unwell. His skin had a grey pallor, and there was an aura of melancholy about him.

Jimmy picked up his mug of tea and a slice of cake and said, "Well, I'll leave you all to it," before leaving the room and closing the door.

Peter addressed the three Brothers, "First," he said, "I'd like to thank you all for allowing me to interview you. As Oliver and Jimmy told you, I'm writing a series of articles for The West Australian. I've been researching British child migrants who were sent to Western Australia in the 1940s and 1950s.

"I recently returned from the UK, where I researched the policies and schemes that made such deportation possible. I understand the children were sent under the Catholic child migration scheme."

"Correct. They came through the Catholic Episcopal Migration and Welfare Association, which was the receiving agency here in Perth at that time," Brother Daniel said. "It's the Catholic Family Welfare Bureau now."

"And did the Association coordinate the placement of the children to Baile?"

"That's right."

"I see. So, would the Association have kept all the records of children who came to Western Australia? Would all correspondence from the UK have been sent there?"

"Quite possibly. The only records we kept were about the subsidies paid and an admission form and discharge card for each boy."

"So you kept no personal case files with the boy's history or ongoing record of matters affecting the child, such as medical records?"

"No, when they left, it was up to them to get any documents or information they needed. We referred them to the Association and the Child Welfare Department."

"I see. I want to ask you about schooling Brother Daniel. I've been told that it was virtually non-existent. There were no functioning classrooms and facilities here at Baile. Instead, the boys were forced to work on the building sites daily. They virtually built this place. The lack of a proper education would have had a significant impact on the young men's ability to get decent jobs once they left here."

"Well, you have to understand, Peter, that Baile was never set up, never fitted out to be run as a conventional school program with classrooms and lessons. None of us were trained as teachers. Many of us entered the Order before we finished secondary school.

"Baile was a *Farm* and *Trade* School intended to give the boys *practical skills* through farm work and training so they could get a job on a farm once they left us. And that's what we did. We taught them how to clear land, build fences, and undertake the construction of buildings as part of our Apprenticeship Scheme.

"The boys looked after the dairy herd and worked in the piggery, the vegetable garden, and with the chickens. They participated in general farm labour, such as ploughing fields and planting and harvesting. Of course, they also had their daily chores, such as collecting firewood."

"But Brother Daniel, Oliver was eight when he came here, and Jimmy was only six."

"We weren't supposed to have primary school children here, but we fulfilled our primary obligation to ensure the children practised their faith daily as members of our Catholic family. That was Brother Nolan's key concern, which informed *our* child-care policy. We followed his instructions to the letter, teaching the boys religion down to their very souls," Brother Daniel said.

"The men have also spoken of sexual abuse and violent, daily physical punishment."

"It was our moral duty to discipline them. I knew from the beginning that the boys from the UK would be trouble. And as for the sexual abuse, we'd been warned that the British children were prone to boy-on-boy sex. So it was our mission, our responsibility, to do what was needed to safeguard their eternal souls," Brother Bernard said, glaring at Peter.

Peter stared at Brother Bernard in shock. "So are you saying the boys were to blame for the sexual abuse, Brother?"

But before Brother Bernard could answer, Brother Mathew stepped in, saying, "I'm not sure I agree with Brother Bernard's view. But what I would say is that we are human too, you know Peter, and have our frailties."

"Child sexual abuse is a crime, Brother Mathew. And despite that, there don't seem to have been any reports made to the police by any St Isidore Brothers about boys being sexually abused by brothers, priests, and even older students at Baile. Yet now, there are men telling stories of sexual abuse taking place over decades. How do you explain that?"

"Well, none of *us* knew about it. Anyway, reporting would be up to the Superior, whoever that was at the time," Brother Mathew said.

"The thing is, Peter, there were one or two brothers here doing things that we knew nothing about at the time. It's unfortunate that it happened. But I'm sure it's not any worse than in any other religious group and probably far less frequent than out in the general population."

"Brother Mathew, it was far more than 'unfortunate'. A victim says that it was a devastating experience, and the trauma and emotional problems he's suffered since have ruined his entire life."

"Well, Peter, we were never trained to look after children. We weren't social workers. We knew nothing about childrearing or children's needs. We didn't have any women here to help with the younger ones. The women we did have only worked in the infirmary, laundry, and kitchen. We just had to figure it out on our own, out here, completely isolated," Brother Mathew said.

"And *we* were working morning, noon, and night ourselves. We had very little by way of holidays or time off or recreation or leisure activities," Brother Daniel added.

"So are you saying that being an all-male institution and having no time for yourselves were factors that contributed towards the sexual and physical abuse of the boys?"

"Well, now that you put it like that, yes, quite possibly. But Peter, we had plenty of people coming to check up on us over the years, and no one *ever* wrote up a complaint about sexual abuse or harsh physical punishment, and none of the boys ever said anything," Brother Daniel said.

The complete lack of understanding of the total power and control their positions of authority gave them over the boys left Peter gobsmacked.

Finally, Peter said, "Do you have anything you would like to add in terms of your understanding of how the boys might have been affected emotionally and psychologically by the alleged excessive physical punishment and sexual abuse?"

"Standards were different then, Peter and reflected the social mores and values at the time. We did our best under very challenging circumstances," Brother Daniel said.

Peter shook his head, "Brother Daniel, I'm not talking about corporal punishment that was standard in schools then; I'm talking about alleged *excessive* physical punishment and *sexual abuse*. Both these forms of abuse were as illegal in the 1940s and 50s as they are now in the 1970s."

The three Brothers stared at Peter in silence.

Peter closed his notebook, put his biro away and said, "I think that concludes the interview. Thank you, brothers."

***

"How did it go?" Jimmy asked.

"Jesus, Jimmy, I need a bloody drink. It was like talking to people from another planet."

"Yeah, know what you mean."

"It's unbelievable that two governments could get together and send kids there. I feel so bad for how it must have been for you all, suddenly finding yourselves in such a cold, harsh environment with nobody to turn to for help or comfort. Don't know how you survived it, Jimmy."

"Wouldn't have without Ollie. We were sad, lonely kids torn away from everything we knew and with no way of escape."

"And the Catholic Church, shameful, just shameful. Picking you up and dumping you there out in the middle of nowhere with a bunch of men who had no clue, no fucking clue, how to look after kids. It just takes my breath away, the total lack of any forethought or regard for your well-being.

"Not one of them had an ounce of understanding of the damage, the havoc, they've caused Jimmy. No sympathy for the victims of their abuse. They don't care. All I got was explanations and justifications and, *Oh My God*, Brother Bernard!"

"Yeah, he was a violent bastard."

***

The day after their arrival in Canberra, William, Jean, and Tiana were keen to start their research and headed straight to the National Archives. It didn't take them long to realise that the Archives were set up with a fantastic series system that would make it much quicker and easier for them to find relevant documents.

They decided to split up. William would focus on child migration policy files and the various schemes and agreements with government and private organisations. Jean and Tiana would search the files for other documentation related to child migrants, such as reports or newspaper articles.

"Let's break for lunch at one o'clock and then share our findings," William said.

***

Four hours later, after returning to the hotel and ordering lunch, Jean said, "So tell us what you found out, darling."

"Well, before World War II, child migrant matters were primarily handled by the individual States. Each state government entered into immigration agreements with the British Government under the Empire Settlement Act, which Pete told us about.

"It was all about the number of child migrants and financial subsidy arrangements between the state governments and the sending agencies and receiving agencies. These schemes provided rural farm training for boys and domestic skills for girls. They were taking children from the slums and turning them into farmers and domestic servants.

"But after World War II, the rationale for child migration shifted with, as Pete outlined, the aim of increasing Australia's population with good British stock. Assisted child migration was considered a potentially valuable element of the *broader* immigration policy."

"That's an important shift," Jean said.

"Exactly, and towards that end, in July 1945, the Australian Department of Immigration was created by the Executive Council. Ben Chifley, the Prime Minister, was particularly enthusiastic about making early arrangements for the resumption of child migration.

"In 1946, the Australian Immigration's Guardianship of Children Act gave the Minister for Immigration legal control over unaccompanied minors until they came of age at twenty-one. Once the children started to arrive, there was a provision within the Act to enable the Minister to delegate his functions and powers of legal guardianship to any officer or authority of the State that received the immigrant children."

"So we're back to the individual States handling the set-up," Jean said.

"Correct. Specifically, regarding Perth, an appointment was made in February 1946 for the new position of Migrant Officer. Child migration to WA was encouraged. Once children arrived, indentures would be drawn up between the Child Welfare Department and the receiving agencies detailing their respective responsibilities for the care of the migrant children.

"The Catholic Episcopal Migration and Welfare Association was the Catholic receiving agency in Perth. The Archbishop of Perth and the Abbot of New Norcia were actively involved in setting it up and enthusiastic advocates for child migration.

"The St Isidore Brothers had always run the four Catholic orphanages in WA, so I'm assuming the CEMWA would have assigned each child to one of the four institutions, and that's how Oliver ended up with them at Baile.

"Put simply, that's how the relationship developed between the Commonwealth Government, the State Governments, the Catholic Church and the child immigration schemes they administered and the institutions the children were subsequently sent to."

"Excellent work, darling. It's exactly what Pete needs for his articles. Tiana and I found some interesting reports that tie in with your research. One of them, recorded by the Department of External Affairs, discussed child migration being given 'special consideration'.

"The question was asked, 'Where will the children be obtained?'. 'Obtained', like they were a commodity sitting on a shelf in storage somewhere. The answer was even worse, and I quote, 'Must be, and always had been, institutions and poor families'. That was in 1944, and it confirms what you've said and what Pete told us.

"Amazingly, Australia was hoping to have fifty thousand child migrants, war orphans, sent here after the war ended. Then Tiana found a copy of an article that appeared in the Sydney Morning Herald on Monday, February 5, 1945, in which Sir James Womersley, the Minister for Pensions in the UK, was quoted as stating that war orphans would not be sent to the Dominion until they were fifteen or sixteen and able to decide for themselves.

"He said he spoke as a father and grandfather and would not want to send his little orphaned grandson away until he was old enough to decide for himself."

"Pity he didn't have more clout," William said

"Well, Australia was in for a big disappointment. In February 1946, a report made it clear to the government officials that the massive number of child migrants they'd hoped for simply wasn't going to happen," Jean said.

"Now it makes perfect sense why they decided to encourage the organisations already in existence, the charities, the churches with previous experience of handling child migration, to become involved again," William said.

"Yes," Tiana said. "And in the case of the Catholic Church, they had access to the most vulnerable children. The ones nobody cared about or those stolen from their families. It makes me so mad."

"Me too, Tiana," Jean said. "They targeted poor, vulnerable working-class kids because clearly, they were not going to get their hands on any middle or upper-class ones."

"Good work, you two. Well, I think we've probably found enough information for Pete's needs right now, especially since we can't get access to files from 1947 onwards. That's when all the action started with the arrival of the first boatload of post-war child migrants. What do you think?"

"Yes, I agree," Jean said. "And maybe Pete can gain access to more articles and photos in the archives of The West Australian."

"I wonder if there was a Catholic newspaper reporting on what was happening then in Perth, especially since the Archbishop of Perth was involved. If there was, it might give us more information if we could get hold of back copies," Tiana said.

"That's an excellent idea, Tiana. Let's check it out once we get back," Jean said.

"Well, now our job is done here; we can spend this afternoon and tomorrow morning sightseeing before we fly out in the afternoon. And first on the agenda has to be the Australian War Memorial," William said.

"I can't wait to get back and find out how Pete's interview with the brothers went," Tiana said. And I hope Ollie's plans for Bali are still on track."

PART SIX

THE BISHOP

CHAPTER TWENTY

W hen Bishop Gagnon arrived in Melbourne in January 1976, he received a warm welcome from the Archbishop. "I'm delighted to have you here finally, Philippe," he said.

"You'll be pleased to know there is great enthusiasm for including a Graduate Diploma in Canon Law at St Thomas Theological College. You have the full support of the Master, Brian Malloy. Brian was formerly the Rector at St John's. You can expect the same level of support from Donald Baker, St John's current Rector."

"That's good to hear, Excellency. I plan to begin by understanding their expectations of the programme and what they see as its critical components."

"And excellent approach, Philippe," Archbishop Walsh said, nodding in approval.

"Now, regarding your accommodation, we've assigned you one of our properties in the parish of Waverly, which I think you'll find extremely comfortable. You'll also use one of our diocesan cars to get yourself around."

***

His Excellency quickly settled into his new life. He was pleasantly surprised to discover that Melbourne was far more cosmopolitan than anticipated. Nor did it take him long to get a general overview of his new surroundings. He learnt that St Thomas Theological College opened in 1972, and the St John's College Seminary had opened a year later. The two colleges were next door to each other, not far from Williamson University.

Since the early seventies, the Theological College had become the academic hub for the Seminary. His Excellency was informed that this innovative collaboration between the two colleges positively impacted priestly formation.

The Master of the Theological College, The Very Reverend Dr Brian Molloy, was delighted at the prospect of adding a Graduate Diploma in Canon Law to the curriculum, which already included a Bachelor of Theology, philosophical studies and a wide range of postgraduate courses and higher degrees by research.

After greeting His Excellency, he explained, "We are organising an office for you at the college, Philippe. In addition to our offices, we have a lecture theatre, tutorial rooms and common rooms for students and staff. Once you're settled into your office, we'll hold an official Welcome Party."

The Very Reverend Dr Donald Baker invited His Excellency to take a guided tour of the Seminary. He told His Excellency, "Our students live in units or blocks of twenty-five students per unit, together with one or two staff members, far removed from the era of dormitories, I'm happy to say. Our large dining room and common rooms were specifically designed to encourage the community's social life.

"You'll also be happy to see we have an extensive library. Our collection of books and historical artefacts dates back to the first century." His Excellency was impressed.

***

The week following his arrival, the Archbishop invited His Excellency to attend a meeting of the Curia, where he was introduced to the Archbishop's Vicar General and his four auxiliary bishops, who assisted him in running the Archdiocese of Melbourne and the Western, Northern, and Southern Regions of the huge State of Victoria.

"Michael Campbell is the Bishop for the diocese that includes the parish where you're staying, Philippe. I'll arrange for us to get together for a meeting once he gets back from leave."

The Archbishop followed the introductions by enthusiastically describing his aspirations for the proposed new course on canon law.

This was followed by a brief discussion of general administration matters and the issue of what to do about two presbyteries in dire need of repair.

"This is a key area we need to look at Philippe in respect to church law and the role the parish takes in the care of property and finance," Archbishop Walsh stated.

A final matter, which had not been included on the agenda, was briefly mentioned by the Vicar General. "Excellency," he stated, "there is just one further matter about a complaint I've received regarding Father Finlay, who is 'not in good standing'. This is in respect to *special issues*."

"Yes, thank you, Monsignor Burke. I've heard all about Father Finley, and the matter is being dealt with," Archbishop Walsh replied, closing any further discussion.

***

In the first week of February, His Excellency moved into his office at the Theological College and made it known that his door was always open to staff and students alike.

Over the next month, he consulted extensively with teaching staff members at both the Seminary and Theological College. Eventually, it was agreed that the diploma should focus on the relevance of canon law to parish life, and consensus was quickly reached on the subject matter to be included in each of the four modules. Module Four would focus on canon law and the temporal administration of parish property and finance.

"The Archbishop will be delighted with module four," The Master said, "given his keen interest in asset protection."

In all the discussions, there had been no mention of clergy child sexual abuse or the failure of bishops to correct the grave injury to victims through the rule of canon law. However, the reference at the meeting of the Curia to the case of Father Finley and the somewhat oblique reference to 'special issues' had not escaped His Excellency's notice. He was biding his time until he met someone he trusted sufficiently to ask what this curious term might mean, although he had already made an educated guess.

***

Following the welcoming party in his honour held by the Theological College, His Excellency was invited to be the guest of honour at dinner with the seminarians at St John's College. His Excellency had already observed the seminarians at several informal meetings and, by the end of the dinner, had confirmed his suspicion that there was an overtly homosexual group amongst the students.

After years of living in Vatican City with gay priests, not to mention his own experience of life in the seminary, he had become adept at reading body language and decrypting the codes. He observed *the looks*, the subtle displays of *tenderness* between those appearing to share a 'special friendship', and the generalised homoerotic atmosphere that emanated from certain groups of students, none of which escaped his discerning eye.

Soon after the dinner, His Excellency received a visit from Father Christopher Roe, one of the junior teachers at the Seminary. Father Roe's reputation had proceeded him. His Excellency had been told he was one of the up-and-coming academics on staff. The following year, he would go to Rome to study for his doctorate at the Pontifical Gregorian University before returning to lecture at the Theological College.

Father Roe had been raised in Melbourne by his Irish father and Italian mother. He was himself a St John's College graduate, having attended the college when it was at its previous location.

When they had talked briefly at dinner, His Excellency had taken an immediate liking to Father Roe. He had a ready smile and a keen sense of humour.

His Excellency had been told that his skill on the tennis court supported stories that he could have turned professional had he chosen to do so. It wasn't hard to see why he was so popular with his students.

"I'm told you'll be studying at my alma mater next year," His Excellency said, opening the conversation once Father Roe was seated in a chair.

"Yes, Your Excellency and I'm hoping you can give me a few pointers on what to expect when I get to Rome. I'm a little nervous about such a big move overseas and what it will be like studying at such a prestigious university."

"I understand completely, having gone through the same experience myself. I grew up in America and didn't know a soul when I arrived in Rome. But you'll find that many students are in the same boat, and you'll soon make friends and form your own study group. You also have the advantage of speaking Italian."

Following a more detailed discussion about the subjects he would be studying, Father Roe said, "Excellency, there is something else I would like to talk to you about, something concerning the current students at St John's."

"Go ahead, Christopher, anything you say will be held in the strictest confidence."

"Em, well, I'm sure I'm not telling you anything new when I say that we are experiencing an issue with some of our students, an issue regarding 'special friendships'."

"It's an issue as old as the priesthood itself," His Excellency said with a wry smile.

"Yes, Excellency, it was an issue when I attended the seminary and no doubt when you did as well. But in this case, it's rumoured that a group of senior students are having '*particular* friendships', active homosexual relationships, with each other. And one of them is also said to have a liaison with the parish priest who regularly visits the seminary."

"I see. And this is common knowledge?"

"Yes, Excellency. It's a hot topic of gossip, especially amongst senior students. It seems they don't like or trust the parish priest."

"Have you spoken to anybody else about this matter?"

"Yes, I spoke to the Rector, but he said it was idle gossip and I should ignore it. He told me to focus on my teaching."

"But it's something that still worries you."

"Yes, on many levels, Excellency. The priest's behaviour is the most terrible example for the students. What message is it giving them about priestly identity, celibacy, not to mention morals and ethics."

"And what is the name of this priest, Christopher?"

"Father Finlay. But there's something else that worries me even more, Excellency. Yesterday, one of the senior students came to see me and said the other day he saw Father Finlay bring a boy with him when he came into the seminary."

His Excellency was stunned. This was the priest who had been the subject of discussion at the meeting of the Curia. Why was he still active in the parish when the Archbishop had said the matter was being dealt with? Clearly, this was not the case.

Finally, he said, "I can only imagine how you felt when the student told you that, Christopher."

"I just didn't know what to do, Excellency, given the response I got before from the Rector. And that's why I came here, to see you," Father Roe said, his voice trailing off.

"Leave it with me, Christopher. This has to be handled with the greatest care."

"Of course, thank you, Excellency."

So here it is, the moment I've been dreading.

***

After considerable thought and prayer, His Excellency decided to make an official visit to the parish priest to meet him and assess the situation for himself.

He dictated a letter to be addressed to the Pastor of the Waverly Parish. After briefly introducing himself, he explained that he was currently in residence at St Thomas Theological College as part of a team creating a new diploma on the relevance of canon law to parish life.

He wrote that he would greatly appreciate meeting with the parish priest and his assistant priests to get their feedback on what they saw as important issues to be included in the new diploma. He stated that this would be of great help to the team, and he would be happy to meet either at the college or wherever would be most convenient for them.

Three days later, the parish secretary called to invite His Excellency to join Father Finlay and his two assistant priests for lunch at the presbytery the following Wednesday. He accepted the invitation.

***

Father Finlay greeted His Excellency and introduced him to his assistant priests, Father Morris and Father Walker.

It wasn't hard for His Excellency to see why Father Finlay might not appeal to students. He was muscular and heavy-built and had an abrupt manner. His initial fleeting smile quickly disappeared, and it soon became apparent that his customary expression was a scowl.

But it was his stare that was the most off-putting. When someone was talking to him, Father Finlay would focus on them with his large, blue, bulging eyes and stare for an inordinate length of time without blinking. His Excellency found it disconcerting and could imagine how the look might impact a young person.

Father Morris was the youngest of the three priests. He had a slim build, a rather angelic face and spoke very softly. His handshake could best be described as 'delicate'. His Excellency had no doubt that he was gay.

Father Walker quickly took on the role of host, inviting His Excellency to join them in the dining room for lunch. His Excellency judged him to be in his mid-forties, and his reddish skin and nose were strong indicators of a drinking habit. Father Walker was the most hospitable of the three, making light conversation while pouring everyone a glass of wine.

"And how are you finding our beautiful city of Melbourne, Your Excellency?" Father Walker asked.

"I'm thoroughly enjoying my stay here, especially the wonderful coffee!"

"Ah yes, we have the Italians to thank for that. Have you managed to get out of the city at all?"

"Regrettably not yet, Father."

"We have our coastal regions, of course, but what I like best are the lakes. Next week, I'll take a group of underprivileged boys camping at Lake Eildon. The lake was dammed in the 1950s, you know, and now it's bigger than Sydney Harbour. It's a popular spot with lots of boating, swimming, and fishing. The boys love it."

"It looks like you take a keen interest in the youth of your parish, Father. I noticed a pool table when I came in."

"Yes, it gives the boys somewhere to hang out after school and prevents them from getting into mischief."

"So, how can we assist you with this new diploma?" Father Finlay said, abruptly stopping the conversation.

***

After he visited the presbytery, His Excellency's anxiety was sky-high. *There's something terribly wrong there. Far too many opportunities for boys to be unsupervised while in the company of these priests. Looks like a deliberate setup. I need more information about why Father Finlay is 'not in good standing' and whether 'special issues' is a euphemism for 'child sexual abuse'. And I'd love to know who made the complaint to the Vicar General before I go and speak to him.*

The answer came in circumstances he could never have anticipated.

***

On Sunday, His Excellency decided to take the afternoon off to try and clear his head before contacting the Vicar General. He drove to Mario's, his favourite café, where he could chat with the owner and staff in Italian. The café was usually filled with Italians, which made him feel at home. He wore a black suit with his Roman collar and sat in a corner, hoping to be inconspicuous.

Suddenly, he heard a voice behind him say, "Your Excellency, I do hope you'll forgive me for interrupting your leisure time, but may I speak with you?"

Turning, he saw a woman, possibly in her early thirties, standing there. "My name is Mary Russo," she said. "I work in the office at the Theological College."

"Well, Mary Russo, why don't you take a seat and tell me what I can do for you? Are we giving you too much work with the new diploma?"

"Thank you, Your Excellency. Oh no, it's nothing to do with that. It's about my sister-in-law Eileen and my nephew Mark. You see, Mark was an altar boy in the Waverly Parish church, St Patrick's."

"Was?"

"Yes, Excellency, he doesn't go to St Patrick's Church anymore."

"Mary, I suspect this will be a serious conversation. Let's go to my office at the college, where what you have to tell me can be treated with the utmost confidentiality. What do you say?"

"Yes, Excellency, It's a very private matter. I'll follow you in my car."

***

Once Mary was settled in a comfortable chair, His Excellency said, "So something happened to your nephew, Mary?"

"Yes, with the parish priest, Father Finlay. He was, well, he was touching him and - and then, he wanted Mark to touch him - down there."

"Mary, this must have been a terrible shock to you. Who did your nephew tell? Was it his mother?"

"Not at first. But one day, he became hysterical when it was time for him to attend church. He flatly refused to go, saying he would 'never go to church again'. She finally managed to get out of him what had happened. He said it had happened several times before, and he couldn't take it anymore."

"What happened next?"

"She told her husband, my brother Paul. Paul was so angry that he wanted to go straight to the church and punch Father Finlay. But Eileen managed to stop him. Ultimately, they decided to go and see Bishop Campbell, but he was away on leave. So instead, they went to speak to the Vicar General, hoping he'd speak to the Archbishop and that Father Finlay would be removed."

"I see. And did the Vicar General advise your brother not to speak to anyone about the allegation?"

"Not that I'm aware of, Excellency."

"Did your brother Paul make a statement to the police?"

"Good heavens, no. This has shaken Paul and Eileen's faith, but they would never dream of doing anything that might damage the church. Although I must tell you, Excellency, that there is talk in the parish. One evening, Paul was down at the pub, and he overheard a couple of men talking about Father Finlay. It turns out Mark is not the first one to have been abused by him.

"I see."

"And then, once Mark told his mother what had been happening and he knew she'd told his father, Mark opened up and told Paul what was happening at his primary school. All the boys know about Father Walker. They know not to be in a situation where they'll be alone with him because he 'makes them do things'. Mark also says one of his best friends said Father Walker did horrible things to him when he went to one of his camps.

"It just beggars belief, Excellency. When Eileen first told me about Mark, my first question was, 'Are you sure?' I hate myself for that now. But it's just so hard to believe that a priest, someone you trust completely, could do such terrible things to little children."

"I'm so glad you felt you could come and tell me about this, Mary. This has been a devastating experience for you, too. I wonder, would you know what impact this abuse has had on your nephew?"

"Eileen told me that she was worried about Mark's sudden change of behaviour before she knew what had happened. He used to be a happy, confident child, but then he suddenly became withdrawn and anxious and started having nightmares, which had never happened before.

"He used to love school. He was a good student. But then he became moody and lost all interest in his schoolwork. His teacher told Eileen that Mark was having angry outbursts at school, so unlike him. And then, after he told Eileen what had been happening, he said, 'God is so angry with me, Mum.' It shocked her to the core, Excellency, that he blamed himself for what had happened. It broke her heart."

Mary paused, looking visibly upset. "My poor nephew, it's so wrong that he should suffer like this."

"I couldn't agree more, Mary. Can you continue, or would you like a break?"

"No, no, I'm fine, Your Excellency, thank you. Eileen told her parents what had happened to Mark. But they both flatly refused to believe her. Her father said Mark must be confused or lying or something, as no priest would *ever* do such a terrible thing. Eileen was devastated, and now there's a huge rift in the family. Thank God our parents were supportive when Paul went and told them, although it was an awful shock to them both."

"I'm so sorry, Mary, for the two priests' actions and the aftermath that has touched all your lives."

"Thank you, Your Excellency."

"I'm wondering if your brother went to the school and complained after Mark told him about Father Walker."

"Oh yes, I forgot that part. Paul went to see the principal of St Aloysius Primary School, and he said he would write a letter to the Melbourne Catholic Education Office reporting Paul's complaint. But again, there has been no follow-up, just like with Monsignor Burke. Paul spoke to him a couple of weeks ago, but so far, nothing has happened.

"Paul is an accountant, and he's currently looking for a job somewhere else to move the family away from this parish and its school and church."

"I see. It's tragic that he and the family must leave their community, friends, and family. But I can see that it will positively affect Mark, knowing how his father is protecting him. I hope there is also counselling that Mark can get. For my part, I will personally follow through on this whole situation. And again, thank you for telling me, Mary, it took great courage."

"Thank you, Excellency, for listening to me."

"By the way, how did you know where to find me?"

Mary laughed. "Well, Excellency, Melbourne can be a small place, especially when you have a large family. One of my cousins works at Mario's café and mentioned that you occasionally dropped in. So I rang in the afternoon on the off-chance that you might be there and spoke to my cousin. He said that you'd just arrived. So I drove over, praying you'd still be there and willing to speak with me."

"God moves in mysterious ways, Mary."

CHAPTER TWENTY ONE

The following day, His Excellency telephoned the Vicar General and made an appointment to see him that afternoon.

As soon as he arrived, His Excellency didn't waste any time getting to the point. He informed Monsignor Burke that 'no', he had not come to talk to him about the new diploma. He had come to inform him that he had been told about an allegation of child sexual abuse made against Father Finlay.

"It is alleged Monsignor that he sexually abused one of his altar boys on several occasions. There are also rumours that this boy was not the first victim of Father Finlay."

Monsignor Burke looked shocked and took several moments to respond.

"I see. And where did you hear about this allegation and these rumours, Excellency?"

"From a concerned citizen who informed me that a complaint had been made and forwarded to you Monsignor. As for the rumours, Father Finlay's alleged abuse of altar boys is a topic of discussion in the local pub.

"I've also heard rumours from an entirely different source that Father Finlay is currently involved in a liaison with a senior student at the seminary. Even more disturbing is a report that a senior student has seen him taking a young boy into the seminary with him."

"Excellency, it's hard to know where to begin."

"With Father Finlay Monsignor. I'm bringing this allegation and these rumours to you since you were the one who raised the subject of Father Finlay at the Curia meeting."

"Yes, Excellency. Well, at the meeting of the Curia, I *was* referring to a recent allegation that Father Finlay had sexually abused an altar boy."

"And would that be the same boy that I've been told about, do you think?"

"Yes, I believe so."

"So I take it that *'special issues'* stands for 'child sexual abuse'?"

"Correct. This term is used to avoid any mention of sexual abuse of minors by clergy, the reason being that any hint, any leak, to the press would inevitably lead to scandal."

"So this naming has become policy."

"Well, yes, I suppose you could put it like that."

"Hmm, so I assume that's also why the item did not appear on the Agenda at the meeting."

"Yes, Excellency."

"You stated that Father Finlay was 'not in good standing'. What did you mean by that?"

"Well, you are correct in saying the boy was not the first. Father Finlay has been the subject of other complaints concerning his behaviour, which is why he is termed 'not in good standing'."

"By 'behaviour', I take it you mean the sexual abuse of minors."

"Correct."

"Then what I do not understand is why Father Finlay is still active in the parish and not under preliminary investigation or, at the very least, placed on administrative leave," His Excellency said, fearing the explanation would confirm his worst fears.

"The Archbishop spoke to Father Finlay, Excellency. He admitted to the Archbishop that he has had moral lapses but said he was sure he could overcome them given another chance in a new environment. The Archbishop is strongly in favour of the rights of his priests. So now the Archbishop is finding out who will accept him and where he can send him."

"As in, send him to another parish?"

"Yes, like he was sent here or to another alternative option."

"Are you saying he was 'not in good standing' when sent here?'

"Yes, well, we didn't know that then."

"In that case, surely there is enough evidence to proceed to a preliminary investigation or an application for an administrative laicisation."

"The thing is, Excellency, Archbishop Walsh takes a more *fatherly* approach to his priests. He believes he has a responsibility to Father Finlay, and he deserves the opportunity to prove, to redeem, himself with a fresh start."

There it is, just as Edmund and the Archbishop described it – the pastoral approach, a 'father-son' relationship.

Staring hard at the Monsignor, he said, "But he had a fresh start when he came here, Monsignor, and yet he is still offending against young boys, not to mention his alleged liaison with a seminarian. All of these rumours about Father Finlay should be investigated, including the one about a boy being taken to the seminary."

"I couldn't agree more Excellency. But it's the Archbishop who has the final say. It's his decision."

He's right, of course.

But His Excellency persisted. "Monsignor, I have also been told that it's general knowledge amongst all the students at the St Aloysius Primary School that Father Walker is a sexual predator. The children warn each other to avoid any situation where they will be alone with this priest. I have seen with my own eyes that there is a pool table set up at the presbytery, which I regard as highly inappropriate. Have there been any official complaints about Father Walker from St Aloysius?"

"Yes, the Principal wrote a letter to the Melbourne Catholic Education Office to report the various complaints about Father Walker's behaviour. Several parents and one teacher had complained about him to the Principal. One of the parents even went to the office of their son's teacher and asked if he was aware that Father Walker had been molesting half the boys in the school."

"That's shocking, and it backs up the story about the boys warning each other."

"It does, yes."

"So what was the follow-up to that letter?"

"Well, by then, Bishop Campbell was on leave, so it was forwarded with a covering letter to Archbishop Walsh."

"I see. So, no further action. Has anything been said about Father Walker and the camps and the pool table set-up at the presbytery?"

"The letter from the Principal also mentioned that Father Walker was taking boys to the presbytery during play time."

"Unbelievable. And the camps? I've been told that there was an allegation that Father Walker abused a boy whilst they were away on a camp."

"A complaint was made to the Bishop before he went on leave by a father who said that Father Walker molested his son on a camping trip."

"Good lord, and what action, if any, did the Bishop take against Father Walker?"

"Well, he did get me to pick Father Walker up and take him to see him."

"What happened then?"

"After their meeting, Bishop Campbell told me, 'He has to go he can't stay in this diocese'. So now, since the Bishop is still on leave, the Archbishop is trying to find somewhere to send Father Walker."

His Excellency sat back abruptly and stared at Monsignor Burke, shaking his head in stunned silence.

Finally, he said, "Monsignor Burke, child sexual abuse is a canonical crime, and the Church in Australia should be dealing with it as such. The offenders must be held accountable.

"If this is not done, and it comes out in the press that the Church is harbouring sex offenders, I dread to think what the scandal might do to the Church. It's a miracle none of the parents have reported either of these two priests to the police already, which *they* have every right to do."

Monsignor Burke was silent, staring down at his clasped hands.

Finally, looking up, he said, "The issue is of deep concern to me, too, Excellency. But the Archbishop believes it's just a 'disastrous coincidence' that there are two priests here who have these weaknesses and, basically, he wants both priests moved to avoid any hint of scandal in his Archdiocese."

"And do you believe there are only two priests, Monsignor?"

"Well…"

"Oh, good lord, don't tell me there are more."

"There are rumours, Excellency, that a parish in the Southern Region of the State is having similar issues with three priests."

"Three?"

"Yes, rumour has it that the three priests were at the same seminary as Father Finlay at the same time."

"And what seminary was that?"

"St John's College."

"This is beyond belief. The seminary has turned out a cluster of child sex offenders. Heaven help us."

The two men sat in silence, each deep in their own thoughts.

Finally, His Excellency said, "If these child sex offenders are not brought to justice, Monsignor, there will come a time when the Church will be held to account. The Church hierarchy *must* be seen as taking immediate action to bring offenders to justice within our canonical trial processes or through an administrative laicisation.

"Failure to do so will inevitably see clerics being hauled before criminal courts. The Church needs *to be seen* to be both holding offenders accountable *and* protecting children from sexual abuse."

"I appreciate what you are saying, Excellency. But honestly, I cannot see the Archbishop taking a different approach to the issue."

***

After leaving Monsignor Burke, His Excellency went home and poured himself a double whiskey. As he sipped his drink, the full impact of what he'd learnt from his meeting with the Monsignor slowly sank in.

He barely noticed the light fading till he was sitting in semi-darkness.

God, come to my assistance, he prayed. *Lord, make haste to help me.*

***

The following morning, His Excellency made an appointment to meet with the Archbishop, ostensibly to update him on the diploma's progress. He arrived promptly at three o'clock to join the Archbishop for afternoon tea.

"Good afternoon, Philippe," Archbishop Walsh said, indicating to His Excellency to sit at the table. "So do tell me, how is it all going?"

"Extremely well, Excellency. The consensus was that the diploma should focus on the relevance of canon law to parish life. We already have an outline for each of the four modules, and we're now writing content, learning outcomes, assessment requirements and so forth. You'll be happy to know that module four addresses the temporal administration of parish property and finance."

"That's excellent news, Philippe. It will provide the practical assistance needed by the priests who are involved in parish administration. This diploma is long overdue."

"Well, the diploma would not have come together so quickly without Brian and Donald's cooperation. Their input has been invaluable."

"Delighted to hear it."

"There is something that I would like to have your advice on, Excellency. As you know, I have an office at the Theological College, and this has given me the opportunity to get to know many of the students. It won't come as a surprise to you that there is a certain amount of gossip.

"But I was disturbed to hear what is circulating amongst the senior students. They're saying that there is a liaison between one of the senior students and Father Finlay. Father Finlay also took a boy with him when he visited the seminary. Do you think it's something I should bring up with the Rector when we next meet?"

"From my experience, gossip should always be taken with a large grain of salt. I'd stay out of it if I were you, Philippe. Anyway, I've just had it confirmed that Father Finlay has requested leave to go to the United States to study for twelve months. He will not be returning to a parish in this Archdiocese."

"I see."

"And we're about to lose another priest, Father Walker."

"Really."

"Yes, he is being transferred to Western Australia to the parish of Geraldton."

"So now you have to find two replacements."

"Yes, thank goodness Michael is back from leave, and he can deal with it."

***

Leaving the Archbishop's residence, His Excellence drove to the Cathedral. He sat in one of the pews at the back and fell to his knees, his head in his hands. "Oh Lord, the children," his lips murmured. *Children whose bodies will be violated and their faith destroyed by the friendly new priest who comes with offerings of special activities and promises of fun-filled camping trips.*

His Excellency shivered. The pain felt like a steel band around his chest. He watched as a single tear splashed down on the wooden pew and disappeared.

Lord, what have we become?

***

His Excellency had five weeks remaining before he left to go on leave prior to returning to the Vatican. He made two decisions. The first was that he would work around the clock to ensure that the Diploma in Canon Law was ready by the time he left. Once this assignment had been completed, he hoped there would be no reason for him to return to Melbourne.

Secondly, he wrote a letter to Archbishop Armand, informing him that he was happy to report that all had gone well regarding his mission to develop a Diploma of Canon Law for the St Thomas Theological College.

Then he wrote...

Thank you, Excellency, for your briefing before I left for Australia. It was both helpful and highly accurate.

I look forward to providing Your Excellency with a full report of my stay in Melbourne

upon my return to Vatican City in July, following my six-week leave in Bali.

He had no doubt the Archbishop would read between the lines and realise the seriousness of the situation in Australia.

One week later, he learnt that Father Finlay had announced at Mass that he was leaving the parish to study in the United States and, sadly, would not return.

The following week, a letter was sent to all the parents of students at St Aloysius Primary School informing them that Father Walker was moving to Western Australia and would be replaced by Father Saunders, who would arrive within the week.

Both Father Roe and Mary Russo came to visit His Excellency to thank him for his help.

Father Roe said, "I can't thank you enough, Excellency, for your intervention in this challenging situation. It feels like a dark cloud has been lifted from the seminary, and I plan to follow up with the Rector regarding the expulsion of the student involved with Father Finlay."

Mary Russo said, "I want to express my gratitude not only on my behalf, Your Excellency, but also on behalf of my sister-in-law and brother. The fact that they will not have to leave the parish after all, and Mark can return to school feeling safe means everything to us."

The only thing he could say that had a shred of truth was that he had had nothing to do with the outcome. But he could tell that they thought he was being modest, which made him feel even worse.

Silenced by rules that forbade him to speak out and a system of governance that rendered him powerless, he grappled with how to steer a course between the

Church's downfall through scandal and the destruction of innocence through child sexual abuse.

Lord, I cry out to You in my despair, he prayed. *My heart is broken, and my spirit is crushed.*

PART SEVEN

The Devil & The Deep

CHAPTER TWENTY-TWO

Peter was at the airport looking forward to picking up his parents and Tiana, who were flying in on the afternoon flight from Canberra.

He was at the front of the arrival hall when they walked out together. "It's so good to have you all back," Peter said, hugging Jean and grinning at Tiana. How was Canberra?"

"It went well; we got all the information I think you'll need," William said.

"Can't wait to hear Dad. Ollie and I have heaps to tell you, too. If it's okay with all of you, we're going straight over to his place so we can update each other on where we're all at. I'll fill you in on my visit to Baile and my interview with the brothers. And Ollie has all the latest on what's happening with John and the group and our Bali trip."

"Terrific," William said, getting nods from Jean and Tiana. "Better stop at the bottle shop; this could be a long evening."

***

When everyone was finally seated around the dinner table, Peter said, "How about you start, Dad? What did you find out?"

William gave Peter an overview of how the Australian Commonwealth government, the States and the Catholic Church had joined forces over child migration, utilising the child immigration schemes.

"Your mother and Tiana also discovered why charities and churches became so involved after the war. I'll write it all up for you, Pete, so you've got it on hand for your articles."

"That's great, Dad, thanks. So I'll go next and fill you in on my trip to Baile with Jimmy, which was an experience and a half," he said, glancing over at Jimmy.

When Peter had finished describing how the three Brothers had responded to his questions, William said, "So it looks like Baile was still operating on the model set up before World War II, which was all about taking young boys from Britain and turning them into farmers."

"You're absolutely right, Dad. It all makes sense now. They never moved beyond that model to the one operating after the war."

"Well, I think you and Jimmy being here with us, Ollie, is an absolute miracle. I don't know how you survived such horrors," Jean said.

"One of the boys fell off the scaffolding and died, and I swear he fell deliberately. I'd have done it myself if Ollie hadn't been there. I often wonder what happened to all the others that went through with us. Maybe some of them will make contact when your articles appear in the newspaper, Pete."

"I think you're right, Jimmy," Jean said. "Maybe we should put some process in place, Pete, just in case you get a few letters or telephone calls to the newspaper after you've published."

"Yes, good idea, Mum. Andy and I were thinking about that. Maybe you could come up with a plan whilst we're in Bali. We start publishing the articles as soon as we get back."

"Sure, leave it with me; I'll put my social work thinking cap on."

"So, speaking of Bali, what's the latest on that front?" Tiana said.

"Well, John flies out with the group next Wednesday, June sixteenth, and we three fly out the following day. The group will be there for seven days. I've left it for you to book your flight to London, Tiana. I thought you might want to fly from Bali to Singapore first and then on to London from there.

"Pete and I are flying back to Perth on Thursday, the twenty-fourth, the day after John and the group leave. Michael will spend the week with Jimmy here at my place, so we have a backup in Perth in case of an emergency.

"In Bali, John and the group will be staying in Ubud at one of the bungalows owned by Jack Simmons; he's the paedophile. The three bungalows are out of the town centre in a Balinese-style compound with high stone walls, which gives his guests the privacy they want. The whole set-up is just too awful for words.

"Based on Pete's advice, I've booked us into the Bali Hyatt at Sanur Beach, down south-east of the island. It's about an hour's drive from Ubud and up-market, so there's no chance we'll run into anyone from the group there. Also, we wanted you to be somewhere nice for your break, Tiana, before you fly home."

"That's so sweet of you both. How big is the island?"

"Well, you could probably circumnavigate the whole island in two days or drive from one end to the other in three hours on a motorbike," Peter said. "That's the most popular form of transport, by the way, or bicycles. Then there are bemos, tiny trucks with covered benches at the back, great for carrying surfing gear. You flag them down, or you can hire them for the day. There are taxis, of course, and you still see farmers with their horses and carts."

"I'm so looking forward to Bali," Tiana said.

***

Tiana was sad to say goodbye to Jean and William when it was finally time to board the plane for Bali.

"I'm going to miss you both; you've been so kind, putting up with me and Vron and showing us around your beautiful city."

"It's been an absolute pleasure having you here. I do hope you'll return to Perth one day," Jean said, giving Tiana a big hug. "Do stay in touch."

"Oh, I will. I want to know what happens when Pete's articles get published. I'll get Pete to send me copies. Andy will let Vron and me know when they're publishing in The Daily Mail. I'm excited and anxious all mixed up together!"

"I know what you mean," Jean said, smiling.

Four hours later, Tiana, Peter and Oliver landed at Denpasar Airport, Bali.

***

Tiana couldn't explain it, but the minute she walked out of the airport and felt the balmy, tropical breeze on her face, she felt at home. The taxi was at the airport to take them to the hotel, and as they made the twenty-five-minute drive to Sanur, she was enchanted by the scenery.

"The palm trees and the tropical flowers are so beautiful, Pete. I can't believe how green the fields are, and I love the thatched roofs. I didn't realise Bali would be quite so rural."

"I told you you'd love it. You should take a trip to the terraced rice fields in Sideman. They're stunning, lush, and the most unbelievable green, crawling up the hills like stairs to heaven with the backdrop of Mount Agung, the highest mountain in Bali. It towers high above the hills and adds so much to the beauty of the landscape."

"Goodness, you could be a Bali tourist guide! I'll put that on my list."

Peter laughed. "Well, I fell in love with Bali when I came over with a group of Uni friends during the summer break in 1970. Most of the guys were mad keen surfers, and all they wanted to do was get down to Uluwatu and surf at Blue Point Beach, which is on the southern end of the West Coast. Surfing wasn't my thing, so I took off on a motorbike and saw as much as I could of the south of the island, driving over east, up the coast and then inland to Sideman.

"I have to confess I learnt so much about Bali from Starr Black and Hans Hoefer's beautiful book Apa Guide to Bali. It was the first one ever written about the island and was published in 1970. Hans Hoefer was a German artist who took all the stunning photographs himself.

"The hotel we're staying at wasn't open back in 1970. The first international resort hotel, the Bali Beach Hotel, was built in 1962, and it's also in Sanur; you'll see it when we get there. It's a monstrosity. It was built based on the architectural style of modern hotels in Miami, and everyone hated it. Funnily enough, the man who sponsored the Bali guidebook was the general manager of the Bali Beach Hotel."

"It sounds completely out of place, and how awful being stuck with it after it was built!" Tiana said.

"Exactly. In the end, there was so much protest about the hotel that the Indonesian government issued a law that any future buildings in Bali could not exceed the height of the nearby coconut and palm trees. I can't imagine anyone who wanted to experience authentic Bali choosing to stay there. It's probably mainly for conventions. Our hotel, Bali Hyatt, was only opened in 1973 and follows some of the architectural style of the famous Tandjung Sari Hotel.

"Tandjung Sari was also opened in 1962, and it's super expensive, probably in your price bracket, Tiana, but not in Ollie's and mine, I'm afraid. I did go there for a drink in the bar on my way through in 1970. It's built in a coconut grove in the traditional Balinese style and has the most magnificent garden. It's the social centre for the foreign community, very chic, everyone who's anyone goes there. It's hosted many famous musicians, royalty, and world leaders over the years."

"Wow, it sounds wonderful. I'll put it on my list. You certainly know a lot about Bali, Pete."

"That's just the tip of the iceberg, Tiana. Wait till you see the sunrise from Sanur Beach. I'm sure we'll be able to walk straight down there from the hotel. The east coast is famous for its beautiful sunrises, but the west coast is where you see truly magnificent sunsets."

"Can't wait. Oh my gosh, look at that. How do the women balance all those trays and baskets on their heads while walking?" Tiana asked, swivelling around to look out of the taxi window at the row of Balinese women they'd just passed walking in single file along the narrow road."

Peter laughed, "I know, they're amazing and so graceful."

"I've just had the most wonderful idea," Oliver said. "I'm going to bring mum and all the family here for Christmas next year. They'll love it."

"That's a great idea, Ollie. I think Vron and Andy would love it here too, maybe even for their honeymoon."

"Maybe we could all come here together," Peter said, looking at Tiana.

"Oh look, we've arrived," Tiana said.

As they entered the reception area, a gong rang out.

"Oh my goodness," Tiana said, "they do know how to make you feel special."

As Peter had anticipated, the Bali Hyatt was set in lush gardens of native trees, water features, and an elaborate plant design, all leading down to the beach. The guest room area was very modern, but the expansive lobby, which flowed onto open space and then onto the restaurant, was covered by a vast, soaring, thatched roof, giving the whole area a Balinese feel.

"Let's take our gear to our room," Peter said to Oliver, "and then we'll meet you downstairs, Tiana, for a drink before dinner."

"Okay; see you both in ten minutes."

***

Seated in one of the open courtyards with their drinks, Tiana said, "This hotel is so great; thank you both for choosing it."

"You're welcome," Oliver said. "Let's go down to the beach after dinner."

"The sun sets at about six-fifteen Ollie, and it gets dark. How about we have an early night and get up tomorrow and go down to the beach to see the sunrise before breakfast."

"Oh, alright, much better idea."

"So, what are you both planning regarding John and the group?"

"Well, John is going to ring here and leave a message for me at reception, telling me where we can meet up in Ubud. It might be tricky for him to get away on his own, but that's the plan so far. He knows we get in today, so hopefully, he'll make contact tomorrow."

"I was thinking, Ollie, once we hear from John, we could hire a motorbike and drive up to Ubud and stay a couple of nights in a Losmen. That's a cheap, one-star guesthouse providing 'bed and breakfast'. That would give us somewhere to meet and chat rather than on the main drag where we might be seen by one of the group.

"Nobody knows me, so it would also allow me to drive around and take photos of the orphanage, Jack Simmons' place if I can find it, and the outside of the compound where his 'guests' stay. If we're lucky, we might meet some people in Ubud who know something about the orphanage. Maybe they've heard rumours about what's going on. What do you think?"

"That's a great plan, Pete. Yes, once we hear where John wants to meet, let's do it. We can drive up, and you can go and pick him up and bring him back to where we're staying. How long will it take for us to get to Ubud?"

"An hour, give or take."

"That sounds great, but be careful, you two. Who knows what kind of contacts this guy Simmons has? Word might get back to him that people are asking about him."

"Okay, Mother, we'll be careful," Oliver said, grinning at Tiana.

"Are you okay with being alone for a couple of days?"

"Absolutely, Pete, I'm going to spend tomorrow lazing on the beach and then take it from there. I'm sure the hotel has many day trips they can organise for me, including Sideman."

"That's settled then. Here's hoping we hear from John tomorrow," Peter said.

***

The following morning, after watching a glorious sunrise on the beautiful long stretch of almost deserted white sand, Tiana, Oliver, and Peter headed to the restaurant for breakfast. Just as they were about to leave, a receptionist walked into the restaurant and handed Oliver a message.

"This telephone message just arrived for you, Sir."

"Thank you."

Oliver read the message and said, "So we're going to meet John at a small restaurant called Murni's Warung. It's at the northern end of Jalan Raya Ubud, the main street that runs through the centre of Ubud. He'll be there at noon.

"So we should probably leave here about nine-thirty, Pete, so we can get to Ubud and give ourselves time to find somewhere to stay before the meeting with John."

"Right, so that gives us time to put some clothes in a bag; then I'll go and hire a motorbike and meet you both back here for a coffee before we head off."

***

After Peter left, Tiana and Oliver wandered back down to the beach.

Oliver hesitated before saying, "Now that we've got this time together, Tiana, there's something I want to talk to you about."

"Oh, what's that, Ollie?"

"Well, you do know Pete's crazy about you. He has been since you first met in London."

"Did he say that?"

"Yes, surely you can tell?"

"Well, yes. The thing is, Ollie, I don't feel that way about him. I care for Pete, but just as a friend."

"Just as a 'friend', well, that's the death knell for any romance, isn't it."

"I feel so bad, Ollie, but I have tried to always keep the relationship on a friendship basis. The last thing I want to do is hurt Pete; he's such a great guy."

"I think he thought you wanting to come to Bali with us was a sign that there might be hope for something more."

"Oh, I had no idea that's what he was thinking. What should I do?"

"Well, I think you should put the poor guy out of his misery and tell him how you feel, or rather how you don't feel. Try and let him down gently. It's going to be a huge disappointment. He's fallen very hard, I'm afraid."

"Okay, I'll speak to him when you return from Ubud. I'm so sorry, Ollie; Pete's the last person I'd want to hurt."

"It's not your fault, Tiana; you either feel it or you don't. It's just such a shame you don't. You'd make a great couple."

"Oh, Ollie, I wish I felt the same way. I suppose Vron and Andy getting engaged hasn't helped either."

"No."

"Merd."

"Yep."

***

Once Peter and Oliver left for Ubud, Tiana went for a long walk along the beach. The tide was out, so she sat and gazed out over the lagoons of crystal-clear water formed by the long string of offshore reefs.

I've got two and a half days to find out where The Bishop is staying on this island. I didn't want Pete to fall for me; that wasn't part of the plan. Now he's going to be hurt, and I hate myself for that. Oh, why does it have to become so darn complicated?

When Tiana returned to her hotel room, she had a plan. She took a long bath to try and relax and then put on one of her prettiest long cotton sun dresses, a floral print of soft greens, dusty pinks, blues, yellows, and white daisies. She finished the look with her favourite diamond heart pendant and gold sandals. She left her hair loose, clipping it back on one side and planned to add a frangipani behind her ear before she headed out. She then went to the hotel restaurant for a light lunch.

Peter had mentioned how all the ex-pats met at the Tandjung Sari, so she planned to go there in the afternoon and see if anyone had met The Bishop and knew where he was staying on the island.

***

Tiana loved Tandjung Sari the minute she saw it. If she had had the choice, she would have preferred to stay there. She decided to start by ordering tea and then planned to move into the bar area later. She went out and sat at one of the tables, looking over the grass towards the beach and sea beyond.

"Magnificent view, isn't it," the man sitting at another table said.

"It certainly is."

"Your first time in Bali?"

"Yes, it is."

"May I join you?"

"Yes, please do."

"I'm Michael Fitzsimons."

"How do you do, Michael, Tiana Manning."

Tiana guessed that Michael would be approximately the same age as The Bishop. He seemed very English, very aristocratic, and very charming.

Just as he sat down, a young woman about Tiana's age walked towards the table.

"So there you are, darling, just like you to find a beautiful woman to talk to the minute I turn my back."

Michael laughed, "Come and join us, darling. Let me introduce Tiana Manning, who is on her first visit to Bali. Tiana, my wife, Elizabeth."

Tiana immediately took to Elizabeth, who seemed a lot of fun. With her fringe and long blond streaked hair that fell straight to her shoulders, she looked like she'd stepped out of Vogue magazine. She wore an off-the-shoulder, loose maxi dress in a blue and taupe print, cinched at the waist with a wide leather belt, and was barefoot. Tiana couldn't help but admire her Cartier watch and beautiful sapphire and diamond engagement ring.

"So what brings you to Bali," Elizabeth said.

"Well, I've been in Australia, and now I'm returning to London via Bali."

"London, I would have thought Paris with your charming French accent," Michael said.

Tiana laughed, "Well, thank you, Michael. I'm half French and half English. My home is in Paris, and I'm currently flatting in London with my best friend."

"One of my oldest friends is French," Michael said. "We met here in 1954 when we were both thirteen. I was here with my father on one of his business trips, and his father was here on holiday with his family. He had been one of the first from America to discover the magnificent surfing in Bali in 1940."

"So they were French but living in America," Tiana said.

"That's right, LA. It was great because our parents got along well with one another and I got free surfing lessons! We caught up again in 1960 when we were nineteen and, of course, went surfing at Blue Point Beach. His father had bought some land close by in 1948, and over the years, they'd transformed what was initially just a shack into a beautiful Balinese home. We had some wonderful times there.

"Bali was a paradise in the 1950s and 60s. It's starting to change now, and I'm unsure if I like it."

"Well, I love it as it is now. Back then, you didn't even have electricity," Elizabeth said.

"That's exactly why I liked it. Kerosene lamps and candlelight was very romantic."

"Oh, you!"

"Do you still see your friend?"

"Yes, we caught up here yesterday. Every few years or so, we manage to turn up in Bali simultaneously, and yesterday, he suddenly arrived here on his motorbike. He comes here to make his international telephone calls. Neither knew the other was here, so it was a wonderful surprise."

"You should have seen them," Elizabeth said. "It was so funny; it was like Philippe had suddenly appeared out of the jungle after being lost to his brother for ten years. I don't think they stopped talking for the next four hours."

"Well, while I'm here, I thought I'd look up someone I know from Paris. His name is Philippe, too, a popular French name. But he's a bishop.

"Good lord!" Michael said.

"Is something wrong?" Tiana said.

Elizabeth stared at Tiana and said, "Good heavens, Tiana, the person we've been talking about all this time *is* a bishop, Bishop Gagnon. But here in Bali, we all call him Philippe. You'd never know he was a bishop as he's always in shorts and getting around on his motorbike."

"Oh, mon dieu, I don't believe it," Tiana said. "We first met in Paris when I was fifteen. He wasn't a bishop then, of course. I had no idea he was brought up in America."

"Well, this is amazing. They say it's a small world, but this takes the cake," Michael said.

"When did you last see him?" Elizabeth asked.

"Just last year in Paris. My father died, and he was wonderfully supportive of me and my mother. He had moved to Rome, but he just happened to be in Paris, having recently attended his mother's funeral. I don't know how we would have coped without His Excellency being there."

"I'm so sorry, Tiana," Elizabeth said.

"Thank you. I wanted to thank His Excellency for being so kind to my mother and me, but the Vatican had sent him to Australia, so I couldn't catch up with him."

"It's so odd hearing you refer to him as His Excellency. I've never seen him in his bishop's clothes. He's so good-looking; I bet he looks amazing!"

Tiana couldn't help laughing. "So, where is his house?"

"We'll give you his address," Elizabeth said. "We'd drive you over, except we have to go to Denpasar to meet a friend. But we can take you there tomorrow if you can wait."

"That's okay, I'll just get a taxi. How far away is it?"

"About forty minutes."

William wrote down the address and handed it to Tiana.

"Would you like me to order you a taxi from here?"

"Yes, thank you, Michael. I'll stop at my hotel and leave a note for my friends."

"Promise you'll come back and see us after your visit," Elizabeth said.

"Of course, I've so enjoyed meeting you both."

After seeing Tiana off in the taxi, Michael turned to Elizabeth and said, "God, I hope we've done the right thing. Philippe didn't go into details, but once we began talking, it became clear he was struggling with something to do with the Church.

"This could complicate things even further for him. I think she's in love with him."

"I thought that too. She positively glowed each time she talked about him."

"Do you still glow when you talk about me, darling?"

Elizabeth put her arms around his neck, pulled him in close and kissed him tenderly.

"Does that answer your question?"

***

Tiana told the cab driver to wait whilst she rushed inside the hotel to her room. She threw a pair of shorts, jeans, a T-shirt, bra and panties, a bag of toiletries and a pair of sneakers into a small leather backpack. She had no idea what to expect once she got to His Excellency's house, but wanting to be prepared for anything.

She then wrote a note to Oliver. She said she'd bumped into friends from Paris who now lived in Bali, and they'd invited her to stay with them for a couple of days. She thought if she left the note with the receptionist and then got back before Oliver and Peter returned, she could always ask them to give it back.

On her way out, she left the note at reception and asked them to put her passport and jewellery in a safe. By three-thirty, she was back in the taxi and on her way to Uluwatu, filled with excitement and anxiety.

CHAPTER TWENTY-THREE

As Tiana got closer to her destination, the realisation that she would finally see The Bishop hit home, and she had a panic attack.

What if he's shocked to see me and tells me to go away? Would he do that? He may be angry with Michael and Elizabeth for giving me his address and feel I'm invading his privacy. What will I say to him? Merde, this is going to be a terrible disaster. I'm crazy to think he might have feelings for me. Yes. I should turn back ...

The driver stopped the taxi and said, "We're here, but you must walk the rest. Just follow the path."

Tiana took a deep breath and thought, *Okay, you can do this. Just be casual, like you do this every day!*

She paid the taxi driver and walked up the pathway leading to His Excellency's house.

Oh, mon dieu, what will he say when he sees me?

She turned the corner and saw him sitting on the verandah reading a book. As she continued walking towards the house, he saw her and stood up, dropping his book. He remained motionless, staring at her for what seemed like forever before he said, "Tiana, c'est vous?"

"Oui."

"Good Lord, why are you here?"

"I'm here to see you."

"I mean, why are you *here,* in Bali?"

Then they both laughed simultaneously, remembering a similar conversation at Orly Airport, but in reverse.

"I've been on a visit to Australia, and now I'm on my way home via a stop-over in Bali."

"Good heavens, how on earth did you find me?"

"I ran into your friend Michael and his wife Elizabeth. They gave me your address."

"Did they now."

"Yes, we were talking, and Michael spoke about a friend he'd known for ages, but he didn't mention your name at first. Then Elizabeth said something about 'Philippe', but I still didn't realise they were talking about you. After I mentioned that I wanted to catch up with a bishop of the same name, we suddenly realised we were both talking about you. I hope you're not angry."

"No, no, of course not. I'm still in shock. Come, Tiana, let's go inside. Welcome to my Bali home."

She walked up the stone steps, across the verandah and through a large open doorway with two beautiful carved Balinese doors folded back on either side. Inside was a massive room beneath a high, traditional, open Balinese roof with bamboo rafters covered in alang alang thatching.

His Excellence moved towards the sitting room area, with a long sofa and two oversized armchairs covered in navy blue and brown cotton batik fabric. At each end of the sofa, there was a small teak table with carved legs, and on top of each table sat a teak, bamboo, and wicker lamp. Tiana thought they looked antique.

"What a magnificent room," Tiana said as she looked around. "Michael said your father had built a stunning Balinese house where you all had great times together."

"Yes, Michael and I were blessed to have parents who brought us to this beautiful island before the tourists discovered it. I was only seven when I first came here with my parents.

"My father was an engineer, and initially, this was just a shack with a mud floor that he built to hold his surfing gear. But on subsequent visits, he put down the stereobate, which is the foundation, and eventually put teak flooring throughout the house. Each time my parents returned, they added to the building, and this is how it ended up, a real 'home away from home'."

"Is that your mother in the portrait?" Tiana asked, looking at the beautiful young woman sitting on a carved wooden chair. She wore a long white dress and had flowers entwined in her brown hair, which fell down her back.

"Yes, the portrait was painted by a Balinese artist. My mother was a huge supporter of Balinese art and crafts. She loved collecting objet d'art and Balinese furniture."

Tiana walked over to the long, solid timber, four-door, four-drawer cabinet opposite the portrait.

"Oh, these are exquisite," she said, looking at the two wooden statues of a Balinese couple painted in gold and soft pink that sat on top of the cabinet.

"Thank you, my mother loved them. I think they represented my parents."

Behind the long sofa, covering the entire wall, was a series of shutters opening out from the bottom. They were held open by long brass rods with a hook at the end. Tiana could see the lush green vegetation through the openings.

"I've always loved shutters," she said.

"Me too. I've seen a few of the new places being built for tourists with air-conditioning, and so, of course, they have to have glass for the windows. I love to be able to look straight out at the garden."

"Michael said he wished he could still have kerosene lamps because they were so romantic!"

His Excellency laughed. "That sounds like Michael. If it weren't for health aspect, I'd still have them here, too. I only put electricity in quite recently. I converted the two lamps at either end of the sofa. And then there's just one bamboo pendant at the centre of the room. I like to keep the lighting low-key at night. And then, of course, there are the candles.

"The black ceiling fan suspended from the high beam overhead and the one over the dining room table is also a new luxury. Now that tourism is taking off,

I'm contemplating renting the house while I'm away, so I thought I'd better put in a few modern conveniences."

"I like the whirring sound of overhead fans; it's quite hypnotic," Tiana said.

"It is. Tiana, what can I get you to drink, tea, water?"

"I'd love a glass of water, thank you."

Whilst His Excellency went to get the water, Tiana wandered over to the dining area at the opposite end of the room. It, too, had identical shutters running down the far wall behind the long teak dining table and eight carved dining chairs.

A large brass candlestick held a candle covered in dripped, hardened candle wax toward each end of the table. At the centre of the table, was a large, round, shallow stone bowl full of water with frangipani floating on the surface.

"I can see your candles are well used," Tiana said when His Excellency appeared with two glasses of water and put them on the table.

"Must be something to do with being Catholic," he said, smiling.

"When were you last here with your parents?" Tiana asked.

"When I was nineteen, in 1960. My parents had planned to retire here, but tragically, my father died in 1970 at the age of forty-eight. My mother couldn't bear to come here without him, so she sold our home in Los Angeles and returned to our family home in Paris."

"So she must also have been quite young when she died in 1975. I'm so sorry."

"Yes, she was only fifty-two. She never got over my father's death and just seemed to wither away."

"That must have been so hard for you to see. You must miss them both terribly when you're here."

"I do, Tiana, yes. But I feel their spirits around me all the time, especially when I watch the sunset over the Indian Ocean, which I do every evening. There's no better place to pray and remember."

"I'd love to see the sunset. I'm staying on the East Coast, where I've seen the beautiful sunrise, but I haven't seen the sunset from the West Coast yet."

"Really, well, I'd be delighted to take you to the top of the cliffs to see it. But by the time we return, it will be dark, and I wouldn't want to risk taking you back to the East Coast on the back of my motorbike; it would be too dangerous. Would you feel comfortable staying here, Tiana? It's highly irregular, but due to the exceptional circumstances and since I have a spare bedroom..."

"That would be wonderful, thank you. I wasn't sure how long I'd be here on the West Coast or where I'd be staying, so I brought a change of clothes. I'd better wear jeans and sneakers if I'm riding on the back of a motorbike."

"That's a good idea. I'll show you the bedroom. And I'd better get respectable and put on a T-shirt," His Excellency said, smiling at her.

***

The bedroom was lovely. It had a small four-poster bed with a mosquito net looped up at each corner, ready to be dropped down around the bed. To one side of the bed, there was a teak chest of drawers that had a large bedside table lamp with a bamboo woven shade on top.

On the opposite side of the room was a small teak dressing table and stool. The dressing table was very delicate, with a beautiful oval mirror. Tiana thought it might have belonged to His Excellency's mother. Over the dressing table hung a bell rattan light shade. And to the right of the doorway, there was a small, carved, teak wardrobe.

A row of opened shutters ran the length of the far wall, but unlike those in the main area, these shutters folded out sideways.

Tiana walked over and gazed out at the surrounding garden with its tall palm and coconut trees, dense vegetation, and riots of colour from the red bougainvillaea and hibiscus to the bright orange of the bird of paradise and soft white clusters of jasmine. Closing her eyes, she inhaled the delicate perfume of the frangipani as it wafted towards her in the late afternoon breeze. She listened to the lazy buzz of a dragonfly and the strange cackle of the frogs.

This is what it must be like in paradise.

Becoming aware of how long she'd been standing there, she quickly changed, pulling on her jeans and T-shirt. After tying up her sneakers, she hurried out to join His Excellency.

***

She saw him standing near the doorway, waiting for her. With his blond hair and deep suntan, he looked unbearably handsome. He was dressed in shorts, a white T-shirt, and boots, and she could feel her heart pounding as she walked towards him.

"Come, Tiana, we must hurry to catch the sunset."

They moved quickly down the path to where he had already brought around his motorbike. He swung his leg over the seat in a smooth motion, kicked the kickstand up, pushed the ignition and shouted, "Hop on Tiana and hold on tight."

Tiana did as instructed, wrapping her arms around him and holding herself tight against his back as they took off. She felt the warmth of his body through her T-shirt, and he smelt like freshly cut grass, sweet and slightly musty. Tears stung her eyes as his nearness overwhelmed her. She never wanted to let go.

They sped along the road and down the track leading to the Uluwatu cliffs overlooking the Indian Ocean. They parked the bike and arrived at the cliff's edge just as the sun was about to set. They sat on the grass to watch nature in all her glory. Tiana could hear the waves smashing against the rocks far below and watched in awe as the sun sank into the ocean. The sky was like a giant canvas, splashed with molten gold and fiery orange ripples mixed with tiny splotches of purple and soft grey.

She turned and saw that His Excellency had closed his eyes, so she closed hers and prayed, *please let him love me.*

When she opened her eyes, he was looking at her intently.

"Did you enjoy the sunset Tiana?"

"I did; it was glorious and one I will never forget."

"Well, let's get back and get something to eat; you must be hungry. My pembantu, my Balinese housemaid, leaves me a meal she's already prepared for the evening, and there's always far more than I can eat."

"That would be wonderful, thank you."

As they walked towards the bike, Tiana said, "When I spoke to Michael and Elizabeth, they thought it so odd that I referred to you as 'His Excellency'. They said nobody called you that in Bali; everyone just called you Philippe."

"Well, that's because I've known people here forever, and I've known Michael since we were thirteen, twenty-odd years or so."

"I was wondering if you would mind if I called you Philippe? 'Excellency' does seem rather out-of-place here, especially since you're dressed in shorts and a T-shirt," Tiana said, hastily adding, "just whilst we're here in Bali."

He smiled, "I get your point. I'd like that, Tiana, whilst we're in Bali."

On the ride back, she clung to him again, closing her eyes and laying her cheek against his warm back.

By the time they got back, it was dark, so he asked Tiana to wait on the verandah whilst he put the motorbike away. When he returned, they went inside, and he put on the single overhead light and the two table lamps on either side of the sofa.

Then he said, "Tiana, there is another update you might enjoy. In the beginning, we always had a cold shower outside, but when I had the electricity installed, I also upgraded the bathroom to include hot water and a new shower. I saw one of the bathrooms in a villa Michael was renting and thought I'd better do something similar if I were going to put the house on the rental market. Maybe you'd like to go and take a shower, Tiana, whilst I check out what Kamala has prepared in the kitchen and get things started."

"Thank you, I'd love that."

The bathroom was full of surprises. The handbasin was a giant shell, and the shower was outside in a small courtyard with rustic stone walls and square flagstones underfoot. Tiana had never had a shower under the night sky before and thought it was amazing.

When she emerged barefoot in her long summer dress, he grinned at her. "Did you enjoy your outside shower?"

"It was superb, a real surprise."

"If you'll excuse me, Tiana, I'll leave you with a glass of wine whilst I take a quick shower myself."

Tiana curled up on the sofa and sipped her wine whilst listening to the night sounds of Bali. She could hear the wind rattling the leaves of the coconut palms and thought she heard an owl whooping above the chorus of frogs. *I could live here forever.*

Philippe returned after taking his shower, a glass of wine in hand. He, too, was barefoot and now wore jeans with a fresh white T-shirt.

He placed his wine glass on the dining room table, where he had laid two settings, and lit the candles.

"Would you like to come into the kitchen with me whilst I cook dinner," he said. "Kamala has prepared everything, so all I have to do is heat the charcoal under the grill to the right temperature in the terracotta cooker. But I must warn you, the kitchen hasn't been touched, and it's basic. I will need an expert to upgrade it as Kamala would like."

"Absolutely," Tiana said, picking up her wine and following him to the kitchen.

"As you can see, the cooking is done on the wood-fired stove top. The Balinese don't have ovens, and they've never needed refrigerators as the meals are always cooked fresh daily and eaten immediately. That is, until now, follow me, Tiana."

She followed him through the kitchen out to the back verandah, and there, humming away, sat an olive-green refrigerator."

Tiana couldn't help laughing at how incongruous it looked.

"Kamala goes to the markets first thing in the morning and then comes here every day to look after the house and cook the main meal for lunch," His Excellency explained. "But I prefer to eat in the evening, so now she can prepare the meal and leave it in the refrigerator for me to finish cooking later. I enjoy doing that as it's not something I get to do when living at the Vatican."

Philippe opened the refrigerator door and handed Tiana a bowl of jukut urab, which he told her meant Balinese mixed vegetables combined with grated coconut. "It's a kind of salad," he said.

He then removed a dish of sate lilit. "The key ingredient for this satay is minced chicken, mixed with all the other ingredients and then wrapped around lemongrass sticks, which add to the flavour. I think you'll find them tasty."

The charcoal had reached the desired heat in the kitchen, so he brushed the satay sticks with oil and put them on the grill. The aroma of the garlic, shallots, nutmeg, and cloves filled the room as Philippe slowly turned them, making sure not to burn the seagrass sticks. It made Tiana's mouth water.

Philippe handed Tiana his wine glass and said, "Would you like to top up our wine, Tiana? And could you please bring me a platter from the cabinet in the dining room?"

The long buffet cabinet was similar to the one in the sitting room. It had a large wooden bowl of fruit on top, four blue and white china bowls, a bottle of malt whisky and two crystal whiskey glasses on a brass tray.

Tiana topped up their two glasses of wine, sat them on the table, found the platter in the cupboard and returned to the kitchen.

Philippe arranged the satay sticks on the platter, handed Tiana the salad bowl, and said, "Let's eat."

***

Philippe said Grace, raised his glass, and said, "Santé Tiana, bon appétit."

"Santé Philippe."

He smiled when she said his name.

"So tell me, how is your mother?"

"She's doing so well. She was amazing after papa died; she was truly inspirational."

"And you, Tiana, how are you doing?"

"Well, it was tough at first without him. But it got easier once I started flatting in London with my best friend, Veronica. We're both going up to Oxford next year.

"Then, in May this year, we flew to Perth to see a friend. Afterwards, we went to Melbourne, where I did some family business. We returned to Perth, and now

I'm going home via Bali. Whilst we were in Melbourne, Veronica's boyfriend proposed over the telephone, so she flew home early. She couldn't wait to get back to him."

"Good lord, when were you in Melbourne?"

"From May thirtieth to June first."

"That's amazing. I was in Melbourne for five months and flew out on May twenty-ninth, the day before you arrived."

Tiana took another sip of her wine, biding time while deciding whether to tell him she had gone looking for him in Melbourne. She wasn't sure how he'd take it.

Then suddenly, he said, "Do you remember the first time we met Tiana?"

"Oh please, don't remind me," Tiana said, laughing. "I made such a fool of myself. Look, I'm blushing even now just at the thought of it."

Philippe burst out laughing. "I thought you were adorable," he said.

"And I thought you were so handsome; I told Veronica you could have been a movie star if you hadn't been a priest."

That made him laugh even more.

"But when I saw you again at Orly Airport, and you looked so lost, so, well..."

She waited for him to continue, holding her breath.

Philippe stood up, topped up Tiana's wine glass, picked up the bottle of whiskey and a glass, and brought them back to the table.

Tiana watched as he poured himself a shot of whiskey.

"You were about to say, Philippe..."

CHAPTER TWENTY-FOUR

Philippe took a sip of whiskey before looking at Tiana. "I was about to say." Again, he hesitated. "I was about to say you were in so much pain, and I wanted to make it all go away for you."

"Oh, Philippe, I wanted you to hold me. As soon as I got to London, I called the Vatican to try to speak to you and tell you how I felt about you. But you'd already left for Melbourne.

"And there's something else I need to tell you. I did go to Melbourne for business, but it was also to try to see you. Archbishop Armand had told me when I rang the Vatican and ended up speaking to him instead of you that you had gone to Australia. That's because I told him maman and I wanted to thank you for being so kind to us when papa died.

"He suggested that maman could write you a letter care of the Archdiocese of Melbourne. That's how I knew where to find you. But when I got there, as you've said, you'd already left."

Philippe stared at Tiana, speechless and finally said, "So you're saying you flew across the world to see me in Melbourne."

"Primarily yes, and that's when I found out you'd gone on leave to Bali."

"Mon dieu, so you came to Bali to find me, having no idea where I might be on the island."

"Yes, I came to Bali for another reason, too, but yes. If I hadn't been told you were here, I probably would have flown straight home from Perth. I planned to contact you at the Vatican before you returned to Melbourne."

"Good lord, Tiana. So are you here by yourself then?"

"No, I came with two friends, but they're away in Ubud for the next two days."

"And then you met Michael and Elizabeth."

"Yes."

"Did you tell them you were looking for me?"

"No, it just came out in the conversation as an extraordinary coincidence that I knew you. I did tell them we met in Paris when I was fifteen."

"I'm at a loss for words, Tiana."

Philippe got up, picked up the whiskey bottle and glass, and said, "Bring your wine, Tiana and let's go and sit on the front verandah."

"You take the chair," he said as he sat down on the verandah's edge and poured himself another shot.

The garden and surrounding vegetation were bathed in moonlight, and the sounds of Bali nightlife and the whisperings of the palms filled the tropical air.

"If you look up there, Tiana, you can see the Milky Way,"

Tiana gazed at the sky above and said, "I think this must be one of the most beautiful places on earth."

Philippe turned towards her, and she could see he was smiling. "Bali seduces everyone who comes here," he said.

"Now, there's something I have to say to you, Tiana."

"Are you going to tell me off for coming here?"

Philippe laughed, "No, Tiana, but it isn't every day that a beautiful young woman turns up at a priest's door and tells him she's been looking for him from one side of the world to the other."

"Too extreme?" she asked with a wicked grin.

Philippe burst out laughing. "Tiana, you're incorrigible, but as I said, you're a young woman."

"I'm nearly twenty, Philippe."

"I know. But I am so much older than you."

"Yes, sixteen years."

He laughed. "Tiana, please stop interrupting; I'm trying to say something important here."

"And I'm sure there's just the same age difference between Michael and Elizabeth."

"Tiana!"

"Okay, okay, please continue," Tiana said, putting her hand over her mouth.

"So what are we to do? Do I wish to send you away, right now, right here, sitting so close to you? No, I do not."

"Oh, Philippe," Tiana whispered.

"It's a lie that all priests remain celibate. From my observation, I'd say at least fifty per cent do not, and it's probably far more. And in the Vatican, well, I won't go into details about that. But I don't think you understand what is involved, Tiana."

"Well, I think celibacy is unnatural, and I did my research. It's only a Church rule, not like one of the Ten Commandments set in stone."

"Yes, that's correct, it's a church-created law, universally imposed in 1123 and confirmed in 1139. And if I'm frank with you, Tiana, I have to admit that I now believe that celibacy should be an option.

"This is especially true for young men coming out of the seminary who are not mature enough emotionally or sexually to make such a promise before the bishop. They have no concept of what's involved in leading a celibate life. Celibacy should be a choice for those who genuinely believe it's their calling, not mandatory for all. But as things stand, I can't see any Pope changing the law any time soon.

"So, returning to the subject of a priest having a relationship with a woman, what I was going to say is that you have no understanding of what such a relationship involves, Tiana. The Church knows that this is going on; it's been happening for centuries. However, liaisons have to be kept secret for fear of scandal. The Church doesn't want the laity to know about it. That's the hypocrisy of it. It gets back to the celibacy issue."

"But how would they find out with us here in Bali, for example?"

"Believe me, they have their ways."

"What do they do if they find out?"

"Well, in the 1950s, it was brutal. When a priest was discovered to be having a relationship with a woman, he would be moved instantly and forbidden to contact the woman ever again. He'd be closely monitored, and the woman would not know what had happened to him. Dispensations were very rarely given then.

"Oh, how *cruel*."

"Yes, it was. Technically, once a man is ordained, he cannot resign his priest-hood; he can never be 'un-ordained', just like you cannot ever be 'un-baptised'. But because so many priests have been leaving the Church this decade, our current Pope generally grants dispensations to those who request them, so long as there's sufficient cause.

"What that means is that the priest is still a priest but is released from the clerical state—that is, from his priestly duties and responsibilities. Then there's the dispensation from celibacy. This is a separate request and can only be granted by the Pope.

"If dispensation from celibacy isn't granted, then it's likely the man will not receive permission to marry. If he decides to get married anyway, he's suspended and loses any ecclesiastical office he may have.

"He cannot marry in a Catholic Church, and any marriage in a non-Catholic ceremony will not be recognised by the Church. He's ostracised, may lose the support of his family and friends and will not be able to continue living in the same area for fear of causing a scandal for the Church."

"That's unbelievable. And what happens if a priest has an affair, and they have a child?"

"You won't like this either. Again, it's all kept secret and out of the public eye. There's no provision by the Church for emotional or financial support for the mothers or children involved. The Church doesn't see this as a widespread, hidden problem but as isolated incidents. And canon law is silent on the issue.

So it's up to the priest to make arrangements, according to his conscience and whether or not he takes his responsibilities seriously."

"So it's the women and children who suffer."

"Yes. But it's also hard for a priest if he leaves the Church and doesn't come from a wealthy family. The Church doesn't give him a pension, and it can be tough for an ex-priest to get a job in the outside world. It's a rude awakening and hard to adjust."

"But you have your home here and your inheritance from your family in France."

"Yes, I do. I'm very fortunate and an exception in that regard. But the expectation is that I will use my worldly goods for evangelisation and helping the poor, which I do, of course."

"So, are you telling me all this to scare me off?"

"Of course not. But if we should take steps leading to an intimate relationship, you must understand what you're letting yourself in for. When you leave Bali, you'll be returning to your life and studies, and I will be returning to the Vatican.

"I must be sure I'm not taking advantage of your vulnerability, Tiana."

"Well, that's extremely gallant of you, Philippe. But have you forgotten that I've been chasing you for the past six months?"

"I know, chérie, but..."

"What did you just say?"

'I said, I know chérie, but..."

Tiana got up and went and sat next to Philippe. "So I'm chérie now?"

Philippe laughed and put his arm around her.

"So you're sure that this is what you want, chérie, for us to be together in Bali."

"I'm sure. I love you, Philippe. I have done since I was fifteen."

Philippe took her hands and said, "Then now I can tell you a secret I've held in my heart with no expectation that I would ever be able to say the words to you. On that drive home from Orly Airport, not only did I want to take all your pain away, but I also fell in love with you, Tiana. It took all my self-control and more not to reach out and touch you. I love you too, chérie."

Tiana turned and wrapped her arms around him as tears filled her eyes, and he stroked her hair.

"Tiana," he said, "my love," and then he raised her chin and kissed her.

***

Philippe stood up, "Come, chérie," he said, pulling her up and leading her to his bedroom. He lifted her onto the side of his king-size four-poster bed and then proceeded to turn on the bedside table lamp and light the two large candles sitting on the dresser. Next, he walked around the bed and let down the mosquito net on one side and then at the foot of the bed. Tiana could now see the candles flickering through the netting. *Oh my gosh, this is so romantic.*

"This used to be my parents' bedroom," he said.

"It's beautiful, Philippe."

"Come, stand up," he said, holding out his arms. "Are you nervous?"

"No, well, yes, just a little."

He took her face in his hands and kissed her forehead, then her eyelids, then her lips with a long, lingering kiss. His closeness and the touch of his lips on hers flooded her body with sensations that left her heart pounding and her legs feeling weak.

He trailed his fingers across her left shoulder and slowly undid the ties holding up her dress. He undid the ties on the other side, and her dress fell to the floor.

"Well!" he said when it was revealed that Tiana had not been wearing underwear.

Tiana thought she was going to faint before he lifted her back onto the bed.

Philippe then quickly removed his T-shirt, jeans, and boxer shorts.

Tiana gazed down at him. *So that's what it looks like.*

"Move to the centre of the bed, chérie," he said as he switched off the bedside lamp, climbed onto the bed and lowered the mosquito net.

Tiana's eyes adjusted to the moonlight through the open shutters and the candlelight as she looked up at him.

"I love you, Philippe," she said.

"I love you too, chérie," he murmured, tracing his finger around the hollow of her neck.

"This is your first time?"

"Yes."

"I'll be gentle."

He kissed her again, and the touch of his tongue on hers sent shivers rippling down through her body.

"You're so beautiful," he said as he bent to kiss her breast.

Tiana gasped as she felt her nipple rise as his lips circled it.

He then moved between her legs, gently moving them apart. He kissed her other breast and sucked her raised nipple.

Tiana started losing control of her body as it responded to his touch, pressing hard towards him.

His hand slid down over her stomach and further down until he felt her soft hair. He began by gently massaging her before parting her and inserting his finger, sliding it up and down. Then, in circles of increasing pressure, he rubbed the tiny nub of flesh where the lips joined. Her hips began to writhe, and she was moaning as he moved over her in one smooth movement; he guided himself in, moving rhythmically back and forth, back and forth, before pulling himself out.

Tiana cried out, "Oh, Philippe, please."

He moved in again, deeper with his thrusts, and she felt a small jolt of pain before a warm wave of pleasure pulsated through her, leaving her quivering. She heard Philippe groan as he pressed hard against her.

After they drew apart, Philippe looked down on her and gently brushed away a tear that slid from the corner of her eye.

"What is it, chérie?"

"Oh, Philippe, I've wanted you for so long. I didn't know it could be like this, so - I don't have the words."

"As one."

"Yes."

"Did you feel any pain?"

"Only a little, just for a second."

"It'll be even better next time," he said, holding her as she drifted to sleep in his arms.

Merci Rosemarie, he thought before he, too, fell asleep.

***

The following day, Tiana woke to the sound of birds outside and faint voices inside.

She got up, picked up her dress, and ran to the other bedroom. After pulling on her shorts and T-shirt, she walked to the main room.

Philippe came through from the kitchen. "Good morning, chérie; I couldn't bear to wake you. You looked so peaceful. Kamala is making us a huge omelette, and I have the coffee on."

"Oh, mon dieu, is she shocked that someone is here with you?"

"Surprised, more likely. The Balinese are very relaxed about sex."

"Yes, but it's different, you being a priest."

"I've known Kamala for the past twenty years, and I think she's just happy to see me happy. It's a big change from the last few weeks."

Tiana smiled at him and said, "And I'm happy to see you happy."

"And you chérie, are you?"

"This is the happiest I've ever been in my life."

She wrapped her arms around his neck and pulled him down to kiss her.

"So this morning," he said. "I was thinking we could go to a small beach I know. Nobody else will be there as it's not well known. The sea is calm there and perfect for swimming. And then we could have lunch at my favourite Balinese warung, a traditional family restaurant. What do you think, chérie?"

"Wonderful. And then this afternoon, we should go and watch the sunset again, come home, drink wine, have dinner, and make love."

Philippe laughed, "Now that," he said, "sounds like the perfect plan."

"There's just one thing: I didn't bring a swimsuit."

"You won't need it. There won't be anyone else there."

***

After breakfast, Philippe said he had a small errand to do. "I'll be back in half an hour, chérie, and then we should head straight to the beach. It's a bit of a hike down from the top of the cliff."

After he left, Tiana took her second shower in the open air, put on her shorts, T-shirt and sneakers, and picked up a couple of towels before heading out to the verandah to wait for Philippe.

The minute he returned on his motorbike, she ran down the path with the towels and got on behind him. Twenty minutes later, they arrived at the cliff top. Tiana could see the beach far below and a long line of steps hewn into the rock leading down to it.

Philippe took a bottle of Reef Coconut Sun Tan Oil out of the small bag on the back of the motorbike. They grabbed a towel each and started the long climb down.

"Only three hundred and twenty-six steps to go," Philippe said.

When they reached the bottom, Tiana said, "Oh, this is heavenly," as she gazed at the small white-sand beach and crystal-clear water that was a glorious turquoise blue.

"And not a soul to disturb us," Philippe said.

They spread out the two towels, slipped out of their shorts and T-shirts, and Philippe said, "Lie down on your stomach, chérie, and I'll put the sun tan oil on your back."

Tiana did as she was told. He started at her shoulders, massaging in the oil, and gradually worked his way down her body and legs with long, lingering strokes, sending tingles down her spine. Putting more oil on his hands, he slipped them around her waist and over her stomach and lifted her to a kneeling position. Then, grasping her by the hips, he whispered, "I'm going to take you from behind," and he entered her.

Tiana gasped, and then, as Philippe moved slowly in and out, she became more and more turned on, pressing herself into him. Philippe picked up the pace, and she matched him, her hips rolling back into him, pushing him to go deeper and deeper until he shouted out. She was swept up into a delirious spiral that bore her up and up till she reached the peak and then dissolved into a feeling of blissful satisfaction.

"Oh my lord, Philippe!" she said as they collapsed onto the towels.

Philippe grinned at her, saying, "I told you it would get better." He then stood up, bent down and pulled her up. "Come," he said, "let's cool off with a swim."

While floating together in the ocean, Tiana put her arms around Philippe's neck and said, "Philippe, I have a question."

"Oh."

"Well, I have no previous experience in love-making, obviously. But I have seen films, and, well, you're an amazing lover."

"Ah, so you're wondering 'how does he know these things?'"

"Yes."

"I suspected that at some point you would ask me this question," he said. "So the time has come for me to tell you about Rosemarie."

"Rosemarie?"

"Don't look so horrified, chérie. I'll tell you what happened."

As Tiana listened to Philippe tell her how Rosemarie had seduced and educated him, a wave of jealousy overwhelmed her.

He said, "She told me that one day I might be grateful to her for what she had taught me, and I am chérie if our love-making has been as incredible for you as it has been for me."

"Oh, so I guess I should be grateful to Rosemarie, too, then."

Philippe kissed her. "It's you I love chérie."

***

For the rest of that day, night, and the next day, they were in a world of their own, eyes only for each other and always within touching distance.

Philippe said, "I hadn't realised just how desperately lonely I was till I slept in bed next to you, chérie."

Tiana's heart ached for him.

"I was thinking I'd purchase an apartment in Rome, Philippe, or a villa somewhere to be together in secret. I don't care that it has to be like that."

"Oh, chérie, after a while, you'd hate it, and then you'd begin to hate me for putting you in such a position. And you have your studies, and at some stage, you'll want to have your own family with children."

"Not without you, Philippe. There must be some who've made this work."

"But at what cost, chérie."

"Well, I'm coming to see you in Rome as soon as you return, and we can talk about it then."

***

Philippe and Tiana were sitting on the verandah before heading off to see the sunset when they heard a car approaching.

"That's odd. Who could it possibly be," Philippe said.

The sound of the car stopped, and eventually, two men appeared around the corner. Tiana suddenly recognised Peter and Oliver.

"Merd," she said.

"Do you know them chérie?"

"Yes, they're the two friends I came to Bali with, the ones who've been in Ubud."

"How did they know you were here?"

"I don't know. I just left a message that I'd bumped into friends from Paris, and they'd invited me to stay with them."

As Peter and Oliver walked up the path, they suddenly stopped. "Good heavens, is that Tiana?" Peter said to Oliver.

"Yes, it is. What on earth is she doing here?"

They continued walking towards the verandah, and when they got there, Peter said, "Good afternoon. My name's Peter, and this is Oliver. We're here to see Bishop Gagnon. What are you doing here, Tiana?"

Philippe stood up. "I'm Bishop Gagnon," he said. "How can I help you."

Peter was confused. "Tiana?" he said.

Tiana looked from Peter to Philippe and back to Peter. "Well..." she said.

Philippe interrupted, "Can I ask why you're here?" he said.

Peter dragged his eyes away from Tiana and said, "Somebody in Ubud told us that you might be able to help us."

"Help you, in what way?"

"There's a priest here," Oliver said, "His name is Father William Carson, and he's here on a child sex tour."

"Good lord," Philippe said. "Will you excuse me for a moment? Please come inside and take a seat. Tiana, maybe you could get them both a glass of water."

Philippe walked inside, indicated the seating area, and disappeared through the house.

Tiana said, "I'll just get you both a glass of cold water," and left them to sit down. She walked through the kitchen and then out to the back verandah and the refrigerator. She took out the bottled water, found two glasses in the kitchen and poured the water out. Her hands were shaking, and she had no idea what she would say to Peter and Oliver to explain the situation.

She walked back into the main room and over to Peter and Oliver, sitting on the sofa's edge. "Thank you," Oliver said, staring hard at Tiana.

Peter said, "Tiana, I..."

But before Tiana could say anything, Philippe returned. He was dressed in black trousers and shoes, a purple clerical shirt and collar and over the shirt hung his Pictorial Cross.

Everyone stared at him in amazement.

Philippe sat down in one of the chairs and said, "So you're alleging that Father Carson is here in Bali to have sex with children."

"Yes," Oliver said.

"And how do you know this?"

"I've had him under surveillance for months, and my private detective, John, signed up for the tour too, so we could continue to watch him. We went to see John in Ubud to get an update on what's been happening."

"And where is Father Carson based? What parish?"

"Victoria Park in Perth, Western Australia."

"And why have you come to me?"

"We were told that you've been coming to Bali for quite a few years and have helped many people. It was suggested that you might know someone in the police force or government who has influence and could look into what's happening. This whole child sex tour thing has been set up by an Australian paedophile who's been living here for three years and runs the whole disgusting business through an orphanage he opened up."

"And why do you have an interest in this priest?"

"Peter here is a journalist, and he's doing a whole series of articles for a Perth newspaper about British child migrants sent to Australia. I was one of the kids sent to Western Australia, and William Carson, Billy, came out on the same ship as me and went to the same institution outside of Perth. He went on to become a priest and sexually abused an altar boy."

"In Perth?"

"Yes"

"And was this allegation taken to the Bishop?"

"Yes, the mother of the altar boy Father Carson sexually abused reported him to the Bishop, and he sent Father Carson away for a couple of years, and now he's back at his old parish as if nothing happened," Oliver said.

"I see; well, I'm very sorry to hear that, Oliver. But I regret that I can't help you with the allegation regarding Father Carson here in Bali. Once an allegation is made against a priest, the matter is held in the strictest confidence and cannot be spoken about to anybody outside those handling his case. I cannot speak to the police or anybody else."

Oliver and Peter stared at Philippe in dead silence.

"But this priest is engaged in crimes against children right here in Bali," Peter finally said, his voice rising. "Surely there's something you can do, someone who can help."

"If what you are alleging is correct, then Father Carson is committing a crime. But the case must be taken to his bishop. He is the only one who must handle the allegation and take action to bring him to justice."

"But Philippe," Tiana said, totally confused by Philippe's response. "What about the children? Surely, the police should be involved."

Philippe turned to Tiana and said, "There's nothing to stop any of you going to the police, Tiana, but strict rules bind me."

"And what do your strict rules say about having an affair?" Peter said, glaring at Philippe. "You two are more than just friends. I thought you people were supposed to be celibate."

Tiana felt sick to her stomach. "Peter," she said, I can't believe you're saying this. What's got into you?"

"Well, it looks pretty obvious to me."

"Peter," Philippe said, "You are a guest in my house, and my relationship with Tiana is none of your business."

"Bloody hell, it's not," Peter said, jumping off the sofa.

Philippe stood up, too, and then Oliver and Tiana.

Tiana looked at Peter and said, "Pete, you don't understand; I'm the one who came to Bali to find Philippe, Bishop Gagnon."

"Good lord Tiana, what are you saying?"

"Damn it, Pete, I'm saying I came to find him because I'm in love with him. I have been since I was fifteen."

"Jesus, Tiana, I can't believe you're saying this. And how the hell did you know he was here in Bali?"

"I found out in Melbourne."

"Oh...So *that's* why you were so keen to come to Bali. And that's why you wanted to know where Melbourne was in Australia and fixed it so you could go there for business.

"Bloody hell, Tiana, *that's* why you wanted to go to Australia in the first place and why you offered to fly to Perth with Ollie's mum. Jesus Tiana, how *could* you? You used me, and you used Ollie."

Tiana was crying now. "No, no, Pete, it wasn't like that. It wasn't. I wanted to fly out to Perth with Enid, I did. And I wanted to meet Ollie. It's just that everything's all mixed up together."

"I don't believe a damn word you're saying, Tiana."

"That's quite enough," Philippe said as he moved towards Tiana.

Peter lunged towards Philippe to push him away, "You've no bloody right to touch her," he shouted.

Oliver jumped forward to restrain Peter, and Tiana screamed.

"Jesus, Pete, you need to calm down," Oliver said, pulling Peter back. "This isn't bloody helping."

"Can everybody please sit down," Philippe said. "I understand you're upset, Peter, but this is getting completely out of hand."

Tiana turned to Philippe and said, "Philippe, please, you must be able to do something to protect the children."

She could see the pain etched on his face and had to lean forward to hear him say, "I cannot chérie; the Pontifical Secret binds me."

"What binds you?" Peter said.

"The *Pontifical Secret*. It is the Church's strictest rule of confidentiality outside the confessional. To break this rule can mean excommunication."

"Well, now I've heard everything," Oliver said. "So Church cover-ups even have a bloody name. Bastards. I should have known it was a waste of time coming here."

"Oh, Philippe, I can't bear it. The Church has trapped you in another one of its cruel rules," Tiana said, looking distraught. "And now you're protecting the Church instead of the children."

Oliver stepped forward, "Tiana, we should go; there's nothing we can do here. You need to come with us."

Tiana looked at Philippe, who looked broken. He nodded.

"You must go; it's best for you," he said, his voice barely audible.

***

As they walked away, Tiana turned to take one last look. He stood on the verandah, frozen, the fading rays of sun glinting off his Pictorial Cross.

EPILOGUE

When Tiana arrived back at the flat, she was relieved that Veronica wasn't home. She took her luggage to her bedroom, lay down on her bed for a moment, and promptly fell asleep.

She awoke two hours later, hearing sounds coming from the kitchen, and reluctantly got up. *I wonder if she's heard anything.*

She walked into the kitchen, where Veronica was chopping vegetables.

Not looking up, Veronica said, "Oh, you're finally awake. Andy's coming over for dinner later, so I'm doing a roast." Then, finally, looking at Tiana, she said, "Feeling better after your sleep? You look terrible, by the way."

"Thanks," Tiana said. "I didn't get much sleep on the plane."

"Pete rang Andy at the paper this morning."

"Oh..."

"Then Andy rang me, of course."

Tiana just stared at Veronica, dreading what was coming.

"Pete told him what happened in Bali," Veronica said, her voice flat.

"I see."

"Bloody hell, Tiana, why didn't you listen to me? I told you, way back when, that falling for a priest was a dead-end street."

"I know, Vron, I know."

"I knew your sudden interest in Australia was sus and the whole 'Melbourne' thing. Pete's devastated."

"Oh, don't, Vron; I never meant to hurt him. I tried to be clear that we were just friends. What else did Pete say?"

"He said after you all left the Bishop and returned to the hotel, you just disappeared."

"I had to Vron. I was in so much pain and so confused. Michael, one of Philippe's oldest friends, pulled a few strings and got me on the next evening flight out of Bali.

"Did Pete say anything else?"

"Not about you. But he told Andy what happened when his first article on British child migrants appeared in The West Australian if you're interested."

"Of course I'm interested. What happened?"

"Well, the article was published the day after he and Ollie returned to Perth. Heaps of people got in touch with the newspaper afterwards, and they expect even more to contact the paper when the next one about Baile comes out in a week.

"Andy said they'll start running the articles in The Daily Mail in a couple of weeks, so there could be an avalanche of people contacting the paper this end, too."

"I'm so proud of them. Did Pete say what happened with Billy, Father Carson?"

"Pete told Andy that Ollie and John are putting together all the information they have about him, his abuse of the altar boy and the sex tour set up, and then they're going to hand it all over to the police. After what your Bishop said about the secrecy thing, they're not going to even bother going to see the Bishop in Perth."

"Oh Vron, at first I was in shock when Philippe said he couldn't help. And then, when he told us about the secrecy rule, it made it so much worse. But I could see saying 'no' was tearing him apart. When we left, his face was ashen, and he could barely speak."

"Then why on earth *did* he say 'no'? I don't get it."

"He was trapped, Vron, by the secrecy rule and the threat of excommuni-cation, and you know what that means. Suppose he had gone to the police or some other official like Ollie and Pete wanted. There's no way it wouldn't have got into the newspapers and become a huge scandal. Can you imagine what the Church would have done to Philippe for being involved, for airing the Church's dirty linen in public, exposing the Church's dirty secrets? They'd have destroyed him.

"The Church has been his life, and in the heat of the moment, going against the Church, it was just too much to ask. But I'm scared of how this will affect him, Vron."

"God, I hadn't thought of it like that. You're still in love with him, aren't you."

"Yes," Tiana said, tears welling up.

"Oh, Tiana, I'm sorry," Veronica said, her voice softening. "What are you going to do?"

"First, I have to go and see maman and tell her what's happened. I can't have secrecy in my life anymore; look what damage it's done to my relationships with everyone. I'm not sure how she'll take it. I pray she won't be too angry with me. After that, I'll return to London and try to pick up the pieces.

"I've got to try and make things right with Pete and Ollie. I've been thinking; maybe I can meet with Ollie when he comes over for Christmas and with Pete when he comes back for Michael and Jenny's wedding."

"Yes, give them time. I'm sure they'll come around. And the Bishop?"

"Oh, Vron, the pain is still so raw."

"Come here; let me give you a hug."

"Don't know what I'd have done if I'd lost you too, Vron."

"Just as well. I love you then. So when are you planning to go over to Paris?"

"The day after tomorrow."

***

"Come and sit next to me on the sofa, darling," Adelia said. What's happened? I thought you'd be so happy after your successful trip to Australia and your holiday in Bali, but you look terrible."

"So everyone keeps telling me," Tiana said with a weak smile.

"Shall I get a fresh pot of tea, or maybe you'd like a sherry or a brandy?"

"A brandy, please, Maman."

"So what's this all about? What happened in Australia?"

Tiana said, "Please try to understand Maman. Please don't hate me." Then she told her mother the whole story, starting with when The Bishop met her at Orly Airport and ending with her flying out of Bali.

Adelia sat listening without saying a word, and when Tiana finished, she said, "I could never hate you, darling, and I knew you had strong feelings for him."

"How did you know, Maman? And you're so calm. I thought you would be so angry with me, so disappointed in me."

"The signs were all there, and I couldn't be angry or disappointed with you, darling, because, well, I need to tell you something now, no more secrets. I also fell in love with a priest."

Tiana couldn't believe what she was hearing and said, "*What?* How is that possible? When Maman?"

"In the mid-1950s, when I was seventeen. Before I met your father."

"Oh My God, Maman."

"I got pregnant, Tiana, and I had a miscarriage. That's why I was terrified when I saw that you had a crush on Bishop Gagnon, Father Gagnon, then. I did everything I could to ensure you didn't see him again.

"And then, of course, he suddenly reappeared and was so wonderful when your papa died. My greatest fear was that he'd become your 'Knight in Shining Armour'."

"Oh, Maman, I can't even begin to imagine how that must have been for you, losing a baby. Thank God you met papa. Now I understand why you were sad sometimes. You never told papa, did you."

"No darling, Aunt Vivienne was the only one who ever knew. She felt so bad lying to you that time you went to see her on the yacht to ask if she knew what made me sad."

"Philippe told me what happened to priests in the 1950s when the Church found out they were having an affair with a woman."

"What do you mean, Tiana? What did he say?" Adelia said, her voice suddenly hushed.

"Oh my lord, Maman, of course, you don't know. I shouldn't have said anything."

"Tell me," Adelia whispered.

"It was cruel Maman. Once the Church found out about the relationship, the poor priest was hauled away. He was forbidden to contact the woman ever again, and he was watched. Philippe said it was virtually impossible to get a dispensation, and basically, the priest had no choice but to stay trapped in the Church or be kicked out with nothing. And then, of course, he could never marry in a Catholic Church."

Adelia's hand flew up to her mouth, and she just stared at Tiana, shaking her head. "Oh mon dieu, my poor Nicolas," she finally managed to say. "Imagine his torment thinking about me waiting and waiting to hear from him and then imagining that I'd be thinking he'd abandoned me. Oh, I can't bear it," and Adelia began to cry.

Tiana put her arms around her mother, and the two women held each other and wept together.

When they drew apart, Adelia said, "Do you still love him, darling?"

"Yes, Maman, and when we were in Bali, I thought I could live with having a secret relationship. But Philippe said after a while I'd hate it, and then I'd start to hate him. I'd never hate him, but I do hate that the Church forces people to live a lie like that. I hate that the Church isn't protecting children against priests like Father Carson. It's cruel, and it's wrong.

"But that leaves us nowhere to go, except if..."

"Oh, darling, don't torture yourself with 'What ifs'; they will destroy you; I know only too well. You have to accept—" Adelia suddenly stopped talking and said, "Did you hear that? Is it the doorbell?"

"Yes, it is."

"Who could be visiting so late?"

After a few minutes, there was a gentle knock on the door.

"Entrez," Adelia said.

"Good evening, Madame; there's a gentleman to see Mademoiselle Tiana," Dominique said.

"A gentleman? To see Mademoiselle Tiana at such a late hour? Did he tell you his name?"

"No, Madame. He apologised for the late intrusion and said he had an urgent message for Mademoiselle. He's waiting in the study."

"I see; well, when you go downstairs, Dominique, please ask André to come up and wait in the hall whilst Mademoiselle Tiana goes into the study."

"He's there already, Madame. He answered the door."

"Oh, but he sent you up?"

"Yes, Madame."

Tiana stared at her mother, and by now, her heart was almost beating through her chest. *Oh God—a*ll she could do was look at her mother and shake her head in a daze.

"Well, it can't be anybody you know," Adelia said, "or he would have given his name. You'd better go down and see who it is."

Tiana raced down the stairs to the hall, barely seeing André, who said, "Good evening, Mademoiselle," as he watched her fly by.

She threw open the study door. The gentleman in the navy blue suit was standing by the window. He turned as she stood framed in the doorway and said, "Chérie".

ABOUT THE AUTHOR

KISANE SLANEY

Kisane Slaney became one of Sydney's top photographic models in the 1960s before retiring in the 1970s to spend the next twelve years caring full-time for her four children. When her youngest was four, Kisane took a new path, entering Murdoch University as a mature-age student. After completing her BA and whilst working in the fields of child sexual abuse and domestic violence, she went on to achieve First Class Honours, an APRA Scholarship and her PhD. In 2006, Kisane returned to academia as a Senior Lecturer in Counselling at the School of Social Work, Curtin University, Perth.

Following the self-publishing of her first novel, *The Heiress,* Kisane plans two more. The next one, *The Three Sisters*, is inspired by the extraordinary lives of three of her great-aunts. She has three very cool grandchildren, is an avid movie fan and lives with her bossy cat, Venus, in the beautiful city of Perth.

https://kisaneslaney.com.au

A Final Note from Kisane:

Getting books noticed nowadays is challenging, especially for self-published authors. If you enjoyed The Heiress, please consider leaving a review, just a sentence or two, at your favourite ebook store. I will read them all and would be extremely grateful.

FURTHER READING

I have included three resources for those who would like to know more about what happened to British child migrants and how many historical residential institutions failed to protect children from child sexual abuse and harsh physical punishment perpetrated by those responsible for their care.

My Pinterest Page

Here, you will find links to newspaper articles and government websites showing children being shipped out to Australia and labouring at the Catholic *Bindoon Farm & Trade School*.

https://www.pinterest.com.au/kisaneslaney/bindoon-the-real-catholic-institution

Empty Cradles by Margaret Humphreys

Empty Cradles is a remarkable true story by Nottingham social worker Margaret Humphries. In the late 1980s, Margaret discovered that an estimated 150,000 children had, in fact, been deported from Britain. They had been shipped off to Australia and elsewhere in the British Empire to start a new life, where they were told they would get an excellent education. Before Humphreys' expose, this practice of deportation was a shocking secret.

https://www.childmigrantstrust.org:

This organisation provides family research, access to records, specialist counselling and a family restoration fund.

Royal Commission into Institutional Responses to Child Sexual Abuse:

The Final Report – Volume 11: Historical Residential Institution – copyright © Commonwealth of Australia 2017.

https://www.royalcommission.gov.au/system/files/2021-08/carc-final-report-volume-11-historical-residential-institutions_1.pdf

Content Warning:

This PDF contains information about child sexual abuse that may be distressing to some readers.

This volume presents an overview of the experiences of child sexual abuse survivors who had been placed in Australian institutions post-World War II.

Child abuse casts a shadow the length of a lifetime.

Herbert Ward

RESOURCES

Australia

Survivors & Mates Support Network, NSW 1800 472 676
    https://www.samsn.org.au
Alliance for Forgotten Australians, Victoria. 0488 460 646
    https://forgottenaustralians.org.au
RIGHTSIDE Legal
    https://www.rightsidelegal.com.au/abuse-claims
Perth & Melbourne. 08 6461 6166/1300 765 702

24 Hour Helpline

Lifeline 13 11 14

United Kingdom

Ministry & Clergy Sexual Abuse Survivors.
    https://www.macsas.org.uk
Helpline: 08088 010 340

National umbrella agency for over 125 voluntary sector agencies in the UK & Ireland

https://thesurvivorstrust.org

Helpline 08088 010 818

Supporting survivors of church-related abuse in England & Wales

https://safespacesenglandandwales.org.uk

Helpline 0300 303 1056

United States

Survivors Network of Those Abused by Priests

https://snapnetwork.org

24 Hour Suicide & Crisis Line 1-877-762-7432 General Information (312) 321-4770

National Sexual Violence Resource Centre – Directory of Organizations

https://www.nsvrc.org/organizations

Toll-Free 877-739-3895

Clergy Sexual Abuse Lawyer

https://www.whitelawpllc.com/sexual-abuse-lawyer/clergy-sexual-abuse/

24/7 Helpline (517) 628-4452